Charles Staniland Wake

Serpent-worship and other essays

With a chapter on totemism

Charles Staniland Wake

Serpent-worship and other essays
With a chapter on totemism

ISBN/EAN: 9783337282264

Printed in Europe, USA, Canada, Australia, Japan

Cover: Foto ©Andreas Hilbeck / pixelio.de

More available books at **www.hansebooks.com**

SERPENT-WORSHIP,

AND OTHER ESSAYS

WITH A CHAPTER ON

TOTEMISM

BY

C. STANILAND WAKE

LONDON

GEORGE REDWAY

YORK STREET COVENT GARDEN

1888.

CONTENTS.

CHAPTER IX.

CHAPTER X.

CHAPTER XI.

CHAPTER XII.

CHAPTER XIII.

CHAPTER I.

THE lines of development of the religious faiths of mankind have been aptly termed by Major-General Forlong " Rivers of Life."   The streams of faiths are marvellously depicted by this writer in a chart which shows " the rise and fall of the various religious ideas, mythologies, and rites which have at any time prevailed among nations."   This chart ingeniously shows, moreover, " the degrees of intensity manifested at stated periods by any particular wave of doctrine or worship, and the mode in which the tributary streams of mythological or theological thought become in turn absorbed in the central River of Life."   The views adopted by General Forlong have much in common with those embodied in the works of Godfrey Higgins and some later writers, but they have a special value as being based on personal observation.   The author of " Rivers of Life" had the inestimable advantage of being admitted to shrines and of receiving instructions in sacred mysteries which are generally closed to European inquirers, and of having made " a diligent exploration of ruined temples, pillars, and mounds, and all such traces of a primitive symbolism, which lie scattered over the East and West, as religious fossils underlying the superficial crust of theological strata."

Rivers of religious life have a beginning, like other streams, and what are the sources to which man's primitive faiths may be traced? The early "symbolic objects of man's adoration" are arranged by General Forlong in the following order: First, Tree; 2nd, Phallic; 3rd, Serpent; 4th, Fire; 5th, Sun; 6th, Ancestral. The first "breathings of the human soul" were manifested under the sacred tree or grove, whose refreshing shade is so highly valued in the East. All nations, particularly the Aryan peoples, have considered tree-planting a sacred duty, and the grove was man's first temple, "and became a sanctuary, asylum, or place of refuge, and as time passed on, temples came to be built in the sacred groves." If tree-worship had such an origin as this, its origin ought to be shown in the ideas associated with it. What, then, are those ideas? General Forlong, after referring to Dr. Fergusson's statement that the tree and serpent are symbolised in every religious system which the world has known, says that the two together are typical of the reproductive powers of vegetable and animal life. The connection between tree and serpent-worship is often so intimate that we may expect one to throw light on the other. The Aryans generally may be called " tree-worshippers," and according to Fergusson they as a rule destroyed serpents and serpent-worshipping races. Yet at Athens and near Rome both those faiths flourished together, as they appear to have done also in many parts of Western Asia. They are intimately associated with religious notions of many Buddhist peoples. This is shown curiously in the early legends of Kambodia. These are said by General

Forlong to present two striking features. First, a holy tree, which the kingly race, who came to this serpent country, reposed under, or descended from heaven by; secondly, that this tree-loving race are captivated by the dragon princess of the land. It is the serpent king, however, who builds the city of *Nakon Thom* for his daughter and her stranger husband. It is not improbable that Buddhism originated among a people who were both tree and serpent-worshippers, although the former became more intimately and at an earlier period associated with its founder.

Let us now see what ideas are symbolised by the serpent. We are told that he is "an emblem of the Sun, Time, Kronos, and Eternity." The serpent was, indeed, the Sun-God, or spirit of the sun, and therefore Power, Wisdom, Light, and a fit type of creation and generative power. Dr. Donaldson came to the conclusion that the serpent has always a Phallic significance, a remark which exactly accords with General Forlong's experience, "founded simply upon *close observation* in Eastern lands, and conclusions drawn by himself, unaided by books or teachers, from thousands of stories and conversations with Eastern priests and people." The testimony of a competent and honest observer is all important, and we must believe when we are told that the serpent, or the constant early attendant on the Lingam, is the special symbol which veils the actual God. The same may be said, indeed, of Tree Worship, and as tree-worship and serpent-worship embrace the Phallic faith, the first three streams of faiths are represented by them. It is evident, however, that Phallic ideas are at the foundation of both tree and serpent-worship, and the Phallic stream of faith should be given the first place as the actual source of the Rivers of Life. General Forlong does, indeed, affirm that Phallic worship enters so closely into union with *all* faiths to the present hour that it is impossible to keep it out of view. We can well understand how this should be as to the tree, serpent, and solar cults, but it is not so evident at first sight in relation to fire-worship. If fire was, however, regarded as the servant of Siva, and all creating gods, there is no difficulty in accepting the position. The object of the worship offered to the sacred fire is consistent with that view. Thus Greeks, Romans, and Hindoos "besought Agni by fervent prayers for increase of flocks and families, for happy lives and serene old age, for wisdom and pardon from sin." General Forlong appears to see in the worship of fire essentially a household faith, and this was undoubtedly so if his explanation of the Lares and Penates is correct. These symbols represented " the *past* vital fire or energy of the tribe, as the patriarch, his stalwart sons and daughters did that of the *present* living fire the sacred hearth." General Forlong states, indeed, that everything relating to blood used to be connected with fire, and he supposed, therefore, that *agnatio* may have been *relation by fire*, for the *agnati* can only be those of the fire or father's side.

If the father derived his authority in the household from the sacred hearth-fire, we can understand why General Forlong has assigned to ancestor-worship the last place in his scheme. He says, moreover, that ancestor-worship is " a development and sequence of that idiosyncracy of man which has led him to worship and deify even the living—that which, according to the teaching of Euemerus, accounts for all the mythological tales of the gods and god-like men of Greece." The ancestor was worshipped in the great chief, the Father of Fathers, each of whom was worshipped in the *Dii Gentiles* of his own class, and this not only during the comparatively modern Roman sway, but during the ages of serpent, fire, and solar faiths. In the still earlier faiths he was represented in the rude pillar, as well as in the little Lares and Penates of the hearths. In this case, however, ancestor-worship would seem to be entitled to stand on the same level as tree-worship and serpent-worship as a phase of the Phallic faith. In fact, it is in a sense identified with serpent-worship. General Forlong remarks that among the Greeks and Romans "the ancestor came to be honoured and worshipped only as the Generator, and so also the serpent as his symbol." This agrees with the conclusion I have elsewhere endeavoured to establish, that the serpent is really regarded as the representative of the ancestor, in which case ancestor-worship is a very primitive faith, although, in a specialised form, it may possibly, as asserted by General Forlong, come later than fire-worship.

It can hardly now be doubted that the same ideas underlie all the early faiths. This view is entertained by General Forlong, who says : "So imperceptibly arose the serpent on pure Phallic faiths, fire on these, and sun on all, and so intimately did all blend with one another, that even in the ages of true history it was often impossible to descry the exact God alluded to."

The foundations of all those faiths, and of ancestor-worship as allied to them, must therefore be sought in the ideas entertained by mankind in the earliest times, "when the races lived untaught, herded with their cattle, and had as their sole object in life the multiplication of these and of themselves." The question arises, however, whether the simple faith which man then entertained was the earliest he had evolved. General Forlong answers this question in the negative, for he says, then referring to the serpent Buddhism of Kambodia, that "Fetish worship was the *first* worship, and to a great extent is still the *real* faith of the ignorant, especially about these parts." He finds that nearly one quarter of the world yet deifies, or at least reverences, sticks and stones, rams' horns and charms, a practice not unknown even to later faiths. The fundamental belief which furnishes the key to those phenomena, as well as to the animal-worship which is so closely associated with one or other of the great faith streams, should not be lost sight of. Jacob Grimm pointed out, in his "Teutonic Mythology,"[1] that all nature was thought of by the heathen Germans as living. Gods and men transformed themselves into trees, plants, or beasts; spirits and elements attained animal forms; and therefore we cannot wonder at the heavenly bodies, and even day and night, summer and winter, being actually personified. These ideas lend themselves as well to fetishism as to sun-worship, and all the ancient faiths alike may justly, therefore, be regarded as phases of one universal nature-worship. Mankind prays only for that which is thought good,

[1] Eng. Trans., vol. ii., p. 647.

and if one man seeks to obtain his desire through the agency of a stick or a stone, and another through a serpent or planetary god, the difference between them is purely objective. The prayers which were offered to the Vedic gods would be equally appropriate in the mouth of a native of Western Africa. They had relation simply to temporal needs, and were, says Mr. Talboys Wheeler,[1] for plenty of rain, abundant harvests, and prolific cattle, for bodily vigour, long life, numerous offspring, and protection against all foes and robbers. Moreover, the observances of the more advanced faiths have little practical difference from the fetishist. All alike have for their object the compelling the good countenance, or counteracting the evil designs, of the gods or spirits, and the real difference is to be sought in the symbols under which they are represented. Thus the Vedic Aryans regarded their deified abstractions as personified with human wants, and invoked them with rites which " may have formed an accompaniment to every meal, and may have been regarded almost as a part of the cooking." Mr. Wheeler adds[2] that " Sometimes a deity is supposed to be attracted by the grateful sound of the stone and mortar by which the *soma* juice was expressed from the plant, or by the musical noise of the churning-sticks by which the wine was apparently stirred up and mixed with curds ; and the eager invokers implore the god not to turn aside to the dwelling of any other worshipper, but to come to them only, and drink the libation which they had prepared, and reserve for them all his favours and benefits."

[1] " The History of India," vol. i., p. 8.   [2] Ditto, p. 13.

CHAPTER II.

PHALLISM IN ANCIENT RELIGIONS.

DR. FABER, when treating of the ancient mysteries in opposition to Bishop Warburton's views of their original purity, says : " Long before the time of Apuleius, whom he (Warburton) would describe as quitting the impure orgies of the Syrian Goddess for the blameless initiations of Isis, did the Phallic processions, if we may credit Herodotus and Diodorus, form a most conspicuous and essential part, not only of the mysteries in general, but of these identical Isiac or Osiric mysteries in particular. Nor is there any reason to doubt their accuracy on this point. The same detestable rites prevailed in Palestine among the votaries of Siton, or Adonis, or Baal-Peor, long before the exodus of Israel from Egypt. The same also, anterior at least to the days of Herodotus, in Babylonia, Cyprus, and Lydia. The same likewise from the most remote antiquity in the mountains of Armenia, among the worshippers of the great mother Anais; and the same, from the very first institution of their theological system, as we may fairly argue from the uniform general establishment of this peculiar superstition, among the Celtic Druids both of Britain and of Ireland. Nor do we find such orgies less prevalent in Hindostan. Every part of the theology of that country . . . . . is inseparably blended with them, and replete with allusions to their fictitious origin."[1] It will not be necessary for me to give details of the rites by which the Phallic superstition is distinguished, as they may be found in the works of Dulaure,[2] Richard Payne Knight,[3] and many other writers. I shall refer to them, therefore, only so far as may be required for the due understanding of the subject to be considered, the influence of the Phallic idea in the religions of antiquity. The first step in the inquiry is to ascertain the origin of the superstition in question. Faber ingeniously referred to a primitive universal belief in a Great Father, the curious connection seen to exist between nearly all non-Christian mythologies, and he saw in Phallic worship a degradation of this belief. Such an explanation as this, however, is not satisfactory, since not only does it require the assumption of a primitive divine revelation, but proof is still wanting that all peoples have, or ever had, any such notion of a great parent of mankind as that supposed to have been revealed. And yet there is a valuable germ of truth in this hypothesis. The Phallic superstition is founded essentially in the family idea. Captain Richard Burton recognised this truth when he asserted that "amongst all barbarians whose primal want is progeny, we observe a greater or less development of the Phallic worship."[4] This view, however, is imperfect.

---

[1] "Origin of Pagan Idolatry," vol. iii., p. 117.

[2] "Histoire abrégée de differens Cultes," vol. ii.

[3] "A Discourse on the Worship of Priapus."

[4] "Memoirs of the Anthropological Society of London," vol. i., p. 320.

There must have been something more than a mere
desire for progeny to lead primitive man to view the
generative process with the peculiar feelings embodied
in this superstition. We are, in fact, here taken to
the root of all religions—awe at the mysterious and
unknown. That which the uncultured mind cannot
understand is viewed with dread or veneration, as it
may be, and the object presenting the mysterious
phenomenon may itself be worshipped as a fetish or
the residence of a presiding spirit. But there is
nothing more mysterious than the phenomena of
generation, and nothing more important than the final
result of the generative act. Reflection on this result
would naturally cause that which led to it to be
invested with a certain degree of superstitious significance. The feeling generated would have a double
object, as it had a double origin—wonder at the phenomenon itself and a perception of the value of its
consequences. The former, which is the most simple,
would lead to a veneration for the organs whose
operation conduced to the phenomena, hence the
superstitious practices connected with the phallus and
the yoni among primitive peoples. In this, moreover,
we have the explanation of numerous curious facts
observed among Eastern nations. Such is the respect
shown by women for the generative organ of der-
vishes and fakirs. Such also is the Semitic custom
referred to in the Hebrew Scriptures as the putting of
the hand under the thigh, which is explained by the
Talmudists to be the touching of that part of the body
which is sealed and made holy by circumcision ; a
custom which was, up to a recent date, still in use

among the Arabs as the most solemn guarantee of truthfulness.[1]

The second phase of the Phallic superstition is that which arises from a perception of the value of the consequences of the act of generation. The distinction between this and the preceding phase is that, while the one has relation to the organs engaged, the other refers more particularly to the chief agent. Thus the father of the family is venerated as the generator, and his authority is founded altogether on the act and consequences of generation. We thus see the fundamental importance, as well as the Phallic origin, of the family idea. From this has sprung the social organisation of all primitive peoples. An instance in point may be derived from Mr. Hunter's account of the Santals of Bengal. He says that the classification of this interesting people among themselves depends "not upon social rank or occupation, but upon the family basis." This is shown by the character of the six great ceremonies in a Santal's life, which are, "admission into the family; admission into the tribe; admission into the race; union of his own tribe with another by marriage; formal dismission from the living race by incremation; lastly, a reunion with the departed fathers."[2] We may judge from this of the character of certain customs which are widespread among primitive peoples, and the Phallic origin of which has long since been lost sight of. The value set on the results of the generative act would naturally make the arrival at the age of puberty

---

[1] Dulaure, *op. cit.*, vol. ii., 219.
[2] "Rural Bengal," p. 203.

an event of peculiar significance. Hence we find various ceremonies performed among primitive, and even among civilised peoples, at this period of life. Often when the youth arrives at manhood other rites are performed to mark the significance of the event. Marriage, too, derives an importance which it would not otherwise possess. Thus, among many peoples, it is attended with certain ceremonies denoting its object, or at least marking it as an event of peculiar significance in the life of the individual or even in the history of the tribe. The marriage ceremonial is especially fitted for the use of Phallic rites or symbolism, the former among semi-civilised peoples often being simply the act of consummation itself, which appears to be looked on as part of the ceremony. The symbolism we have ourselves retained to the present day in the wedding-ring, which had undoubtedly a Phallic origin, if, as appears probable, it originated in the Samothracian mysteries.[1] Nor does the influence of the Phallic idea end with life. The veneration entertained for the father of the family, as the "generator," led in time to peculiar care being taken of the bodies of the dead, and finally to the worship of ancestors, which, under one form or another, distinguished all the civilised nations of antiquity, as it does even now most of the peoples of the heathen world.

There is one Phallic rite which, from its wide range, is of peculiar importance. I refer to circumcision. The origin of this custom has not yet, so far as I am

[1] Ennemoser's "History of Magic" (Bohn), vol. ii., p. 33.

aware, been satisfactorily explained. The idea that, under certain climatic conditions, circumcision is necessary for cleanliness and comfort,[1] does not appear to be well founded, as the custom is not universal, even within the tropics. Nor is the reason given by Captain Richard Burton, in his "Notes connected with the Dahoman," for both circumcision and excision, perfectly satisfactory. The real origin of these customs has been forgotten by all peoples practising them, and therefore they have ceased to have their primitive significance. That circumcision at least had a superstitious origin may be inferred from the traditional history of the Jews. The old Hebrew writers, persistent in their idea that they were a peculiar people, chosen by God for a special purpose, asserted that this rite was instituted by Jehovah as a sign of the covenant between Him and Abraham. Although we cannot doubt that this rite was practised by the Egyptians and Phœnicians[2] long before the birth of Abraham, yet two points connected with the Hebrew tradition are noticeable. These are, the religious significance of the act of circumcision—it is the sign of a covenant between God and man—and its performance by the head of the family. These two things are indeed intimately connected; since, in the patriarchal age, the father was always the priest of the family, the officer of the sacrifices. We have it on the authority of the Veda that this was the case

---

[1] Dr. Fernand Castelain, in his work, "La Circoncision est-elle utile?" comes to the conclusion (p. 14) that it is both hygienic and moral. The value of circumcision may be admitted, without ascribing its origin to a sanitary motive.

[2] Herodotus, "Euterpe," sec. 104.

also among the primitive Aryan people.[1]   Abraham,
therefore, as the father and priest of the family, performed the religious ceremony of circumcision on the
males of his household.

Circumcision, in its inception, is a purely Phallic
rite,[2] having for its aim the marking of that which
from its associations is viewed with peculiar veneration, and it connects the two phases of this superstition,
which have for their objects respectively the *instrument*
of generation and the *agent*. We are thus brought back
to the consideration of the simplest form of Phallic
worship, that which has for its object the generative
organs, viewed as the mysterious instruments in the
realisation of that keen desire for children which
distinguishes all primitive peoples. This feeling is so
nearly universal that it is a matter of surprise to find
the act by which it is expressed stigmatised as sinful.
Yet such is the case, although the incidents in which
the fact is embodied are so veiled in figure that their
true meaning has long been forgotten. Clemens
Alexandrinus tells us that "the bacchanals hold their
orgies in honour of the frenzied Bacchus, celebrating
their sacred frenzy by the eating of raw flesh, and go
through the distribution of the parts of butchered
victims, crowned with snakes, shrieking out the name

[1] De Coulanges, "La Cité antique," 6th ed., pp. 36, 100.

[2] M. Elie Reclus, in a remarkable paper presented in 1879 to
the Anthropological Institute, affirms (p. 16, *et seq.*) that circumcision is derived from the custom of emasculation practised on
captives, which is equivalent to death, and that it is a substitute
for human sacrifices. He admits, however (p. 32), that, among
the Semites at least, circumcision was a "consecration of the
sexual organ to a Phallic divinity."

of that Eva by whom error came into the world."
He adds that "the symbol of the Bacchic orgies is a
consecrated serpent," and that, "according to the
strict interpretation of the Hebrew term, the name
Hevia, aspirated, signifies a *female serpent*."[1] We have
here a reference to the supposed fall of man from
pristine "innocence," Eve and the serpent being very
significantly introduced in close conjunction, and
indeed becoming in some sense identified with each
other. In fact, the Arabic word for serpent, *hayyat*,
may be said also to mean "life," and in this sense the
legendary, first human mother is called Eve or *Chevvah*,
in Arabic *hawwa*. In its relations, as an asserted fact,
the question of the fall has an important bearing on
the subject before us. Quite irrespective of the im-
possibility of accepting the Mosaic Cosmogony as a
divinely-inspired account of the origin of the world
and man—a cosmogony which, with those of all other
Semitic peoples, has a purely "Phallic" basis[2]—the
whole transaction said to have taken place in the
Garden of Eden is fraught with difficulties on the
received interpretation. The very idea on which it is
founded—the placing by God in the way of Eve of a
temptation which he knew she could not resist—is
sufficient to throw discredit on the ordinary reading
of the narrative. The effect, indeed, that was to
follow the eating of the forbidden fruit appears to an
ordinary mind to furnish the most praiseworthy motive

---

[1] "Ante-Nicene Christian Library," vol. iv. (Clement of
Alexandria), p. 27.

[2] The Hebrew word *bara* translated "created" can be used
in a different sense.

for not obeying the commandment to abstain. That the "eating of the forbidden fruit" was simply a figurative mode of expressing the performance of the act necessary to the perpetuation of the human race—an act which in its origin was thought to be the source of all evil—is evident from the consequences which followed and from the curse entailed.[1] As to the curse inflicted on Eve, it has always been a stumbling block in the way of commentators. For what connection is there between the eating of a fruit and sorrow in bringing forth children? The meaning is evident, however, when we know that conception and child-bearing were the direct consequences of the act forbidden. How far this meaning was intended by the compiler of the Mosaic books we shall see further on.

The central feature of the Mosaic legend of the "fall" is the reference to the tree of knowledge or wisdom. It is now generally supposed that the forbidden fruit was a kind of *citrus*,[2] but certain facts connected with *aborolatry* clearly show this opinion to be erroneous. Among peoples in the most opposite regions of the world various species of the fig-tree are considered sacred. In almost every part of Africa the *banyan* is viewed with a special veneration. Livingstone noticed this among the tribes on the Zambesi and the Shire,[3] and he says that the banyan is looked upon with veneration all the way from the

[1] "Jashar," by Dr. Donaldson, 2nd ed. (1860), p. 45, *et seq.*
[2] Smith's "Dictionary of the Bible"—Art., "Apple-tree." Inman's "Ancient Faiths," vol. i., p. 274.
[3] "Zambesi and its Tribes," p. 188.

Barotse to Loanda, and thought to be a preservative from evil.[1] Du Chaillu states that in almost every Ishogo and Ashango village he visited in Western Equatorial Africa there was a large *ficus* "standing about the middle of the main street, and near the mbuiti or idol-house of the village." The tree is sacred, and if it dies the village is at once abandoned.[2] Captain Tuckey found the same thing on the Congo, where he says the *ficus religiosa* is considered sacred.[3] Again, according to Caillié, at Mouriosso, in Western Central Africa, the market was held under a tree, which, from his description, must have been the banyan, and he noticed the same thing in other towns.[4] It is evident from Dr. Barth's "Travels in Central Africa," that superstitious regard for certain trees is found throughout the whole of the region he traversed, and among some tribes the fig-tree occupies this position. Thus, he says, "the sacred grove of the village of Isge was formed by magnificent trees, mostly of the *ficus* tribe."[5] Nor is this superstition unknown among other dark races of the Southern Hemisphere. A species of the fig-tree is planted by the New Zealanders close to the temples of their gods. The superstition is traceable, according to Mr. Earle, even among the aborigines of Northern Australia, certain peculiar notions connected with the banyan tree being common to the inhabitants of the

---

[1] " Missionary Travels in South Africa," p. 495.
[2] " Journey to Ashango Land," p. 295.
[3] " River Zaire," p. 181.
[4] " Travels through Central Africa," p. 394, 407.
[5] " Travels," vol. ii., p. 391 ; and vol. iii., p. 665.

Coburg Peninsula and of the Indian Islands.[1] Mr. Marsden met with this superstition among the Sumatrans, and we learn from Mr. Wallace that in one of the towns of Eastern Java the market is held under the branches of a tree allied to the sacred fig-tree.[2] If we turn to India, we find that while the banyan is venerated by the Brahmans, it is the bo-tree which is held sacred by many of the followers of Gautama Buddha. This may be because, under the name of the *Pilpel,* it was the peculiar tree of the first recorded Buddha, of whom Gautama was supposed by his disciples to be an incarnation. Both of these trees belong to the genus *ficus,* and it is curious that, although probably in consequence of Semitic influence, the *ficus sycamorus* was the sacred tree in ancient Egypt, of which it was the symbol, its place appears ultimately to have been taken by the banyan (*ficus indica*),[3] so highly venerated in other parts of Africa. Now, what is the explanation of the peculiar character ascribed to these trees by peoples who must, on any hypothesis, have been separated for thousands of years? The bo-tree of the Buddhists itself derived a more sacred character from its encircling the palm—the Palmyra Palm being the *kalpa-tree,* or " tree of life," of the Hindu paradise.[4] The Buddhists term this connection "the bo-tree united in marriage with the palm." The Phallic significance of the palm is well known, and in its connection with the bo-tree we have the perfect idea of

<hr>

[1] Journal of R. Geog. Society, vol. xvi., p. 240.
[2] " The Malyan Archipelago," vol. i., p. 158.
[3] Wilkinson, vol. iv., p. 260, 313.
[4] Tennent's " Ceylon," vol. ii., p. 520.

generative activity, the combining of the male and female organs, a combination intended by the Hebrew legend when it speaks of the tree of life, and also of " the knowledge of good and evil."[1] "The palm-tree," says Dr. Inman, " is figured on ancient coins alone, or associated with some feminine emblem. It typified the male creator, who was represented as an upright stone, a pillar, a round tower, a tree stump, an oak-tree, a pine-tree, a maypole, a spire, an obelisk, a minaret, and the like."[2] As we have just seen, the Palmyra Palm is the *kalpa-tree,* or the "tree of life" of the Hindu paradise, and this was not the only kind of tree with which the idea of life was thus associated.

In the mythologies of more northern peoples the place of the palm is supplied by the more stately, if less upright, oak. The patriarch Jacob hid the idols of his household under the oak near Shechem,[3] and his descendants afterwards made burnt offerings under every thick oak.[4] Among the Greeks and Romans this tree was sacred to Zeus, or Jupiter, the Father of Gods and men. With the Russians, the Prussians, and the Germans, the oak was equally sacred. The sacred oak was the form under which the Druids worshipped the Supreme Being *Hœsus,* or Mighty. According to Davies,[5] it was symbolised by the

[1] M. Littré sees in the two trees of Genesis only the *soma,* which was introduced into the Brahmanical Sacrifices, which, with the Iranians, was transformed into *two* mystic trees.— *La Philosophie Positive,* 3rd vol., p. 341, *et seq.*

[2] *Op. cit.,* vol. ii., p. 448.

[3] Gen., xxxv. 4.   [4] Ezek., vi. 13.

[5] "Celtic Researches," p. 446.

letter D, which forms the consonantal sound of the word denoting God in many languages, as it does of the name of the mythical father *Ad*, of the Adamic stock of mankind.   In Teutonic mythology the great oak forms the roof-tree of the Volsung's hall, spreading its branches far and wide in the upper air, being the counterpart, says Mr. Cox, of the mighty Yggdrasil.[1] This is the gigantic ash-tree, whose branches embrace the whole world, and which is thought to be only another form of the colossal Irminsul.   Mr. Cox observes on this : " The tree and pillar are thus alike seen in the columns, whether of Herakles or of Roland ; while the cosmogonic character of the myth is manifest in the legend of the primeval Askr, the offspring of the ash-tree, of which Virgil, from the characteristic which probably led to its selection, speaks as stretching its roots as far down into earth as its branches soar towards heaven.[2] The name of the Teutonic Askr is also that of the Iranian *Meschia*,[3] and the ash, therefore, must be identified with the tree from which springs the primeval man of the Zarathustrian cosmogony.[4] So Sigmund of the Volsung Tale is drawn from the trunk of a poplar tree,[5] which thus occupies the same position as the ash and

---

[1] " Aryan Mythology," vol. i., p. 274*n*.

[2] Ditto, vol. ii., p. 19.

[3] See Grimm's " Teutonic Mythology," p. 571, *et seq*.

[4] Cox, *op. cit.*, vol. i., p. 274*n*.

[5] According to Gen., ii. 23, the name *isha* (woman) was bestowed by Adam on the first woman, because she was taken out of man (*Ish*)—terms which were used in reference to man and wife. This is shown by the subsequent reference to marriage (v. 24). See Smith's " Dictionary of the Bible "—Art. " Marriage."

the oak as a "tree of life." The poplar was, indeed, a sacred tree among many nations of antiquity. This may, doubtless, be explained by reference to its "habit," which much resembles that of the sacred Indian fig-tree, with which the trembling movement, as well as the shape, of its leaves have caused it to be thus compared.

That the ideas symbolised by the various sacred trees of antiquity originated, however, with the fig-tree is extremely probable. No other tree has been so widely venerated as this. The sycamore (*ficus sycamorus*) was sacred to Netpe, the mother of Osiris, whose statue was generally made of its wood. In relation to that subject, Sir Gardner Wilkinson says :[1] " The Athenians had a holy fig-tree, which grew on the ' sacred road,' where, during the celebration of the Eleusinian mysteries, the procession which went from Athens to Eleusis halted. This was on the sixth day of the ceremony, called Jacchus, in honour of the son of Jupiter and Ceres, who accompanied his mother in search of Prosperine; but the fig-tree of Athens does not appear to have been borrowed from the sycamore of Egypt, unless it were in consequence of its connection with the mother of Osiris and Isis, whom they supposed to correspond to Ceres and Bacchus."[2] According to Plutarch, a basket of figs formed one of the chief things carried in the processions in honour of Bacchus, and the sacred phallus, like the statue of Priapus, appears to have been generally made of the wood of the fig-tree.[3] These

---

[1] " Ancient Egyptians," vol. iv., p. 313.   [2] Ditto, p. 313.

[3] Dulaure's " Histoire abregée de differens Cultes," vol. ii., p. 169.

facts well show the nature of the ideas which had come to be connected with that tree. To what has been already said may, however, be added the testimony of a French writer, who, after speaking of the *lotus* as one of the many symbols anciently used to represent the productive forces of nature, continues: " Il faut y joindre, pour le règne végétal, le figuier indien, ou l'arbre des Banians, le figuier sacré ou religieux (ficus indica, bengalensis, ficus religiosa, &c.), *vata*, *aswatha*, *pipala*, et bien d'autres, idéalisés de bonne heure, dans le mythologie des Hindous, sous la figure de l'arbre de vie, arbre immense, colonne de feu, énorme et orgueilleux phallus, l'abord unique, mais depuis devisé et dispersé, et qui n'est peut-être pas sans rapport, soit avec l'arbre de la connaissance du bien et du mal, soit avec d'autres symboles non moins fameux."[1]

That the *ficus* was the symbolical tree "in the midst of the garden" of the Hebrew legend of the fall is extremely probable. That notion would seem, indeed, to be required by reference to the fig leaves[2] as the covering used by Adam and Eve when, after eating the forbidden fruit, they found themselves to be naked. The fig-tree, moreover, meets the difficulty in distinguishing between the tree of life and the tree of knowledge. These, according to the opinion above expressed, as to the meaning of the "fall," would represent the male and female principles, as do the bo-tree and palm, "united in marriage,"

---

[1] See Guigniaut's " Religions de l'Antiquité" (1825), vol. i., p. 149.

[2] See on this, Inman, *op, cit.*, vol. ii., p. 462.

of the Buddhists, the palm deriving more sacredness from being encircled by the ficus. Probably, however, the double symbol was of later introduction. The banyan of itself would be sufficient to represent the dual idea, when to the primitive one of "knowledge" was added that of "life." The stately trunk would answer to the "tree of life," while its fruit was the symbol of that which was more especially affected by the act of disobedience. This was the eating of the fruit, which, as conveying the forbidden wisdom, is evidently the essential feature of the legend, and the *fig* had anciently just that symbolical meaning which would be required for the purpose.[1] Throughout the East, from the earliest historical period, the fruit of the fig-tree was the emblem of virginity. Dr. Inman says: "The fruit of the tree resembles in shape the virgin uterus; with its stem attached, it symbolises the *sistrum* of Isis. Its form led to the idea that it would promote fertility. To this day, in Oriental countries, the hidden meaning of the fig is almost as well known as its commercial value."[2]

That we have in the Mosaic account of the "fall" a Phallic legend, is evident also from the introduction of the serpent on the scene, and the position it takes as the inciting cause of the sinful act. We are here reminded of the passage already quoted from Clemens Alexandrinus, who tells us that the serpent was the special symbol of the worship of Bacchus. Now this animal holds a very curious place in the religions

[1] The Hindu legend expressly mentions the fig. See *infrà*.

[2] *Op. cit.*, vol. i., p. 108, 527. In the East the pomegranate symbolises the full womb.

of the civilised peoples of antiquity. Although, in consequence of the influence of later thought, it came to be treated as the personification of evil, and as such appears in the Hebrew legend of the fall, yet originally the serpent was the special symbol of wisdom and healing. In the latter capacity it appears even in connection with the Exodus from Egypt. It is, however, in its character as a symbol of wisdom that it more especially claims our attention, although these ideas are intimately connected—the power of healing being merely a phase of wisdom. From the earliest times of which we have any historical notice the serpent has been connected with the gods of wisdom. This animal was the especial symbol of *Thoth* or *Taaut*, a primeval deity of Syro-Egyptian mythology,[1] and of all those gods, such as *Hermes* and *Seth*, who can be connected with him. This is true also of the 3rd member of the Chaldean triad, *Héa* or *Hoa*. According to Sir Henry Rawlinson, the most important titles of this deity refer "to his functions as the source of all knowledge and science." Not only is he "the intelligent fish," but his name may be read as signifying both "life" and a "serpent," and he may be considered as "figured by the great serpent which occupies so conspicuous a place among the symbols of the gods on the black stones recording Babylonian benefactions."[2] The serpent was also the symbol of the Egyptian *Kneph*, who resembled the *Sophia* of the Gnostics, the divine wisdom. This animal, moreover, was the *Agatho-*

---

[1] See Bunsen's "Egypt," vol. iv., p. 225, 255, 288.
[2] "History of Herodotus," vol. i., p. 600.

dæmon of the religions of antiquity—the giver of happiness and good fortune.[1] It was in these capacities, rather than as having a Phallic significance, that the serpent was associated with the sun-gods, the Chaldean *Bel*, the Grecian *Apollo*, and the Semitic *Seth.*

But whence originated the idea of the wisdom of the serpent which led to its connection with the legend of the "fall?" This may, perhaps, be explained by other facts, which show also the nature of the wisdom here intended. Thus, in the annals of the Mexicans, the first woman, whose name was translated by the old Spanish writers, "*the woman of our flesh,*" is always represented as accompanied by a great male serpent. This serpent is the sun-god *Tonacatle-coatl*, the principal deity of the Mexican Pantheon, while the goddess-mother of primitive man is called *Cihua-Cohuatl*, which signifies "*woman of the serpent.*"[2] According to this legend, which agrees with that of other American tribes, a serpent must have been the father of the human race. This notion can be explained only on the supposition that the serpent was thought to have had at one time a human form. In the Hebrew legend the tempter speaks, and " the old serpent having two feet," of Persian mythology, is none other than the evil spirit Ahriman him-

---

[1] Wilkinson's "Ancient Egyptians," vol. iv., p. 412, 413; and King's "Gnostics," p. 31. See also Bryant's "Ancient Mythology," vol. iv., p. 201. The last-named work contains most curious information as to the extension of serpent-worship.

[2] See "The Serpent Symbol in America," by E. G. Squier, M.A.—"American Archæological Researches," No. 1 (1851), p. 161, *et seq.*; "Palenqué," by M. de Waldeck and M. Brasseur de Bourbourg (1866), p. 48.

self.[1]   The fact is that the serpent was only a symbol, or at most an embodiment of the spirit which it represented, as we see from the belief of several African and American tribes, which probably preserves the primitive form of this superstition. Serpents are looked upon by these peoples as embodiments of their departed ancestors,[2] and an analogous notion is entertained by various Hindoo tribes. No doubt the noiseless movement and the activity of the serpent, combined with its peculiar gaze and marvellous power of fascination, led to its being viewed as a spirit embodiment, and hence also as the possessor of wisdom.[3]   In the spirit character ascribed to the serpent, we have the explanation of the association of its worship with human sacrifice noted by Mr. Fergusson—this sacrifice being really connected with the worship of ancestors.

It is evident, moreover, that we find here the origin of the idea of evil sometimes associated with the Serpent-God.   The Kafir and the Hindu, although he treats with respect any serpent which may visit his dwelling, yet entertains a suspicion of his visitant.   It may perhaps be the embodiment of an *evil* spirit, or for some reason or other it may desire to injure *him*. Mr. Fergusson states that "the chief characteristic of the serpents throughout the East in all ages seems to

---

[1] Lajard—"Memoires de l'Institut Royal de France" (Acad. des Inscriptions et Belles Lettres), T. xiv., p. 89.

[2] Wood's "Natural History of Man," vol. i., p. 185; also Squier's "Serpent Symbol," p. 222, *et seq.*

[3] I have a strong suspicion that in the primitive shape of the Hebrew legend, as in that of the Mexicans, both the father and mother of the human race had the serpent form.

have been their power over the wind and rain," which
they gave or withheld according to their good or ill-
will towards man.[1]   This notion is curiously confirmed
by the title given by the Egyptians to the Semitic God
Seti or *Seth—Typhon*, which was the name of the
Phœnician Evil principle, and also of a destructive
wind, thus having a curious analogy with the "Ty-
phoon" of the Chinese Seas.[2]   When the notion of a
duality in nature was developed, there would be no
difficulty in applying it to the symbols or embodiments by which the idea of wisdom was represented
in the animal world.   Thus, there came to be not only
good, but also bad serpents, both of which are referred
to in the narrative of the Hebrew Exodus, but still
more clearly in the struggle between the good and the
bad serpents of Persian mythology, which symbolised
Ormuzd or Mithra and the Evil spirit Ahriman.[3]   So
far as I can make out the serpent symbol has not a
direct Phallic reference, nor is its attribute of wisdom
the most essential.   The idea most intimately associated with this animal was that of *life*, not present
merely but continued and probably everlasting.[4]   Thus

---

[1] *Op. cit.*, p. 46.   Rudra, the Vedic form of Siva, the "King
of Serpents," is called the father of the Maruts (winds).   See
infrà as to identification of Siva with Saturn.

[2] The idea of *circularity* appears to be associated with both
these names.   See Bryant, *op. cit.*, vol. iii., p. 164, and vol. ii.,
p. 191, as to derivation of Typhon.

[3] Lajard.   *Op. cit.*, p. 182, "Culte de Mithra," p. 45; also
" Memoire sur l'Hercule Assyrien de M. Raoul-Rochette."

[4] Mr. J. H. Rivett-Carnac suggests that the snake is a
" symbol of the phallus."   He adds, " The sun, the invigorating
power of nature, has ever, I believe, been considered to represent
the same idea, not necessarily obscene, but the great mystery of
nature, the life transmitted from generation to generation, or,

the snake *Bai* was figured as Guardian of the doorways of those chambers of Egyptian Tombs which represented the mansions of heaven.[1] A sacred serpent would seem to have been kept in all the Egyptian temples, and we are told that "many of the subjects, in the tombs of the kings at Thebes, in particular, show the importance it was thought to enjoy in a future state."[2] Crowns, formed of the asp, or sacred *Thermuthis*, were given to sovereigns and divinities, particularly to Isis,[3] and these, no doubt, were intended to symbolise eternal life. Isis was a goddess of life and healing,[4] and the serpent evidently belonged to her in that character, seeing that it was the symbol also of other deities with the like attributes. Thus, on papyri it encircles the figure of Harpocrates,[5] who was identified with Æsculapius; while not only was a great serpent kept alive in the temple of Serapis, but on later monuments this god is represented by a great serpent with or without a human head.[6] Mr. Fergusson, in accordance with his peculiar theory as to the origin of serpent-worship, thinks that this superstition characterised the old Turanian (or let us rather say Akkadian) empire of Chaldea, while tree-worship was more a characteristic of the later Assyrian Empire.[7] This opinion is no

as Professor Stephens puts it, 'life out of death, life everlasting.' "—*Snake Symbol in India* (reprinted from Journal of As. Soc. of Bengal"), 1879, p. 13.

[1] Wilkinson, *op. cit.*, vol. v., p. 65.

[2] Ditto, p. 243.   [3] Ditto, p. 239.

[4] See Ennemoser's "History of Magic" (Bohn), vol. i., p. 253.

[5] Ditto, p. 243.

[6] Guigniaut's "Le Dieu Serapis," p. 19.   [7] *Op. cit.*, p. 12.

doubt correct, and it means really that the older race had that form of faith with which the serpent was always indirectly connected—adoration of the *male* principle of generation, the principal phase of which was probably ancestor-worship; while the latter race adored the *female* principle, symbolised by the sacred tree, the Assyrian " grove." The " *tree* of life," however, undoubtedly had reference to the *male* element, and we may well imagine that originally the *fruit* alone was treated as symbolical of the opposite element.

There is still one important point connected with this legend which requires consideration as throwing light on another very wide-spread superstition. Baron Bunsen says that the nature of the *Kerubim* who were set to keep the way to the tree of life has not yet been satisfactorily explained. He seems to think they have a volcanic reference, although the usual supposition is that they were angels bearing " flaming swords." The latter opinion, however, could only have arisen from the association, in other places, of kerubim with seraphim, who are also popularly supposed to be angelic spirits, but whom Bunsen thinks have reference to flame. All these explanations, however, appear to me to be erroneous. According to one opinion, kerub is compounded of two words, *ke* a particle of resemblance, and *rab*, signifying great, powerful. If this derivation be correct we may safely infer that the *kerub* was simply a representation of the strong deity himself, of whom the flaming sword was also an emblem. This notion is confirmed by the statement of the Jewish Targams that " the glory of God dwelt between the two cherubim at the gate of Eden, just

as it rested upon the two cherubim in the Tabernacle."[1]
It is curious that in the analogous Greek myth of the
Garden of Hesperides, the golden apples were guarded
by a serpent. We have a closer resemblance to the
Hebrew Kerubim in Persian mythology. Delitzsch
says "the kerubs appear here as guards of Paradise,
just as in the Persian legend 99,999—*i.e.*, innumerable
attendants of the Holy One keep watch against the
attempts of Ahriman over the tree Hôm, which contains in itself the power of the resurrection. Much
closer, however, lies the comparison of the winged
lion-and-eagle-formed griffin,[2] which watch the gold-
caves of the Arimaspian metallic mountains, and of
the sometimes more or less hawk-formed, sometimes
only winged and otherwise man-formed-guardians,
upon the Egyptian and Assyrian monuments. The resemblance of the symbols is surprisingly great; and
the comparison of the King of Tyre,[3] to a protecting
kerub with outspread wings, who, stationed on the
holy mountain, walked up and down in the midst of the
stones of fire, justifies us in assuming such a connection."[4]

The real nature and origin of the Hebrew kerub is
apparent on reference to the language used by Ezekiel
in describing his vision of winged creatures. Dr.
Faber shows clearly that these were the same as the
kerubim in the Holy of Holies of the Hebrew temple,

[1] Faber's "Pagan Idolatry," vol. 1, p. 424*n*.

[2] Prof. Max Müller derives cherubim from γρύφες, griffins, the
guardians of the Soma in the Veda and Avesta. "Chips from
a German Workshop," 2nd ed., i. 157.

[3] Ez., c. 28, v. 14-16.

[4] See Colenzo's "Pentateuch" (1865), p. 341.

and he argues, moreover, with great justice, that the latter must have agreed with those who were said to have been stationed before the tree of life in Eden. In fact, the King of Tyre is styled by Ezekiel "the anointed covering kerub of Eden, the garden of God."[1] Now, a curious difference is made by Ezekiel in the two descriptions he gives of the creatures which appeared in his vision. In the one case he describes them as having each four faces—that of a man, that of a lion, that of an ox, and that of an eagle.[2] Subsequently, however, they are described as having each the faces of a *kerub*, of a man, of an eagle, and of a lion.[3] Judging from this discrepancy, the head of a kerub being substituted for that of an ox, it has been suggested that the kerub and the ox are synonymous. Dr. Faber very justly observes on this difficulty, that Ezekiel "would scarcely have called the head of the ox by way of eminence the *head of a kerub*, unless the form of the ox so greatly predominated in the compound form of the kerub as to warrant the entire kerub being familiarly styled *an ox*."[4] This conclusion is the more probable when we consider that in the first vision the creatures are represented with feet like those of a calf.[5] In fact, we have in this vision, as in the *kerubim* of Genesis, animal representations of deity, such as the Persians and other Eastern peoples delighted in, the most prominent being that of the ox—or, rather *bull*, as it would be more properly rendered.

---

[1] See Faber's "Pagan Idolatry," vol. iii., p. 606.
[2] C. i., v. 10.   [3] C. x., v. 14.
[4] *Op. cit.*, vol. i., p. 422.   [5] Ez., c. i., v. 7.

But what was the sacred bull of the religions of antiquity, or rather what its mythological value? Dr. Faber says expressly on this subject: "There is perhaps no part of the Gentile world in which the bull and the cow were not highly reverenced and considered in the light of holy and mysterious symbols."[1] He cites the traditional founder of the Chinese empire, Fohi, as having a son with a bull's head, this personage being also venerated by the Japanese under the title of the "ox-headed prince of heaven." According to Mr. Doolittle, a paper image of a domestic buffalo, as large as life, with smaller images in clay of this animal, are carried in procession at the Great Chinese Festival in honour of spring, while a live buffalo accompanies the procession for some distance.[2] It is curious to find that at the other side of the Europo-Asiatic continent the bull was considered sacred by the Celtic Druids, it being reverenced by the ancient Britons as the symbol of their Great God Hu. Thus also the Kimbri "adored their principal God under the form of a brazen bull;" as the ancient Colchians worshipped brazen-footed bulls which were said to emit fire from their nostrils, which has reference to the sacrifices with which they were propitiated. Dr. Faber says as to the Great Phœnician God, called by the Greek translator of Sanchoniatho Agruerus, from the circumstance of his being an agricultural God, that he "was worshipped by the Syrians and their neighbours the Canaanites, under the titles of *Baal* and *Moloch;* and, as his shrine was drawn by oxen, so he himself was represented by the figure of a man having the head of

[1] *Op. cit.,* vol. i., p. 404.   [2] "Chinese," p. 376.

a bull, and sometimes probably by the simple figure of a bull alone. The Persian *Mithra* is also represented as a bull-god, and it is highly suggestive that in one of the carved grottos near the Campus Marjorum he is figured under the symbol of the phallus surmounted by the head of a bull. Even among the Hebrews themselves the golden calf was, under the authority of Aaron, used as an object of worship, a form of idolatry which was re-established by Jeroboam, if it had ever been abandoned. Dr. Faber, indeed, thinks that the calves worshipped at Samaria were copies of the kerubim in the Temple at Jerusalem. If we turn to peoples kindred to the Hebrews, we find that the Phœnician Adonis was sometimes represented as a horned deity, as were also Dionysos and Bacchus, who were, in fact, merely the names under which Adonis was worshipped in Thrace and Greece. Plutarch says that "the women of Elis were accustomed to invite Bacchus to his temple on the seashore, under the name of 'the heifer-footed divinity,' the illustrious bull, the bull worthy of the highest veneration." Hence in the ceremonies, during the celebration of the mysteries of Bacchus and Dionysos, the bull always took a prominent place, as it did also during the festivals of the allied deity of Egypt—the bull Apis being worshipped as an incarnation of Osiris. In India the bull is still held sacred by the Brahmans, and in Hindu mythology it is connected with both Siva and Menu.[1] A superstitious veneration for this animal is in fact entertained by all pastoral or agricultural peoples who possess it. To seek the explanation

[1] See Faber, *op. cit.*, vol. i., pp. 404-410.

of this curious phenomenon in the traditional remembrance of the kerubic representations of deity which guarded the tree of life would be in the highest degree irrational. These representations were merely copies of symbolical figures, which, like the story of the fall, were borrowed from an Eastern source. The real explanation is found in the fact that the bull was an emblem of the productive force in nature. The Zend word *gaya*, which means "bull," signifies also the "soul" or "life," as the same Arabic word denotes both "life" and a "serpent." A parallel case is that of the Zend word *orouéré*, which means a "tree" as well as "life" or "soul."[1] According to the cosmogany of the Zend-Avesta, Ormuzd, after he had created the heavens and the earth, formed the first being, called by Zoroaster "the primeval bull." This bull was poisoned by Ahriman, but its seed was carried by the soul of the dying animal, represented as an *ized*, to the moon, "where it is continually purified and fecundated by the warmth and light of the sun, to become the germ of all creatures." At the same time the material prototypes of all living things, except perhaps man himself, issued from the body of the bull.[2] This is but a developed form of the ideas which anciently were almost universally associated with this animal, among those peoples who were addicted to sun-worship. There is no doubt, however, that the superstitious veneration for the bull existed, as it still exists, quite independent of the worship of the heavenly

---

[1] Lajard, "Le culte de Mithra," pp. 56, 59.

[2] Lajard, *op. cit.*, p. 50; *infrà*, p. 39.

bodies.[1] The bull, like the goat, must have been a sacred animal in Egypt before it was declared to be an embodiment of the sun-god Osiris. In some sense, indeed, the bull and the serpent, although both of them became associated with the solar deities, were antagonistic. The serpent was symbolical of the *personal* male element, or rather had especial reference to the man,[2] while the bull had relation to *nature* as a whole, and was symbolical of the *general* idea of fecundity. This antagonism was brought to an issue in the struggle between Osiris and Seti (Seth), which ended in the triumph of the god of nature, although it was renewed even during the Exodus, when the golden calf of Osiris or Horus was set up in the Hebrew camp.

The reference made to the serpent, to the tree of wisdom, and to the bull, in the legend of the "fall," sufficiently proves its Phallic character, which was, indeed, recognised in the early Christian church.[3] Judging from the facts above referred to, however, we can hardly doubt that the legend was derived from a foreign source. That it could not be original to the Hebrews may, I think, be proved by several considerations. The position occupied in the legend by the serpent is quite inconsistent with the use of this animal symbol by Moses.[4] Like Satan himself even,

---

[1] This superstition is found among peoples—the Kafirs, for instance—who do not appear to possess any trace of planetary worship.

[2] This is evident from the facts mentioned above, notwithstanding the use of this animal as a symbol of *wisdom*.

[3] In connection with this subject, see St. Jerome, in his letter on " Virginity" to Eustachia.

[4] The turning of Aaron's rod into a serpent had, no doubt, a reference to the idea of *wisdom* associated with that animal.

as the Rev. Dunbar Heath has shown,[1] the serpent had not, indeed, a wholly evil character among the early Hebrews. In the second place, the condemnation of the act of generation was directly contrary to the central idea of patriarchal history. The promise to Abraham was that he should have seed " numerous as the stars of heaven for multitude," and to support this notion the descent of Abraham is traced up to the first created man, who is commanded to increase and multiply.

The legend of the fall is not unknown to Hindu mythology, but here the subject of the temptation is the divine Brahma, who, however, is not only mankind collectively, but a man individually.[2] In human shape he is Sivayambhuva, and to try this progenitor of mankind, Siva, as the Supreme Being, " drops from heaven a blossom of the sacred *vata*, or Indian fig—a tree which has been always venerated by the natives on account of its gigantic size and grateful shadows, and invested alike by Brahman and by Buddhist with mysterious significations, as the tree of knowledge or intelligence (*bodhidruma*).[3] Captivated by the beauty of the blossom, the first man (Brahma) is determined to possess it. He imagines that it will entitle him to occupy the place of the Immortal, and hold converse with the Infinite; and on gathering up the blossom,[4]

---

[1] " The Fallen Angels" (1857).

[2] Moor's " Hindu Pantheon," p. 101.

[3] The Bo-tree. See *suprà*, p. 18.

[4] Probably the *fruit* is really intended. Higgins refers to " a peculiar property which the fig has of producing its fruit from its flowers, contained within its own bosom, and concealed from profane eyes," as a reason why the leaves of the fig-tree were selected by Adam and Eve to cover their nakedness. *Anacalypsis*, vol. ii., p. 253.

he at once becomes intoxicated by this fancy, and believes himself immortal and divine. But ere the flush of exultation has subsided, God Himself appears to him in terrible majesty; and the astonished culprit, stricken by the curse of heaven, is banished far from Brahmapattana, and consigned to an abyss of misery and degradation. From this, however, adds the story, an escape is rendered possible on the expiration of some weary term of suffering and of penance. And the parallelism which it presents to sacred history is well-nigh completed when the legend tells us further that woman, his own wife, whose being was derived from his, had instigated the ambitious hopes which led to their expulsion, and entailed so many ills on their posterity."[1] That parallelism cannot well be the result of mere coincidence, and the reference to the fig-tree in the Hindu legend not only renders it highly probable that this was the tree of knowledge[2] of Hebrew legend, but confirms, by the symbolical ideas connected with it, the explanation of the nature of the "fall" given in the preceding pages. The real meaning of the legend was well understood by the Gnostics and Manicheans, and those Christian Fathers who were brought into contact with Eastern ideas through them.[3]

The Persians, who were indebted to the Chaldeans

---

[1] Hardwicke's "Christ and other Masters," vol. i., p. 305-6.

[2] Mr. Hardwicke states that the sacred Indian fig is endowed by the Brahmans and Buddhists with mysterious significance, as the tree of knowledge or intelligence.

[3] See Beausobre's curious and learned work, "Histoire de Manichée et du Manichéisme," Liv. vii., ch. iii.; "Gibbon's Fall and Decline of the Roman Empire," vol. ii., p. 186.

for many of their religious ideas, possessed the story of the fall in a form agreeing more closely with that which may have been the original of the Hebrew legend. According to the *Boundehesch*, one of the sacred books of the Parsees, a tree gave birth to the primeval man *Meschia*. The body of this androgynous being afterwards became divided, one part being male and the other female—*Meschia* and *Meschiana*,[1] as the man and woman were called—were at first pure and holy, but seduced by Ahriman, who had metamorphosed himself into a serpent, they rendered to the Prince of Darkness the worship which was due only to Ormuzd, the God of Light. Meschia and Meschiana thus lost their primitive purity, which neither they nor their descendants could recover without the assistance of Mithra, the god who presided at the mysteries or at the initiations—that is to say, at the way of rehabilitation which is opened before those who seek earnestly the salvation of their souls.[2] At the instigation of Ahriman, the man and woman had, for the first time, committed, in thought, word, and deed, the carnal sin, and thus tainted with original sin all their descendants.[3] Lajard, referring to this legend, adds in a note: "Le triple caractère que pre-sente ici le péché originel est très nettement indiqué dans le passage cité du Boundehesch. Il y est accompagné de détails que font de ce passage un des morceaux les plus curieux de ce traité. Quelques-uns

---

[1] As already suggested, these may be the *ish* and *isha* of Genesis.

[2] Lajard, "Le culte de Mithra," p. 52.

[3] Ditto, p. 60.

de ces détails . . . . rattache à ce même mot (serpent) ou à sa racine la dénomination des parties sexuelles de la homme et de la femme." The Persian account of the fall and its consequences agrees so closely with the Hebrew story when stripped of its figurative language that we cannot doubt that they refer to the same legend,[1] and the use of figurative language in the latter may well lead us to believe that it was of later date than the former.[2] In Ahriman, who was known to Persian teaching as "the old serpent having two feet," we evidently have the origin of the speaking serpent of Genesis, while in "the seed of the woman who shall bruise the serpent's head," the follower of Zarathustra would have seen a reference to Mithra, just as the Christian finds there a prophecy of Christ. Even the antagonism between the Cherubim and the Serpent can be found in Persian teaching, for it was to the malignant action of the Serpent Az that the death, not only of the first man, but of the "primeval bull," was due.[3] The latter was formed by Ormuzd after the creation of the heavens and the earth, and that from which proceeded the material prototypes of all the beings "who live in the water, on the earth, and in the air."[4]

[1] This is shown by Mr. Gerald Massey in his remarkable work, "The Natural Genesis," and particularly the chapter entitled "Typology of the Fall in Heaven and on Earth."

[2] Lajard, *op. cit.*, p. 49.

[3] "Ormazd et Ahriman," by James Darmesteter, pp. 154, 159.

[4] It may be objected that the "Boundehesch," which gives the above details, is comparatively a modern work. It must be noted, however, that the destruction of purity in the world by the serpent *Dahâka* is mentioned in the 9th Yaçna, v. 27, which is much earlier, and that Dr. Haug supposes the "Boundehesch" to have had a Zend original ("Essays on the Sacred Language,

It is very probable, however, that when the legend was appropriated by the compiler of the Hebrew Scriptures it had a moral significance as well as a merely figurative sense. The legend is divisible into two parts—the first of which is a mere statement of the imparting of wisdom by the serpent and by the eating of the fruit of a certain tree, these ideas being synonymous, or at least consistent, as appears by the attributes of the Chaldean *Héa*.[1] The nature of this wisdom may be found in the rites of the Hindu *Sacti Puja*.[2] The second part of the legend, which is probably of much later date, is the condemnation of the act referred to, as being in itself evil and as leading to misery, and even to death itself. The origin of this later notion must be sought in the esoteric doctrine taught in the mysteries of Mithra, the fundamental idea of which was the descent of the soul to earth and its re-ascent to the celestial abodes after it had overcome the temptations and debasing influences

&c., of the Parsees," p. 29). Windischmann, also, says that " a closer study of this remarkable and venerable book, and comparing it with the original text preserved to us, will induce us to form a much more favourable opinion of its antiquity and contents." (" Zoroastrische Studien," p. 282.) The opinion of this latter writer is that, notwithstanding the striking resemblance between the narrative of the fall of man contained in the " Boundehesch" and that in Genesis, the former is original, although inferior in simplicity to the Hebrew tradition (*idem*, p. 212). The narratives are so much alike, however, that they can hardly have had independent origins, and the very simplicity of the latter is a very strong argument against its priority.

[1] See *suprà*, p. 24.

[2] Memoirs of the Anthropological Society of London, vol. ii., p. 264, *et seq.*, and compare with the Gnostic personification of " Truth," for which see King's " Agnostics and their Remains," p. 39.

of the material life.[1] Lajard shows that these mysteries were really taken from the secret worship of the
Chaldean *Mylitta,* but the reference to " the seed of
the woman who shall bruise the serpent's head," is
too Mithraic for us to seek for an earlier origin for
the special form of the Hebrew myth. The object
of the myth evidently was to explain the origin of
death,[2] from which man was to be delivered by a
coming Saviour, and the whole idea is strictly
Mithraic, the Persian deity himself being a Saviour
God.[3] The importance attached to *virginity* by the
early Christians sprang from the same source. The
Avesta is full of reference to " purity " of life, and
there is reason to believe that in the secret initiations
the followers of Mithra were taught to regard marriage
itself as impure.[4]

The religious ideas which found expression in the
legend of the fall were undoubtedly of late development,[5] although derived from still earlier phases of religious thought. The simple worship in symbol of the
organs of generation, and of the ancestral head of the
family, prompted by the desire for offspring and the
veneration for him who produced it, was extended to
the generative force in nature. The bull which, as we

---

[1] Lajard, *op. cit.,* p. 96.

[2] Jehovah threatens *death,* but the Serpent impliedly promises
life, the former having relation to the *individual,* the latter to
the *race.*

[3] Lajard, *op. cit.,* p. 60, *note.*

[4] Some of the Essenes, who appear to have had connection
with Mithraism, taught this doctrine.

[5] It is well known to Biblical writers that this legend formed
no part of the earlier Mosaic narrative.

have seen, symbolised this force, was not restricted to earth, but was in course of time transferred to the heavens, and as one of the constellations was thought to have a peculiar relation to certain of the planetary bodies. This astral phase of the Phallic superstition was not unknown to the Mosaic religion. A still earlier form of this superstition was, however, known to the Hebrews, probably forming a link between the worship of the symbol of personal generative power and that of the heavenly phallus; as the worship of the bull connected the veneration for the human generator with that for the universal father. One of the primeval gods of antiquity was *Hermes*, the Syro-Egyptian *Thoth,* and the Roman *Mercury.* Kircher identifies him also with the god *Terminus.* This is doubtless true, as Hermes was a god of boundaries, and appears, as Dulaure has well shown, to have presided over the national frontiers. The meaning of the word "Thoth"—*erecting*—associates it with this fact. The peculiar primitive form of Mercury or Hermes was "a large stone, frequently square, and without either hands or feet. Sometimes the triangular shape was preferred, sometimes an upright pillar, and sometimes a heap of rude stones!"[1] The pillars were called by the Greeks *Hermœ*, and the heaps were known as *Hermèan* heaps—the latter being accumulated "by the custom of each passenger throwing a stone to the daily-increasing mass in honour of the god." Sometimes the pillar was represented with the attributes of Priapus.[2]

---

[1] Faber's "Pagan Idolatry."

[2] See Dulaure, *op. cit.*, vol. i., as to the primeval Hermes.

The identification of Hermes or Mercury with Priapus is confirmed by the offices which the latter deity fulfilled. One of the most important was that of protector of gardens and orchards, and probably this was the original office performed by Hermes in his character of "a God of the country."[1] Figures set up as charms to protect the produce of the ground would, in course of time, be used not only for this purpose, but also to mark the boundaries of the land protected, and these two offices being divided, two deities would finally be formed out of one. The Greek Hermes was connected also with the Egyptian *Khem*, and no less, if we may judge from the symbols used in his worship, with the Hebrew *Eloah*. Thus, in the history of the Hebrew patriarchs, we are told that when Jacob entered into a covenant with his father-in-law, Laban, a pillar was set up and a heap of stones made, and Laban said to Jacob, "Behold this heap and behold this pillar, which I have cast betwixt me and thee; this heap be witness, and this pillar be witness, that I will not pass over this heap to thee, and that thou shall not pass over this heap and this pillar unto me for harm."[2] We have here the *Hermæ* and *Hermèan* heap, used by the Greeks as landmarks and placed by them on the public roads. In the *linga* of India we have another instance of the use of the pillar symbol. The form of this symbol is sufficiently expressive of the idea which it embodies, an idea which is more explicity shown when the Linga and the Yoni are, as is usually the case

---

[1] Smith's "Dictionary of Mythology"—Art., "Hermes."
[2] Gen., xxxi. 45-53.

among the worshippers of the Hindu Siva, combined to form the *Lingam*. The stone figure is not, however, itself a god, but only representative of a spirit,[1] who is thought to be able to satisfy the yearning for children, so characteristic of many primitive peoples, this probably having been its original object and the source of its use as an amulet for the protection of children against the influence of the evil eye. In course of time, however, when other property came to be coveted equally with offspring, the power to give this property would naturally be referred to the primitive Phallic spirit, and hence he became, not merely the protector, as above seen, of the produce of the fields, and the guardian of boundaries, but also the God of wealth and traffic, and even the patron of thieves, as was the case with the Mercury of the Romans. The Hebrew patriarchs desired great flocks as well as numerous descendants, and hence the symbolic pillar was peculiarly fitted for their religious rites. It is related even of Abraham, the traditional founder of the Hebrew people, that he "planted a grove[2] (*eshel*) in Beersheba, and called there on the name of Jehovah, the everlasting *Elohim*."[3] From the Phallic character of the "grove" (*ashera*),[4] said to have been in the House of Jehovah, we must suppose that the *eshel* of Abraham also had

---

[1] *Linga* means a "sign" or "token." The truth of the statement in the text would seem to follow, moreover, from the fact that the figure is sacred only after it has undergone certain ceremonies at the hands of a priest.

[2] Or tamarisk tree.   [3] Gen., xxi. 33.

[4] Dr. Inman suggests that *ashera* is the female counterpart of *Asher*. See under these names in "Ancient Faiths," vol. i.

a Phallic reference.[1] Most probably the so-called "grove" of the earlier patriarch, though perhaps of wood, and the stone "*bethel*" of Jacob had the same form, and were simply the *betylus*,[2] the primitive symbol of deity among all the Semitic and many Hamitic peoples.

The participation of the Hebrew patriarchs in the rites connected with the "pillar-worship" of the ancient world, renders it extremely probable that they were not strangers to the later planetary worship. Many of the old Phallic symbols were associated with the new superstition, and Abraham, being a Chaldean, it is natural to suppose that he was one of its adherents. Tradition, indeed, affirms that Abraham was a great astronomer, and at one time at least a worshipper of the heavenly bodies, and that he and the other patriarchs continued to be affected by this superstition is shown by various incidents related in the Pentateuch. Thus, in the description given of the sacrificial covenant between Abraham and Jehovah, it is said that, after Abraham had divided the sacrificial animals, a deep sleep fell upon him as the sun was going down, and Jehovah spoke with him. "Then when the sun went down, and it was dark, behold a smoking furnace, and a burning lamp, that passed between those pieces." The happening of this event at the moment of the sun's setting reminds us of the Sabæan custom of praying to the setting sun, still

---

[1] Even if the statement of this event be an interpolation, the argument in the text is not affected. The statement is not inconsistent with the form of worship traditionally assigned to Abraham.

[2] Bætylia were " stones having souls."

practised, according to Palgrave, among the nomads of central Arabia. That some great *religious* movement, ascribed by tradition to Abraham, did take place among the Semites at an early date is undoubted. What the object of this covenant was it is difficult to decide. It should be remembered that the Chaldeans worshipped a plurality of gods, supposed to have been symbolised by the seven planets. Among these deities the sun-god held a comparatively inferior position—the moon-god *Hurki* coming before him in the second triad.[1] It was at Ur, the special seat of the worship of the moon-god,[2] that Abraham is said to have lived before he quitted it for Haran. This fact, considered in the light of the traditions relating to the great patriarch, may perhaps justify us in inferring that the reformation he endeavoured to introduce was the substitution of a simple sun-worship, for the planetary cultus of the Chaldeans, in which the worship of the moon must to him have appeared to occupy an important place. The new faith was, indeed, a return to the old Phallic idea of a god of personal generation, worshipped through the symbolical *betylus*, but associated also with the adoration of the sun as the especial representative of the deity. That Abraham had higher notions of the relation of man to the divine being than his forerunners is very pro-

---

[1] Rawlinson's "Five Ancient Monarchies," vol. i., p. 617; vol. ii., p. 247.

[2] Dr. Alexander Wilder says: "The later Hebrews affected the Persian religion, in which the sun was the emblem of worship. Abraham evidently had a like preference, being a reputed iconoclast. The lunar religionists employed images in their worship."

bable, but his sojourn in Haran proves that there was nothing fundamentally different between his religious faith and that of his Syrian neighbours. I am inclined, indeed, to believe that to the traditional Abraham must be ascribed the establishment of sun-worship throughout Phœnicia and Lower Egypt in connection with the symbols of an earlier and more simple Phallic deity. Tradition, in fact, declares that he taught the Egyptians astronomy,[1] and we shall see that the religion of the Phœnicians, as, indeed, that of the Hebrews themselves, was the worship of Saturn, the erect, pillar-god who, under different names, appears to have been at the head of the pantheons of most of the peoples of antiquity. The reference in Hebrew history to the *seraphim* of Jacob's family recalls the fact that Abraham's father was *Terah*, a "maker of images." The *teraphim* were doubtless the same as the *seraphim*, which were serpent images,[2] and probably the household charms or idols of the Semitic worshippers of the sun-god, to whom the serpent was sacred.

Little is known of the religious habits of the Hebrews during their abode in Egypt. Probably they differed little from those of the Egyptians themselves, and even in the religion of Moses, so-called, which we may presume to have been a reformed faith, there are many points of contact with the earlier cultus. The use of the ark of Osiris and Isis shows the influence of Egyptian ideas, and the introduction of the new name for God, *Jahve*, is evidence of contact

---

[1] Josephus' "Antiquities of the Jews," ch. viii. 2.
[2] The Serpent-symbol of the Exodus is called "Seraph."

with later Phœnician thought. The ark was doubt-less used to symbolise nature, as distinguished from the serpent and pillar symbols, which had relation more particularly to man. The latter, however, were by far the most important, as they were most inti-mately connected with the worship of the national deity, who was the divine father, as Abraham was the human progenitor, of the Hebrew people. That this deity, notwithstanding his change of name, retained his character of a sun-god, is shown by the fact that he is repeatedly said to have appeared to Moses under the figure of a flame. The pillar of fire which guided the Hebrews by night in the wilderness, the appear-ance of the cloudy pillar at the door of the Tabernacle, and probably of a flame over the mercy seat to betoken the presence of Jehovah, and the perpetual fire on the altar, all point to the same conclusion. The notion entertained by Ewald that the idea connected with the Hebrew Jahve was that of a " Deliverer" or a " Healer" (Saviour)[1] is quite consistent with the fact I have stated. The primeval Phenic deity El or Cronus was not only the preserver of the world, for the benefit of which he offered a mystical sacrifice,[2] but " Saviour" was a common title of the sun-gods of antiquity.

There is one remarkable incident which is said to have happened during the wanderings of the Hebrews in the Sinaitic wilderness which appears to throw much light on the character of the Mosaic cultus and to connect it with other religions. I refer to the use

---

[1] " The History of Israel" (Eng. Trans.), vol i., p. 532.

[2] See " Sanchoniatho" (Cory, *op. cit.*)

of the brazen serpent as a symbol for the healing of
the people. The worship of the golden calf may,
perhaps, be said to be an idolatrous act in imitation
of the rites of Egyptian Osiris worship, although
probably suggested by the use of the ark. The other
case, however, is far different, and it is worth while
repeating the exact words in which the use of the
serpent symbol is described. When the people were
bitten by the " fiery" serpents,[1] Moses prayed for them,
and we read that, therefore, " Jehovah said unto
Moses, make thee a fiery serpent (literally, a *seraph*),
and set it upon a pole ; and it shall come to pass,
that every one that is bitten, when he looketh upon it,
shall live. And Moses made a serpent of brass, and
put it upon a pole, and it came to pass, that if a serpent
had bitten any man, when he beheld the serpent of
brass, he lived."[2] It would seem from this account
that the Hebrew seraph was, as before suggested, in
the form of a serpent; but what was the especial
significance of this healing figure? At an earlier
stage of our inquiry reference was made to the fact of
the serpent being indirectly, through its attribute of
wisdom, a Phallic symbol, but also directly an emblem
of " life," and to the peculiar position it held in nearly
all the religions of antiquity. In later Egyptian
mythology the contest between Osiris and the Evil
Being, and afterwards that between Horus and Typhon,
occupy an important place. Typhon, the adversary of

---

[1] Much discussion has taken place as to the nature of these
animals. For an explanation of the epithet " fiery," see " Sanchoniatho, " *Of the Serpent*" (Cory, *op. cit.*)

[2] Numbers, xxi. 8, 9.

Horus, was figured under the symbol of a serpent, called Aphôphis or the Giant,[1] and it cannot be doubted that, if not a form of, he was identified with the god Seth.   Professor Reuvens refers to an invocation of Typhon-Seth,[2] and Bunsen quotes the statement of Epiphanius that "the Egyptians celebrate the festivals of Typhon under the form of an ass, which they call Seth."[3]   Whatever may be the explanation of the fact, it is undoubted that, notwithstanding the hatred with which he was afterwards regarded, this god Seth or Set was at one time highly venerated in Egypt. Bunsen says that up to the thirteenth century B.C. Set "was a great god universally adored throughout Egypt, who confers on the sovereigns of the eighteenth and nineteenth dynasties the symbols of life and power.   The most glorious monarch of the latter dynasty, Sethos, derives his name from this deity." He adds: "But subsequently, in the course of the twentieth dynasty, he is suddenly treated as an evil demon, inasmuch as his effigies and name are oblite-rated on all the monuments and inscriptions that could be reached."   Moreover, according to this distin-guished writer, Seth "appears gradually among the Semites as the background of their religious conscious-ness;" and not merely was he "the primitive god of Northern Egypt and Palestine," but his genealogy as "the Seth of Genesis, the father of Enoch (the man), must be considered as originally running parallel with that derived from the Elohim, Adam's father."[4]   That

---

[1] Wilkinson's "Ancient Egyptians," vol. iv., p. 435.
[2] Ditto, p. 434.   [3] Egypt, vol. iii., p. 426.
[4] "God in History," vol. i., pp. 233-4.

Seth *had* some special connection with the Hebrews is proved, among other things, by the peculiar position occupied in their religious system by the *ass*— the first-born of which alone of all animals was allowed to be redeemed[1]—and the *red heifer*, whose ashes were to be reserved as a " water of separation" for purification from sin.[2] Both of these animals were in Egypt sacred to Seth (Typhon), the ass being his symbol, and red oxen being at one time sacrificed to him, although at a later date objects of a red colour were disliked, owing to their association with the dreaded Typhon.[3] That we have a reference to this deity in the name of the Hebrew lawgiver is very probable. No satisfactory derivation of this name, Moses, Môsheh (Heb.), has yet been given. Its original form was probably *Am-a-ses* or *Am-sesa*,[4] which might become to the Hebrews Om-ses or Mo-ses, meaning only *the* (god) Ses, *i.e.*, Set or Seth.[5] On this hypothesis we may have preserved, in the first book of Moses (so-called), some of the traditional history said to have been contained in the sacred books of the Egyptian Thoth, and of the records engraved on the pillars of Seth. It is somewhat remarkable that, according to

---

[1] Exodus, xxxiv. 20.   [2] Numbers, xix. 1—10.

[3] As to the god Seth, see Pleyte's " La Religion des Pré-Israelites" (1862).

[4] Fürst renders the name Mo-cese, " Son of Isis," *Inman's* " Ancient Faiths," vol. ii., p. 338.

[5] According to Pleyte, the Cabalists thought that the soul of Seth had passed into Moses (*op. cit.*, p. 124). It is strange that the name of the Egyptian princess who is said to have brought up Moses is given by Josephus as *Thermuthis*, this being the name of the sacred asp of Egypt (see " *suprà*"). We appear also to have a reference to the serpent in the name Levi, one of the sons of Jacob, from whom the descent of Moses was traced.

a statement of Diodorus, when Antiochus Epiphanes entered the temple at Jerusalem, he found in the Holy of Holies a stone figure of Moses, represented as a man with a long beard, mounted on an ass, and having a book in his hand.[1] The Egyptian Mythus of Typhon actually said that Set fled from Egypt riding on a grey ass.[2] It is strange, to say the least, that Moses should not have been allowed to enter the promised land, and that he should be so seldom referred to by later writers until long after the reign of David,[3] and above all that the name given to his successor was Joshua—*i.e.*, *Saviour*. It is worthy of notice that " Nun," the name of the father of Joshua, is the Semitic word for *fish*, the Phallic character of the fish in Chaldean mythology being undoubted. *Nin*, the planet Saturn, was the fish-god of Berosus, and, as may possibly be shown, he is really the same as the Assyrian national deity *Asshur*, whose name and office have a curious resemblance to those of the Hebrew leader, *Joshua*.

But what was the character of the primitive Semitic deity? Bunsen seems to think that Plutarch in one passage alludes to the identity of Typhon (Seth) and Osiris.[4] This is a remarkable idea, and yet curiously enough Sir Gardner Wilkinson says that Typhon-Seth may have been derived from the pigmy Pthath-Sokari-Osiris,[5] who was clearly only another form of Osiris himself. In the Egyptian Book of the

---

[1] " Fragments."   Book xxxiv. (See also in connection with this subject, " King's Gnostics," p. 91.)

[2] Bunsen's " God in History," vol, i., p. 234.

[3] Ewald notices the fact. (See "*op. cit.*, vol. i., 454.")

[4] " Egypt," vol. iii., p. 433.   [5] *Op. cit.*, vol. iv., p. 434.

Dead, Horus, the son of Osiris, is declared to be at the same time Set, "by the distinction made between them by Thoth."[2] However that may be, the Phallic origin of Seth can be shown from other data. Thus it appears that the word *Set* means, in Hebrew as in Egyptian, pillar, and, in a general sense, the erect, elevated, high.[3] Moreover, in a passage of the Book of the Dead, Set, according to Bunsen, is called *Tet*, a fact which intimates that Thoth inherited many of the attributes of Set.[4] They were, however, in some sense the same deities, it being through Thoth that Set was identified with Horus. We have here an explanation of the statement that Tet, the Phœnician *Taaut*, was the snake-god, Esmun-Esculapius, the serpent being the symbol of Tet, as we have seen it to have been that of Seth also. In this we have a means of identifying the Semitic deity Seth with the Saturn of related deities of other peoples. Ewald says that "the common name for God, *Eloah*, among the Hebrews, as among all the Semites, goes back into the earliest times."[5] Bryant goes further, and declares that El was originally the name of the supreme deity among all the nations of the East.[6] This idea is confirmed, so far as Chaldea is concerned, by later researches, which show that Il or El was at the head of the Babylonian Pantheon. With this deity must be identified the Il or Ilus of the Phœnicians, who was born the same as Cronus, who, again, was none other than the primeval

---

[1] "Le Livre des Morts," par Paul Pierret," p. 259.
[2] Bunsen's "Egypt," vol. iv., p. 208.　　[3] Ditto, vol. iii., p. 427.
[4] *Op. cit.*, p. 319.　　　　[5] *Op. cit.*, vol. vi., p. 328.

Saturn, whose worship appears to have been at one period almost universal among European and Asiatic peoples. Saturn and El were thus the same deity, the latter, like the Semitic Seth, being, as is well known, symbolised by the serpent.[1] A direct point of contact between Seth and Saturn is found in the Hebrew idol *Kiyun* mentioned by Amos, the planet Saturn being still called *Kevan* by Eastern peoples. This idol was represented in the form of a pillar, the primeval symbol of deity, which was common undoubtedly to all the gods here mentioned.[2] These symbolical pillars were called *betyli* or *betulia*. Sometimes also the column was called *Abaddir*, which, strangely enough, Bryant identifies with the serpent-god.[3] There can be no doubt that both the pillar and the serpent were associated with many of the sun-gods of antiquity.

Notwithstanding what has been said it is undoubtedly true, however, that all these deities, including the Semitic Seth, became at an early date recognised as sun-gods, although in so doing they lost nothing of their primitive character. What this was is sufficiently shown by the significant names and titles they bore. Thus, as we have seen, *Set* (Seth) itself meant the *erect, elevated, high*, his name on the Egyptian monuments being nearly always accompanied by a stone.[4] The name, *Kiyun* or

---

[1] As to the use of this symbol generally, see Pleyte, *op. cit.*, pp. 109, 157.

[2] On these points, see M. Raoul-Rochette's Memoir on the Assyrian and Phœnician Hercules, in his " Mémoires de l'Institut National de France. Académie des Inscriptions," tom. xvii., p. 47, *et seq.*

[3] *Op. cit.*, vol. i., p. 60 ; vol. ii., p. 201.   [4] Pleyte, *op. cit.*, p. 172.

Kevan, of this deity, said by Amos to have been worshipped in the wilderness, signifies " god of the pillar." The idea expressed by the title· is shown by the name *Baal Tamar*, which means " Baal as a pillar," or " Phallus," consequently " the fructifying god." The title " erect," when given to a deity, seems always to imply a Phallic idea, and hence we have the explanation of the *S. mou* used frequently in the " Book of the Dead" in relation to Thoth or to Set. There is doubtless a reference of the same kind in the Phœnician myth, that " Melekh taught men the special art of creating solid walls and buildings;" although Bunsen finds in this myth " the symbolical mode of expressing the value of the use of fire in building houses."[2] That these myths embody a Phallic notion may be confirmed by reference to the Phœnician *Kabiri*. According to Bunsen, " the Kabiri and the divinities identified with them are explained by the Greeks and Romans as ' the strong,' ' the great ;' " while in the book of Job, *Kabbîr*, the strong, is used as an epithet of God. Again, *Sydyk*, the father of the Kabiri, is " the Just," or, in a more original sense, the Upright ; and this deity, with his sons, correspond to Ptah, the father of the Phœnician Pataikoi. Ptah, however, seems to be derived from a root which signifies in Hebrew " to open," and Sydyk himself, therefore, may, says Bunsen, be described as " the Opener" of the Cosmic Egg.[3] The Phallic meaning of this title is evident from its application to Esmun-

[1] Bunsen's " Egypt," vol. iv., p. 249.

[2] Ditto, p. 217.

[3] See ditto, pp. 226-9.

Esculapius, the son of Sydyk, who, as the snake-god, was identical with Tet, the Egyptian Thoth-Hermes.

The peculiar titles given to these deities, and their association with the sun, led to their original Phallic character being somewhat overlooked, and instead of being the Father-Gods of human-kind, they became *Powerful* Gods, *Lords* of Heaven. This was not the special attribute taken by other sun-gods. As was before stated, Hermes and his related deities were "gods of the country," personifying the idea of general natural fecundity. Among the chief gods of this description were the Phœnician *Sabazius*, the Greek *Bacchus-Dionysos*, the Roman *Priapus*, and the Egyptian *Khem.* All these deities agree also in being sun-gods, and as such they were symbolised by animals which were noted either for their fecundity or for their salaciousness. The chief animals thus chosen were the *bull* and the *goat* (with which the ram[1] was afterwards confounded), doubtless because they were already sacred. The Sun appears to have been preceded by the Moon as an object of worship, but the moon-god was probably only representative of the primeval Saturn,[2] who finally became the sun-god *El* or *Il* of the Syrian and Semites and the *Ra* of the Babylonians. The latter was the title also of the sun-god of Egypt, who was symbolised by the obelisk, and who, although his name was added to that of other Egyptian gods, is said to have been the tutelary

---

[1] The ram appears to have been the first month of the Akkadian calendar. "Law of Kosmic Order," by Mr. Rob. Brown, jun., 1882, p. 36.

[2] Rawlinson's "History of Herodotus," vol. i., p. 620.

deity of the stranger kings of the eighteenth dynasty,[1] whom Pleyte, however, declares to have been Set (Sutech).[2] We are reminded here of the opposition of Seth and Osiris, which has already been explained as arising from the fact that these deities originally represented two different ideas, *human fecundity* and the *fruitfulness of nature*. When, however, both of these principles became associated with the solar body, they were expressed by the same symbols, and the distinction between them was in great measure lost sight of. A certain difference was, nevertheless, still observable in the attributes of the deities, depending on the peculiar properties and associations of their solar representatives. Thus the powerful deity of Phœnicia was naturally associated with the strong, scorching, summer sun, whose *heat* was the most prominent attribute. In countries such as Egypt, where the sun, acting on the moist soil left by inundations, caused the earth to spring into renewed life, the mild but energetic early sun was the chief deity.

When, considering the sacred bull of antiquity, the symbol of the fecundating force in nature, Osiris, the national sun-god of the Egyptians, was referred to as distinguished from the Semitic Seth (Set), who was identified with the detested shepherd race. The association of Osiris with Khem shows his Phallic character,[3] and, in fact, Plutarch asserts that he was everywhere represented with the phallus exposed.[4]

---

[1] Rawlinson's "History of Herodotus," vol. ii., p. 291.

[2] *Op. cit.*, p. 89, *et seq.*

[3] Wilkinson, *op. cit.*, vol. iv., pp. 342, 260.

[4] Bunsen's "Egypt," vol. i., p. 423.

The Phallic idea enters, moreover, into the character of all the chief Egyptian deities. Bunsen says : "The mythological system obviously proceeded from ' the concealed god' Ammon to the creating god. The latter appears first of all as the generative power of nature in the Phallic god Khem, who is afterwards merged in Ammon-ra. Then sprung up the idea of the creative power in Kneph. He forms the divine limbs of Osiris (the primeval soul) in contradiction to Ptah, who as the strictly demiurgic principle, forms the visible world. Neith is the creative principle, as nature represented under a feminine form. Finally, her son Ra, Helios, appears as the last of the series, in the character of father and nourisher of terrestrial beings. It is he, whom an ancient monument represents as the demiurgic principle, creating the mundane egg."[1] The name of Ammon has led to the notion that he was an embodiment of the idea of wisdom. He certainly was distinguished by having the human form, but his hieroglyphical symbol of the *obelisk*, and his connection with Khem, show his true nature. He undoubtedly represented the primitive idea of a generative god, probably at a time when this notion of fecundity had not yet been extended to nature as distinguished from man, and thus he would form a point of contact between the later Egyptian sun-gods and the pillar gods of the Semites and Phœnicians.[2] To

[1] *Op. cit.*, vol. i., p. 388.

[2] In the temple of Hercules at Tyre were two symbolical *steles*, one a pillar and the other an obelisk. See Raoul-Rochette, *op. cit.*, p. 51, where is a reference to a curious tradition, preserved by Josephus, connecting Moses with the erection of columns at Heliopolis.

the Egyptians, as to these other peoples, the sun became the great source of deity. His fecundating warmth or his fiery destroying heat were, however, not the only attributes deified. These were the most important, but the Egyptians, especially, made gods out of many of the solar characters,[1] although the association of the idea of "intellect" with Amun-re must have been of late date, if the original nature of Amun was what has been above suggested.

As man, however, began to read nature aright, and as his moral and intellectual faculties were developed, it was necessary that the solar deities themselves should become invested with co-relative attributes, or that other gods should be formed to embody them. The perception of *light*, as distinguished from heat, was a fertile source of such attributes. In the Chaldean mythology, *Vul*, the son of *Anu*, was the god of the air, but his power had relation to the purely atmospheric phenomena rather than to light.[2] The only reference to light found in the titles of the early deities is in the character ascribed to *Va-lua*, the later *Bur* or *Nin-ip*, who is said to "irradiate the nations like the sun, the light of the gods."[3] But this deity was apparently the distant planet Saturn, if not originally the moon, and the perception of light as a divine attribute must be referred to the Aryan mind.[4] Thus the Hindu *Dyaus* (the Greek *Zeus*) is the shining deity, the god of the bright sky. As such the sun-

---

[1] Wilkinson, *op. cit.*, vol. iv., p. 299.

[2] Rawlinson's "Herodotus," vol. i., p. 608.   [3] Ditto, p. 620.

[4] *Mau*, the name of the Egyptian God of Truth, certainly signifies "light," but probably only in a figurative sense.

gods now also become the gods of intellectual wisdom, an attribute which also appears to have originated with the Aryan peoples, among whom the Brahmans were possessors of the highest wisdom, as children of the sun, and whose Apollo and Athene were noble embodiments of this attribute. The Chaldean gods, *Héa* and *Nebo*, were undoubtedly symbolised by the wedge or arrow-head, which had especial reference to learning. In reality, however, this symbol merely shows that they were the patrons of letters or writing, and not of wisdom, in its purely intellectual aspect. If the form of the Assyrian alphabetical character was of Phallic origin,[1] we may have here the source of the idea of a connection between physical and mental knowledge embodied in the legend of the "fall." In the Persian *Ahurô-mazdâo* (the wise spirit) we have the purest representation of intellectual wisdom. The book of Zoroaster, the Avesta, is literally the "word," the word or wisdom which was revealed in creation and embodied in the divine Mithra, who was himself the luminous sun-god.

The similarity between the symbols of the sun-gods of antiquity and the natural objects introduced into the Mosaic myth of the fall has been already referred to, and it is necessary now to consider shortly what influence the Phallic principle there embodied had over other portions of Hebraic theology. The inquiries of Dr. Faber have thrown great light on this question,

---

[1] The importance ascribed to the mechanical arts may perhaps lead us to look for the formal origin of this character in the "wedge," which was the chief mechanical power the ancients possessed.

although the explanation given by him of the myth of Osiris and of the kindred myths of antiquity is by no means the correct one. Finding a universal prevalence of Phallic ideas and symbolism, Dr. Faber refers it to the degradation of a primitive revelation of the Great Father of the Universe. The truth thus taught was lost sight of, and was replaced by the dual notion of a Great Father and a Great Mother—" the transmigrating Noah and the mundane Ark" of the universal Deluge. Noah was, however, only a reappearance of Adam, and the ark floating on the waters of the Deluge was an analogue of the earth swimming in the ocean of space.[1] There is undoubtedly a parallelism between the Adam and Noah of the Hebrew legends, as there is between the analogous personages of other phases of these legends, yet it is evident that, if the Deluge never happened, a totally different origin from the one supposed by Dr. Faber must be assigned to the great Phallic myth of antiquity. It is absolutely necessary, therefore, to any explanation (other than the Phallic one) of the origin of this myth, to establish the truth of the Noahic Deluge.[2] Accordingly, an American writer has framed an elaborate system of " Arkite symbolism," founded on the supposed influence of the great Deluge over the minds of the posterity of those who survived its horrors. Mr. Lesley sees in this catastrophe the explanation of " phallism,"

---

[1] Faber, *op. cit.*, vol, ii., p. 20.

[2] Bryant, in his " Ancient Mythology," has brought together a great mass of materials bearing on this question. The facts, however, are capable of quite a different interpretation from that which he has given to them.

which, " converting all the older Arkite symbols into illustrations of its own philosophical conceptions of the mystery of generation, gave to the various parts and members of the human body those names which constitute the special vocabulary of obscenity of the present day."[1]

But the priority of these symbols or conceptions is the question at issue. Did the development of "Arkism" precede or follow the superstitions referred to by Mr. Lesley as *Ophism*, *Mithraism*, and *Phallism*, all of which have been shown to embody analogous ideas? If the question of priority is to be determined by reference to the written tradition which furnishes the real ground of belief in a great Deluge, it must clearly be given to the Phallic superstition; for it is shown conclusively, as I think, that almost the first event in the life of man there related is purely Phallic in its symbolism. Nor is the account of the fall the only portion of the Mosaic history of primitive man which belongs to this category. The Garden of Eden, with its tree of life and the river which divided into four streams, although it may have had a secondary reference to the traditional place of Semitic origin to which the Hebrews looked back with a regretful longing, has undoubtedly a recondite Phallic meaning. It must be so, if the explanation I have given of the myth of the fall be right, since the two are intimately connected, and the Garden[2] is essential to the succeeding catas-

---

[1] "Origin and Destiny of Man," p. 339.

[2] Dr. Inman points out that, in the ancient languages, the term for "garden" is used as a metaphor for woman. "Ancient Faiths," i. 52 ; ii. 553.

trophe. That this opinion is correct can be proved moreover by reference to Hindu mythology. "The Hindu,"
says Dr. Creuzer, "contemplates with love his mysterious Merou, a sacred mountain from whence the
source of life spreads itself in the valleys and over the
plains, which separates day from night, reunites heaven
and earth, and finally on which the sun, the moon,
and the stars each repose."[1] But what is this mysterious mountain, the sacred Merou? It is shown by
Dr. Creuzer's own explanation. He says : " It is on
the Mount Merou, the central point of the earth (which
elevates itself as an immense phallus from the centre
of an immense yoni amongst the islands with which
the sea is sown), that the grand popular deity who
presides over the Lingam, *Siva* or Mahadeva, the
father and master of nature, makes his cherished
abode, spreading life to every part under a thousand
diverse forms which he incessantly renews. Near him
is *Bhavani* or *Parvati*, his sister and his wife, the
Queen of the mountains, the goddess of the Yoni, who
carries in her bosom the germ of all things, and brings
forth the beings whom she has conceived by Mahadeva. We have here the two great principles of
nature, the one male and the other female, generators
and regenerators, creators and at the same time de-
stroyers ; but they destroy only to renew; they
only change the forms; life and death succeed in a
perfect circle, and the substance remains in the midst
of all these changes." The sacred mountain is wanting
to the Mosaic legend, but Dr. Faber justly sees[2] in

<hr>

[1] Guigniaut's " Religions de l'Antiquité," vol. i., p. 146.
[2] *Op. cit.*, i. 315.

the Mount Merou, where resides Siva and Bhavani, the Hebrew Paradise, and we find that the Hindu myth affirms that the sacred river not only sprang from the roots of Jambu, a tree of a most extravagant size, which is thought to convey knowledge and to effect the accomplishment of every human wish, but also that, after passing through "the circle of the moon," it divides it into "four streams, flowing towards the four cardinal points."

The priority of the Phallic superstition over "Arkism" is further proved by the undoubted fact that, even in the traditions of the race to whom we are indebted for the precise details of the incidents accompanying the Deluge, the Phallic deities of the Hamitico-Semites are genealogically placed long before the occurrence of this event. The Semitic deity Seth is, according to one fable, the semi-divine first ancestor of the Semites. Bunsen has shown clearly also that several of the antediluvian descendants of the Semitic Adam were among the Phœnician deities. Thus, the Carthaginians had a god Yubal, Jubal, who would appear to have been the sun-god Æsculapius, called "the fairest of the gods;" and so, "we read in a Phœnician inscription Ju-Baal—*i.e.*, beauty of Baal, which Movers ingeniously interprets Æsculapius — Asmun-Jubal." Here, then, adds Bunsen, "is another old Semitic name attached to a descendant of Lamekh, together with Adah, Zillah, and Naamah."[1] Hadah, the wife of Lamekh, as well of Esau, the Phœnician Usov, is identified with the goddess, worshipped at Babylon as Hera (Juno), and, notwithstanding Sir Gardner Wil-

[1] "Egypt," vol. iv., p. 257.

kinson's dictum to the contrary, her names, Hera,
Hadah, point to a connection with the Egyptian *Her
Her*, or *Hathor*, who was the daughter of Seb and
Netpe, as Hera was the daughter of Chronos and
Rhea. The name of the god *Kiyun*, or Kevan, who
was worshipped by the Hebrews, and who in Syria
was said to devour children, seems, from its connection
with the root *kun*, to erect, to point to the antediluvian Kain or Kevan. *Kon*, derived from the same
root, was, according to Bunsen, a Phœnician designa-
tion of Saturn.[1] Even the great Carthaginian sun-
god *Melekh*, who was also " held in universal honour
throughout Phœnicia," seems, although Bunsen does
not thus identify him, to be no other than Lamekh,
the father of Noah, in one of the genealogies of
Genesis. We may, perhaps, have in the sacrifices to
the Phœnician deities, when the first-born sons of the
people were offered on his altars, an explanation[2] of
the passage in Genesis which has so much puzzled
commentators, where Lamekh is made to declare that
he has "slain a man for his wound, and a youth for
his hurt," for which, while Cain was avenged seven
times, Lamekh should be avenged seventy times seven
times.[3] The Phœnicians had a tradition that Kronos
(Saturn) had sacrificed his own beloved son Yadid,
and some ancient writers said that the human sacrifices
to Moloch were in imitation of this act.[4] This reason

[1] " Egypt," vol. iv., p. 209.

[2] Mr. Gerald Massey appears to regard the crime of Lamekh
as the practice of abortion, men not desiring to have children.
Op. cit., ii. 119.

[3] Gen., iv. 23, 24.

[4] Bunsen's " Egypt," vol. iv., pp. 285-6.

may not be the correct one for the use of human sacrifices, but the seventy times seven times in which Lamekh was avenged may well refer to the abundance of the victims offered on the altar of the Phœnician deity.

The priority of the Phallic superstition over "Arkism," or rather the existence of that superstition before the formation of the Deluge legend, is proved, moreover, by its agreement with the myth of Osiris and Isis. This agreement forms the central idea of the explanation of pagan idolatry given by Faber, and yet it conclusively proves that the Noachian Deluge was simply a myth, having, like that of Osiris, a Phallic basis. Bunsen says "the myth of Osiris and Typhon, heretofore considered as primeval, can now be authoritatively proved to be of modern date in Egypt—that is to say, about the thirteenth or fourteenth century B.C."[1] But it is *this* version of the Osirian myth which is said to be founded on the Noachian catastrophe, Typhon or The Evil Being, the persecutor of Osiris, being the Waters of the Deluge. The very foundation of the Hebrew legend is thus cut away, and from the fact, moreover, that the Egyptians had no tradition of a great flood, we must seek for another origin for the legend of which different phases were held by so many of the peoples of antiquity. The fact of Typhon (Seth) having been venerated in Egypt to so late a date as the thirteenth century B.C. is a proof that the myth, according to which he was the cruel persecutor of his brother Osiris, must have been of a later origin.

[1] Bunsen's " Egypt," vol. iii., p. 413.

The primitive form of the myth is easily recognised when it is known that both Osiris and Typhon (Seth) were sun-gods. Thus, according to Bunsen, " the myth of Osiris typifies the solar year, the power of Osiris is the sun of the lower hemisphere, the winter solstice. The birth of Horus typifies the vernal equinox—the victory of Horus, the summer equinox—the inundation of the Nile. Typhon is the autumnal equinox—Osiris is slain on the seventeenth of Athyr (November). . . . The rule of Typhon lasts from the autumnal equinox to the middle of December. He reigns twenty-eight years, or lives as long." [1] Thus the history of Osiris is " the history of the circle of the year," and in his resurrection as Horus we see the sun resuscitating itself after its temporary eclipse during the winter solstice. Here Typhon is also a sun-god, his rule being at the autumnal equinox when the sun has its full power. This was the deity of the Semites and of the inhabitants of Lower Egypt, and his scorching force, doubtless, prepared the Egyptians, who venerated the milder Osiris, to look with abhorrence on Typhon-Seth, who had already, probably under the same influence, become a savage deity, delighting in burnt offerings and human sacrifices. [2] No wonder, therefore, that when the worshippers of the Semitic god were driven out of Egypt, the god himself was treated as an enemy. Thus we are told that the enemies of Egypt and their gods contended with the gods of Egypt, who veiled themselves under the heads of animals in order to save themselves from Typhon.

[1] Bunsen's " Egypt," vol. iii., p. 437.
[2] Ditto, vol. iv., p. 286.

Moreover, when this Semitic god was thus degraded and transformed into an Evil Being, he would naturally come to be looked upon as the enemy of Osiris, seeing that he was already identified with the autumn sun, which during the autumnal equinox triumphs over the sun of Osiris; and we can easily understand how, if the myth of a Deluge, and the consequent destruction of all mankind but the father of the renewed human race, was introduced, Typhon would be the destroying enemy and Osiris the suffering and restored man-god.

If, as Dr. Faber supposes, the Egyptian myth was a form of that which relates to the Noachian Deluge, we can only suppose them to have had a similar basis, a basis which, from the very circumstances of the case, must be purely " Phallic."   This explanation is the only one which is consistent with a peculiarity in the Hebrew legend which is an insurmountable objection to its reception as the expression of a literal fact. We are told by the Mosaic narrative that Jehovah directed Noah to take with him into the ark " of fowls after their kind, and of cattle after their kind, of every creeping thing of the earth after his kind, two of every sort."   Now, according to the ordinary acceptation of the legend, this passage expresses a simple absurdity, even on the hypothesis of a partial Deluge. If, however, we read the narrative in a Phallic sense, and by the ark understand the sacred *Argha* of Hindu mythology, the *Yoni* of Parvati, which, like the moon in Zoroastrian teaching, carries in *itself* the " germs of all things," we see the full propriety of what otherwise is incomprehensible. The Elohim " created" the heavens and the earth, and on its destruction the seeds of all things were preserved in the ark to again cover the earth. Taken in this sense, we see the reason of the curious analogy which exists in various points between the Hebrew legends of the Creation and of the Deluge, this analogy being one of the grounds on which the hypothesis of the Great Father as the central idea of all mythologies has been based. Thus, the primeval ship, the navigation of which is ascribed to the mythological being, is not the ark of Noah or Osiris, or the vessel of the Phœnician Kabiri. It was the moon, the ship of the sun, in which his seed is supposed to be hidden until it bursts forth in new life and power. The fact that the moon was, in early mythologies, a male deity, almost necessitates, however, that there should have been another origin for the sacred vessel of Osiris. This we have in the Hastoreth-*karnaim*, the cow-goddess, whose horns represent the lunar ark, and who, without doubt, was a more primitive deity than the moon-goddess herself.[1] The most primitive type of all, however, is that of the *Argha* or *Yoni* of the Indian Iswara, which from its name was supposed to have been turned into a dove.[2] Thus, in Noah and the ark, as in Osiris and the moon, we see simply the combination of the male and female elements as they are still represented in the Hindu lingam. The introduction of the dove into the myth is a curious.

---

[1] If space permitted, we might trace to their source the developments which the primeval goddess of fecundity underwent. To the ideas embodied in her may be referred nearly all the feminine deities of antiquity.

[2] Faber, *op. cit.*, vol. ii., p. 246.

confirmation of this view. For this bird, which, as
" the emblem of love and fruitfulness," was " consecrated to Venus, under all her different names, at
Babylon, in Syria, Palestine, and Greece ;[1] which was
the national banner-sign of the Assyrians, as of the
earlier Sythic empire, whose founders, according to
Hindu tradition, took the name of *Jonim* or *Yoniyas*,
and which attended on Janus, a diluvian 'god of
opening and shutting ;' was simply a type of 'the
Yoni' or Jonah, or Navicular feminine principle,"
which was said to have assumed the form of a ship
and a dove.[2]

In bringing this essay to a close, some mention should
be made of what may be called the *modern* religions,
Brahminism, Buddhism, and Christianity, seeing that
these still exist as the faiths of great peoples. As to
the first of these, it may be thought that its real
character cannot be ascertained from the present condition of Hindu belief. It is said that the religion of
the *Vedas* is very different from that of the *Puranas*,
which have taken their place. It should be remembered, however, that these books profess to reproduce
old doctrine, the word " Purana" itself meaning *old*,
and that Puranas are referred to in one of the Upanishads, while the *Tantras*, which contain the principles
of the *Sacti Puja*, and which are as yet almost unknown
to Europeans, are considered by the Brahmins to be
more ancient than the Puranas themselves.[3] The

[1] Kenrick's "Phœnicia," p. 307.

[2] See Faber, *op. cit.*; also Note at the end of this chapter.

[3] On this question, see the "Memoirs of the Anthropological
Society of London," vol. ii., p. 265 ; also "Sketch of the Religious

origin of the ideas contained in these books is a difficult question. The germs of both Vishnu-worship
and Siva-worship appear to be found in the Vedas,[1]
and the worship of the linga is undoubtedly referred to
the Mahatharata.[2] It is more probable, as thought by
Mr. Fergusson and other late writers, that they are only
indirectly sprung from the primitive Hinduism. The
similarity between Siva-ism and the Santal-worship of
the Great Mountain pointed out by Dr. Hunter is
very remarkable, and this analogy is strengthened by
intermixture in both cases with river-worship.[3] There
is no doubt that the Great Mountain is simply a name
for the Phallic emblem, which is the chief form under
which Siva is represented in the numerous temples at
Benares dedicated to his honour. Considering the
position occupied by the serpent as a symbol of life
and indirectly of the male power, we should expect to
find its worship connected to some extent with that of
Siva. Mr. Fergusson, however, declares that it is not
so, and, although this statement requires some qualification,[4] yet it is certain that the serpent is also inti-

Sects of the Hindus," in the "Asiatic Researches," vol. xvii.
(1832), p. 216, *et seq.*

[1] This question is fully considered by Dr. Muir in his Sanscrit
Texts, part iv., p. 54, *et seq.*

[2] Ditto, pp. 161, 343.

[3] "Rural Bengal," p. 187, *et seq.*, 152. This association of
the mountain and the river is found also in the Persian Khordah-
Avesta. See (5) Abun-yasht, v. 1-3.

[4] See "Tree and Serpent Worship," p. 70; also Sherring's
"Benares," pp. 75-89. Here the serpent is evidently symbolical
of *life*. In the Mahabharata, Mahadeva is described as having
"a girdle of serpents, ear-rings of serpents, a sacrificial cord of
serpents, and an outer garment of serpent's skin." Dr. Muir,
op. cit., part iv., p. 160.

mately associated with Vishnu. In explanation of this fact, Mr. Fergusson remarks: "The Vaishnava religion is derived from a group of faiths in which the serpent always played an important part. The eldest branch of the family was the Naga worship, pure and simple; out of that arose Buddhism, . . . and on its decline two faiths—at first very similar to one another —rose from its ashes, the Jaina and the Vaishnava." The serpent is almost always found in Jaina temples as an object of worship, while it appears everywhere in Vaishnava tradition.[1] But elsewhere Mr. Fergusson tells us that, although Buddhism owed its establishment to Naga tribes, yet its supporters repressed the worship of the serpent, elevating tree-worship in its place.[2] It is difficult to understand how the Vaishnavas, who are worshippers of the female power,[3] and who hate the *lingam*, can yet so highly esteem the serpent which has indirectly, at least, reference to the male principle. Perhaps, however, we may find an explanation in Mr. Fergusson's own remarks as to the character and development of Buddhism. According to him, Buddhism was chiefly influential among Naga tribes, and " was little more than a revival of the coarser superstitions of the aboriginal races,[4] purified and refined by the application of Aryan morality, and

---

[1] *Op. cit.*, p. 70.   [2] Ditto, p. 62.

[3] Mr. Sellon, in the " Memoirs of the Anthropological Society of London," vol. ii., p. 273.

[4] It should not be forgotten that the Vedic religion was not that of all the Aryan tribes of India (see Muir, *op. cit.*, part ii., pp. 377, 368, 383), and it is by no means improbable that some of them retained a more primitive faith—" Buddhism" or " Rudraism"—*i.e., Siva-ism*.

elevated by doctrines borrowed from the intellectual superiority of the Aryan races.[1]" As to its development, the sculptures on the Sanchi Tope show that at about the beginning of the Christian era, although the *dagoba*, the *chakra* or wheel, the *tree*, and other emblems, were worshipped, the serpent hardly appears; while at Amravati, three centuries later, this animal had become equal to Buddha himself.[2] Moreover, there can be no doubt that the *lingam* was an emblem of Buddha, as was also the *lotus*, which represents the same idea—the conjunction of the male and female elements, although in a higher sense perfect wisdom.[3] The association of the same ideas is seen in the noted prayer *Om mani padmi hum* ("Oh, the Jewel in the Lotus"), which refers to the birth of Padmipani from the sacred lotus flower,[4] but also, there can be little doubt, to the phallus and the yoni. We may suppose, therefore, that whatever the moral doctrine taught by Gautama, he used the old Phallic symbols, although it may be with a peculiar application. If the opinion expressed by Mr. Fergusson as to the introduction into India of the Vaishnava faith by an early immigrant race, be correct, it must have existed in the time of Gautama, and indeed the Ion-

---

[1] *Op. cit.*, p. 62. To come to a proper conclusion on this important point, it is necessary to consider the real position occupied by Gautama in relation to Brahmanism. Burnoux says that he differed from his adversaries only in the definition he gives of salvation (*du salut*). "Introduction à l'Histoire du Buddhisme Indien," p. 155.

[2] Fergusson, *op. cit.*, pp. 67, 222, 223.

[3] See Guigniaut, *op. cit.*, vol. i., pp. 293, 160 *n.*

[4] Schlagenweit, "Buddhism in Tibet," p. 120.

ism of Western Asia is traditionally connected with India itself at a very early date,[1] although probably the early centre of Ion-ism, the worhip of the Dove or Yoni, was, as Bryant supposes, in Chaldea.[2] We see no trace, however, in Buddhism proper of *Sacti Puja*, and I would suggest that, instead of abolishing either, Gautama substituted for the separate symbols of the linga and the yoni, the association of the two in the *lingam*. If this were so, we can well understand how, on the fall of Buddhism, Siva-worship[3] may have retained this compound symbol, with many of the old Naga ideas, although with little actual reference to the serpent itself, other than as a symbol of life and power; while, on the other hand, the Vaishnavas may have reverted to the primitive worship of the female principle, retaining a remembrance of the early serpent associations in the use of the *Sesha*, the heavenly naga with seven heads[4] figured on the Amravati sculptures. It is possible, however, that there may be another ground of opposition between the followers of Vishnu and Siva. Mr. Fergusson points out that, notwithstanding the peculiarly Phallic symbolism of the latter deity, "the worship of Siva is too severe, too stern for the softer emotions of love, and all his temples are quite free from any allusion to it." It

---

[1] Higgins' "Anacalypsis," vol. i., p. 332, *et seq.* See also p. 342, *et seq.*

[2] *Op. cit.*, vol. i., p. 1, *et seq.*, 25.

[3] Dr. Hunter points out a connection between Siva-ism and Buddhism. *Op. cit.*, p. 194.

[4] Mr. Fergusson, *op. cit.*, p. 70. The serpent is connected with Vishnuism as a symbol of *wisdom* rather than of life.

is far different with the Vaishnavas, whose temples
"are full of sexual feelings generally expressed in the
grossest terms."[1]   Siva, in fact, is specially a god of
intellect, typified by his being three-eyed, and although
terrible as the resistless destroyer, yet the recreator of
all things in perfect wisdom;[2] while Vishnu has relation rather to the lower type of wisdom which was
distinctive of the Assyrians, among ancient peoples,
and which has so curious a connection with the female
principle.   Hence the *shell* or *conch* is peculiar to
Vishnu, while the *linga* belongs to Siva.[3]   Gautama
combined the simpler feminine phase of religion with
the more masculine intellectual type, symbolising this
union by the lingam and other analogous emblems.
The followers of Siva have, however, adopted the
combined symbol in the place of the linga alone,
thus approaching more nearly than the Vaishnavas
to the idea of the founder of modern Buddhism.   Gautama himself, nevertheless, was most probably only
the restorer of an older faith, according to which perfect wisdom was to be found only in the typical combination of the male and female principles in nature.
The real explanation of the connection between
Buddhism and Siva-ism has perhaps, however, yet to

[1] *Op. cit.*, p. 71.

[2] Hence Siva, as *Sambhu*, is the patron deity of the Brahman
order, and the most intellectual Hindus of the present day are
to be found among his followers.   See Wilson, *op. cit.*, p. 171.
Sherring's " Sacred City of the Hindus," p. 146, *et seq.*

[3] The *bull* of Siva has reference to strength and speed rather
than to fecundity, while the Rig-veda refers to Vishnu as the
former of the *womb*, although elsewhere he is described as the
fecundator.   Muir, *op. cit.*, part iv., pp. 244, 292, 83, 64.

be given[1]. The worship of the serpent-god is not unknown, even at the present day, in the very stronghold of Siva-ism,[2] reminding us of the early spread of Buddhism among Naga tribes. In the "crescent surmounted by a pinnacle similar to the pointed end of a spear," which decorates the roofs of the Tibetan monasteries,[3] we undoubtedly have a reproduction of the so-called trident of Siva. This instrument is given also to *Sani*, the Hindu Saturn, who is represented as encompassed by two serpents,[4] and hence the pillar symbol of this primeval deity we may well suppose to be reproduced in the linga of the Indian Phallic god.[5] But the pillar symbol is not wanting to Buddhism itself. The columns said to have been raised by Asoka have a reference to the pillars of Seth. The remains of an ancient pillar supposed to be a Buddhist *Lat* is still to be seen at Benares,[6] the word *Lat* being merely another form of the name *Tet*, *Set*, or *Sat*, given to the Phœnician Semitic or deity. In the central pillar of the so-called Druidical circles we have doubtless a reference to the same primitive superstition, the idea intended to be represented being the combination of the male and female principles.[7]

[1] This question has been considered by Burnoux, *op. cit.*, p. 547, *et seq.* But see also Hodgson's "Buddhism in Nepaul," and paper in the "Journal of the Royal Asiatic Society," vol. xviii. (1860), p. 395, *et seq.*

[2] See Herring, *op. cit.*, p. 89.   [3] Schlagenweit, *op. cit.*, p. 181.

[4] Maurice's "Indian Antiquities," vol. vii., p. 566.

[5] As to the identity of Siva and Saturn, see Guigniaut, *op. cit.*, vol. i., p. 167 *n.*

[6] Sherring, *op cit.*, p. 305, *et seq.*

[7] It should be noted that many of the so-called "circles" are in reality *elliptical.*

In conclusion, it must be said that Christianity itself is certainly not without the Phallic element. Reference may be made to the important place taken in Christian dogma by the "fall," which has been shown to have had a purely Phallic foundation, and to the peculiar position assigned to Mary, as the Virgin Mother of God.[1] It must not be forgotten, however, that, whatever may have been the primitive idea on which these dogmas are based, it had received a totally fresh aspect at the hands of those from whom the founders of Christianity received it.[2] As to symbols, too, these were employed by the Christians in the later signification given to them by the followers of the ancient faiths. Thus the fish and the cross symbols orginally embodied the idea of *generation*, but afterwards that of *life*, and it was in this sense that they were applied to Christ.[3] The most evidently Phallic representation used by the Christian Iconographers is undoubtedly the *aureole*, or *vesica piscis*, which is elliptical in form and contained the figure of Christ—Mary herself, however, being sometimes represented in the aureole, glorified as Jesus Christ.[4] Probably

[1] See, on this subject, Higgins' "Anacalypsis," vol. i., p. 315, *et seq*.

[2] We must look to the esoteric teaching of Mithraism for the origin and explanation of much of primitive Christian dogma. The doctrine of "regeneration," which is a spiritual application of the idea of physical generation, was known to all the religious systems of antiquity, and probably the Phallic emblems generally used were regarded by the initiated as having a hidden meaning. I may, perhaps, be allowed to refer to the second volume of my " Evolution of Morality" for information on the subject of the " re-birth."

[3] The serpent elevated in the wilderness is said to be typical of Christ. A Gnostic sect taught that Christ was Seth.

[4] Didron's " Christian Iconography" (Bohn), pp. 272-286.

the *nimbus* also is of Phallic significance, for, although generally circular, it was sometimes triangular, square, &c.[1] The name of Jehovah is inscribed within a radiating triangle.[2] Didron gives an illustration of St. John the Evangelist with a circular nimbus, surmounted by two sun-flowers, emblems of the sun, an idea which, says Didron, "reminds us of the Egyptian figures, from the heads of which two lotus-flowers rise in a similar manner."[3] There is also a curious representation in the same work of the *Divine hand* with the thumb and two forefingers outstretched, resting on a cruciform nimbus.[4] In Egypt the hand having the fingers thus placed was a symbol of Isis, and, from its accompaniments, there can be no doubt, notwithstanding the mesmeric character ascribed to it by Ennemoser,[5] that it had an essentially Phallic origin, although it may ultimately have been used to signify life. There can be no question, however, that, whatever may be thought as to the nature of its symbols,[6] the basis of Christianity is more emotional than that of any other religion now existing. Reference has been made to the presence in Hebraic theology of an idea of God—that of a Father—antagonistic to the Phœnician notion of the "Lord of Heaven." We have the same idea repeated in

[1] It is a curious fact that Buddhist saints are often represented in the *Vesica* and with the *nimbus*. See Hodgson's figures (Plates v. and vi.) in the "Journal of the Royal Asiatic Society," vol. xvi.

[2] Didron, pp. 27, 231.   [3] Ditto, p. 29.   [4] Ditto, p. 215.

[5] "History of Magic" (Bohn), vol. i., p. 253, *et seq.*

[6] As to these, see King's "Gnostics and their Remains," p. 72.

Christ's teaching, its distinctive characteristic being the recognition of God as the Universal Father—the Great Parent of mankind, who had sent His son into the world that he might reconcile it unto Himself. It is in the character of a forgiving parent that Christians are taught to view God, when He is not lost sight of in the presence of Christ, of whom the church is declared to be the bride. In Christianity we see the final expression of the primitive worship of the father as the head of the family—the generator—as the result of an instinctive reasoning process leading up from the particular to the universal—with which, however, the dogma of the "fall" and its consequences—deduced so strangely from a Phallic legend —have been incorporated.[1] As a religion of the emotions, the position of Christianity is perfectly unassailable. As a system of rational faith, however, it is otherwise; and the tendency of the present age is just the reverse of that which took place among the Hebrews—the substitution of a Heavenly King for a Divine Father. In fact, modern science is doing its best to effect for primitive fetishism, or demon-worship, what Christianity has done for Phallic-worship—generalise the powers of nature and make of God a Great Unknowable Being, who, like the Elohim, of the Mosaic Cosmogony, in some mysterious manner, causes

---

[1] In the philosophy of St. Paul, the death of Christ was rendered necessary by the fall. By the first man, Adam, came death, and in Christ the second Adam are all made alive. Mankind reverts to the position occupied by Adam before he sinned; and as in the New Jerusalem there is no marriage, so in the earthly paradise of the Hebrew legend man was at first intended to live alone.

all things to appear at a word. This cannot, however, be the real religion of the future. If God is to be worshipped at all, the Heavenly King and the Divine Father must be combined as a single term, and He must be viewed, not as the unknowable cause of being, but as the great source of all being, who may be known in nature—the expression of his life and energy, and in man who was "created" in his own image.

Note.—M. François Lenormant, in the seventh edition of his "Histoire ancienne de l'Orient" (T. i., p. 91), after considering the traditions of a great deluge preserved by various peoples, concludes that "the biblical deluge, far from being a myth, has been a real and historical fact, which has struck the ancestors of at least the Aryan or Indo-European, the Semitic or Syro-Arab, and the Hamitic or Kouschite races—that is, the three great civilised races of the ancient world, before the ancestors of these races were separated, and in the Asiatic country which they inhabited together." The authority of M. Lenormant is great, but preference must be given on this point to the arguments of M. Dupuis, who, in his "Origine de tous des Cultes" (T. iii., p. 176, *et seq.*), has almost certainly proved the astronomical character of what he terms the "fiction sacerdotale," which, however, may have originated with the common ancestors of the three races referred to by M. Lenormant.

CHAPTER III.

THE ORIGIN OF SERPENT-WORSHIP.

THE subject to be discussed in the present chapter is one of the most fascinating that can engage the attention of anthropologists. It is remarkable, however, that although so much has been written in relation to it, we are still almost in the dark as to the origin of the superstition in question. The student of mythology knows that certain ideas were associated by the peoples of antiquity with the serpent, and that it was the favourite symbol of particular deities; but why that animal rather than any other was chosen for the purpose is yet uncertain. The facts being well known, however, I shall dwell on them only so far as may be necessary to support the conclusions based upon them.

We are indebted to Mr. Fergusson for bringing together a large array of facts, showing the extraordinary range which serpent-worship had among ancient nations. It is true that he supposes it not to have been adopted by any nation belonging to the Semitic or Aryan stock; the serpent-worship of India and Greece originating, as he believes, with older peoples. However this may be, the superstition was certainly not unknown to either Aryans or Semites. The brazen serpent of the Hebrew exodus was destroyed in the reign of Hezekiah, owing to the idolatry to which it gave rise. In the mythology of the Chaldeans, from whom the Assyrians seem to have sprung, the serpent occupied a most important position. Among the allied Phœnicians and Egyptians it was one of the most divine symbols. In Greece, Hercules was said "to have been the progenitor of the whole race of serpent-worshipping Scythians, through his intercourse with the serpent Echidna;" and when Minerva planted the sacred olive on the Acropolis of Athens, she placed it under the care of the serpent-deity Erechthonios. As to the Latins, Mr. Fergusson remarks that "Ovid's 'Metamorphoses' are full of passages referring to the important part which the serpent performed in all the traditions of classic mythology." The superstitions connected with that animal are supposed not to have existed among the ancient Gauls and Germans; but this is extremely improbable, considering that it appears to have been known to the British Celts and to the Gothic inhabitants of Scandinavia. In Eastern Europe there is no doubt that the serpent superstition was anciently prevalent, and Mr. Fergusson refers to evidence proving that "both trees and serpents were worshipped by the peasantry in Esthonia and Finland within the limits of the present century, and even with all the characteristics possessed by the old faith when we first became acquainted with it."

The serpent entered largely into the mythology of the ancient Persians, as it does into that of the Hindus. In India it is associated with both Sivaism and Vishnuism, although its actual worship perhaps belonged rather to the aboriginal tribes among whom Buddhism is thought by recent writers to have originated. The modern home of the superstition, however, is Western Africa, where the serpent is not merely considered sacred, but is actually worshipped as divine. On the other side of the Indian Ocean traces of the same superstition are met with among the peoples of the Indian islands and of Polynesia, and also in China. The evidences of serpent-worship on the American Continent have long engaged the attention of archæologists, who have found it to be almost universal, under one form or another, among the aboriginal tribes. That animal was sculptured on the temples of Mexico and Peru, and its form is said by Mr. Squier to be of frequent occurrence among the mounds of Wisconsin. The most remarkable of the symbolic earthworks of North America is the great serpent mound of Adam's county, Ohio, the convolutions of which extend to a length of 1,000 feet. At the Edinburgh meeting of the British Association, in 1871, Mr. Phené gave an account of his discovery in Argyllshire of a similar mound several hundred feet long, and about fifteen feet high by thirty feet broad, tapering gradually to the tail, the head being surmounted by a circular cairn, which he supposes to answer to the solar disc above the head of the Egyptian uræus, the position of which, with head erect, answers to the form of the Oban serpent-mound. This discovery is of great interest, and its author is probably justified in assuming that the mound was connected with serpent-worship. It may be remarked, in evidence of the existence of such structures in other parts of the old world, that the hero of one of the Yaçnas of the Zend Avesta is made to rest on what he thinks is a bank, but which he finds to be a great green snake, doubtless a serpent-mound. Another ancient reference to these structures is made by Iphicrates, who, according to Bryant, "related that in Mauritania there were dragons of such extent, that grass grew upon their backs."

Let us now see what ideas have been associated with the serpent by various peoples. Mr. Fergusson mentions the curious fact that "the chief characteristic of the serpent throughout the East in all ages seems to have been their power over the wind and rain." According to Colonal Meadows Taylor, in the Indian Deccan, at the present day, offerings are made to the village divinities (of whom the nâg, or snake, is always one) at spring time and harvest for rain or fine weather, and also in time of cholera or other diseases or pestilence. So, among the Chinese, the dragon is regarded as the giver of rain, and in time of drought offerings are made to it. In the spring and fall of the year it is one of the objects worshipped, by command of the Emperor, by certain mandarins. The Chinese notion of the serpent or dragon dwelling above the clouds in spring to give rain reminds us of the Aryan myth of Vritra, or Ahi, the throttling snake, or dragon with three heads, who hides away the rain-clouds, but who is slain by Indra, the beneficent giver of rain. "Whenever," says Mr. Cox, "the rain is shut up in the clouds, the dark power is in revolt against Dyaus and Indra. In the rumblings of the thunder, while the drought still sucks out the life of the earth, are heard the mutterings of their hateful enemy. In the lightning flashes which precede the outburst of the pent-up waters are seen the irresistible spears of the god, who is attacking the throttling serpent in his den; and in the serene heaven which shone out when the deluging clouds are passed away, men beheld the face of the mighty deity who was their friend." Mr. Cox elsewhere remarks that Vritra, "the enemy of Indra, reappears in all the dragons, snakes, or worms slain by all the heroes of Aryan mythology."

Whether the great serpent be the giver or the storer of rain, the Aryans, like all Eastern peoples, suppose it to have power over the clouds. This, however, is only one of its attributes. It is thought to have power over the wind as well as the rain, and this also is confirmed by reference to Aryan mythology. Mr. Cox has well shown that Hermes is "the air in motion, or wind, varying in degree from the soft breath of a summer breeze to the rage of the growing hurricane." In these more violent moods he is represented by the Maruts, the "crushers" or "grinders," who are also the children of Rudra, the "Father of the Winds," and himself the "wielder of the thunderbolt" and the "mightiest of the mighty." Rudra is also "the robber, the cheat, the deceiver, the master thief," and in this character both he and Hermes agree with the cloud-thief Vritra.

Notwithstanding the fact that in the Mahâbharâta, Rudra, like Hercules, is described as the "destroyer of serpents," he is in the same poem identified with Mahadeva, and hence he is evidently the same as Siva, who has the title of King of Serpents. The primitive character of Siva, as the Vedic Rudra, is now almost lost, but the identity of the two deities may be supported by reference to an incident related in the myth of Hermes and Apollo. It is said that, in return for the sweet-sounding lyre, Apollo gave to Hermes the magical "three-leafed rod of wealth and happiness." Sometimes this rod was entwined with serpents instead of fillets, and there is no difficulty in recognising in it the well-known emblem of Siva, which also is sometimes encircled by serpents. It can be shown that the Hindu deity is a form of Saturn, one of the Semitic names for whom was Set or Seth. It was the serpent-symbol of this God[1] which was said to have been elevated in the wilderness for the healing of the people bitten by serpents, and curiously enough Rudra (Siva) was called not only the *bountiful*, the *strong*, but the *healer*. The later Egyptian title of the god Set was Typhon, of whom Mr. Breal says that "Typhon is the monster who obscures the heaven, a sort of Greek Vritra." The myth of Indra and Vritra is reproduced in Latin mythology as that of Hercules and Căcus. Căcus also is analogous to Typhon, and as the former is supposed to have taken his name from, or given it to, a certain wind which had the power of clothing itself with clouds, so the latter bore the same name as a very destructive wind which was much dreaded by the Phœnicians and Egyptians. Moreover, the name Typhon was given by the Egyptians to anything tempestuous, and hence to the ocean; and in Hebrew the allied word "Suph" denotes a "whirlwind." There is another point of contact, however, between Siva and the god Set or Typhon, who was known to the

---

[1] Theodoret did not distinguish between an Egyptian sect called *Sethians* and the Gnostic *Ophites* or serpent-worshippers.

Egyptians also as the serpent Aphôphis, or the giant. An ancient writer states that one of the names of El, or Chronos, was Typhon, and the serpent and pillar symbols of the Phœnician deity confirm the identification between Set or Saturn, and the Siva of the Hindu Pantheon.

One of the leading ideas connected with the serpent was, as we have seen, its power over the rain, but another equally influential was its connection with health. Mr. Fergusson remarks that " when we first meet with serpent-worship, either in the wilderness of Sinai, the groves of Epidaurus, or in the Sarmatian huts, the serpent is always the Agatho-dæmon, the bringer of health and good fortune."[1] The Agatho-dæmon, which in ancient Egypt presided over the affairs of men as the guardian spirit of their houses,[2] was the Asp of Ranno, the snake-headed goddess who is represented as nursing the young princes. That the idea of health was intimately associated with the serpent is shown by the crown formed of the asp, or sacred *Thermuthis*, having been given particularly to Isis, a goddess of life and healing. It was also the symbol of other deities with the like attributes. Thus on a papyri it encircles the figure of Harpocrates, who was identified with the serpent god Æsculapius ; while

---

[1] The heavenly serpent, *Danh*, of the Dahomans, is said by Captain Burton to be the god of wealth. " His earthly representative is esteemed the supreme bliss and general good." The Slavonian Morlacchi still consider that the sight of a snake crossing the road is an omen of good fortune.—Wilkinson's " Dalmatia and Montenegro," vol. ii., p. 160.

[2] Mr. Lane states that each quarter of Cairo is supposed to have its guardian genius, or Agatho-dæmon, in the form of a serpent.—Vol. i., p. 289.

not only was a great serpent kept alive in the temple of Serapis, but on later monuments this deity is represented by a great serpent, with or without a human head. Sanchoniathon says of that animal—"It is long-lived, and has the quality not only of putting off its old age and assuming a second youth, but of receiving at the same time an augmentation of its size and strength." The serpent, therefore, was a fit emblem of Rudra, "the healer;" and the gift which Apollo presented to Mercury could be entwined by no more appropriate object than the animal which was supposed to be able to give the health without which even Mercury's magic-staff could not confer wealth and happiness. It is remarkable that a Moslem saint of Upper Egypt is still thought to appear under the form of a serpent, and to cure the diseases which afflict the pilgrims to his shrine.

Ramahavaly, one of the four national idols of the Malagasy, bears a curious analogy to the serpent gods of wisdom and healing. One of his titles is *Rabiby*, signifying "animal," and denoting "the god of beasts;" and his emissaries are the serpents which abide in Madagascar, and are looked upon with superstitious fear by the inhabitants. Ramahavaly is, moreover, regarded as the Physician of Imerina, and is thought to preserve from, or expel, epidemic diseases. Mr. Ellis says that he is sometimes described "as god, sacred, powerful, and almighty; who kills and makes alive; who heals the sick, and prevents diseases and pestilence; who can cause thunder and lightning to strike their victims or prevent their fatality; can cause rain in abundance when wanted, or can withhold it so as to ruin the crops of rice. He is also celebrated for his knowledge of the past and future, and for his capacity of discovering whatever is hidden or concealed."

It is probable that the association with the serpent of the idea of healing arose from the still earlier recognition of that animal as a symbol of life. We have already referred to the representations in the Egyptian temples of the young princes being nursed by a woman having the head of an asp. It is interesting to find that in India at the present day serpent-worship is expressly resorted to on behalf of children, and "the first hair of a child which is shaved off when it has passed teething and other infantine ailments is frequently dedicated to a serpent." This animal in both cases is treated as the guardian of life, and therefore the crown given to Egyptian sovereigns and divinities was very properly formed of the asp of Rânno. Another snake-headed Egyptian goddess has the name *Hih* or *Hoh*, and Sir Gardner Wilkinson mentions that the Coptic word *Hof* signifies the viper, analogous to the *hye* of the Arabs. The Arabic word *hiya*, indeed, means both life and a serpent. This connection is supported by the association, already pointed out, between the serpent and the gods of the life-giving wind, and by the fact that these also possess the pillar symbol of life. This belongs as well to Siva the destroyer, the preserver, and the creator, as to Set or Saturn, to Thoth-Hermes, and El or Chronos. Both the serpent and the pillar were assigned also to many of the personifications of the sun, the deified source of earthly life. Probably the well-known figure representing the serpent with its tail in its mouth was intended to symbolise endless life rather than eternity, an idea which does not appear to have been associated with that animal by the Egyptians. Agreeably with this view, Horapollo affirms that Kneph-Agatho-dæmon denoted immortality.

One of the best-known attributes of the serpent is wisdom. The Hebrew tradition of the fall speaks of that animal as the most subtle of the beasts of the field; and the founder of Christianity tells his disciples to be as wise as serpents, though as harmless as doves. Among the ancients the serpent was consulted as an oracle, and Maury points out that it played an important part in the life of several celebrated Greek diviners in connection with the knowledge of the language of birds, which many of the ancients believed to be the souls of the dead. The serpent was associated with Apollo and Athené, the Grecian deities of wisdom, as well as with the Egyptian Kneph,[1] the ram-headed god from whom the Gnostics are sometimes said to have derived their idea of the *Sophia*. This personification of divine wisdom is undoubtedly represented on Gnostic gems under the form of the serpent. In Hindu mythology there is the same association between the animal and the idea of wisdom. Siva, as Sambhu, is the patron of the Brahmanic order, and, as shown by his being three-eyed, is essentially a god possessing high intellectual attributes. Vishnu also is a god of wisdom, but of the somewhat lower type which is distinctive

---

[1] Warburton supposes that the worship of the One God Kneph was changed into that of the dragon or winged-serpent Knuphis.

of the worshippers of truth under its feminine aspect. The connection between wisdom and the serpent is best seen, however, in the Hindu legends as to the Nagas. Mr. Fergusson remarks that "the Naga appears everywhere in Vaishnava tradition. There is no more common representation of Vishnu[1] than as reposing on the Sesha, the celestial seven-headed snake, contemplating the creation of the world. It was by his assistance that the ocean was churned and Amrita produced. He everywhere spreads his protecting hood over the god or his avatars; and in all instances it is the seven-headed heavenly Naga, not the earthly cobra of Siva." The former animal, no doubt, is especially symbolical of wisdom, and it is probably owing to his intellectual attributes, rather than to his destructive or creative power, that Siva is sometimes styled the King of Serpents. The Upanishads refer to the science of serpents, by which is meant the wisdom of the mysterious Nagas, who, according to Buddhistic legend, reside under Mount Méru, and in the waters of the terrestrial world. One of the sacred books of the Tibetan Buddhists is fabled to have been received from the Nagas, who, says Schlagentweit, are "fabulous creatures of the nature of serpents, who occupy a place among the beings superior to man, and are regarded as protectors of the law of the Buddha. To these spiritual beings Sâkyamuni is said to have taught a more philosophical religious system than to men, who were not sufficiently advanced to understand it at the time of his appearance." So far as this has any historical basis, it can mean only

---

[1] Vishnu is often identified with Kneph.

that Gautama taught his most secret doctrines to the
Nagas, or aboriginal serpent-worshippers, who were
the first to accept his teaching, and whose religious
ideas had probably much in common with those of
Gautama himself. Mr. Fergusson refers to the fact that
a king of the Naga race was reigning in Magadha when
Buddha was born in 623 B.C.; and he adds that the
dissemination of his religion "is wholly due to the
accident of its having been adopted by the low caste
kings of Magadha, and to its having been elevated by
one of them to the rank of the religion of the state."
It would appear, indeed, that according to a Hindu
legend, Gautama himself had a serpent lineage.

The "serpent-science" of Hindu legend has a curious
parallel in Phœnician mythology. The invention of
the Phœnician written character is referred to the god-
Taaut or Thoth, whose snake-symbol bears his name
Têt, and is used to represent the ninth letter of the
alphabet (*teta*), which in the oldest Phœnician character has the form of the snake curling itself up. Philo
thus explains the form of the letter *theta*, and that
the god from whom it took its name was designated
by the Egyptians as a snake curled up, with its head
turned inwards. Philo adds that the letters of the
Phœnician alphabet "are those formed by means of
serpents; afterwards, when they built temples, they
assigned them a place in the adytums, instituted
various ceremonies and solemnities in honour of them,
and adored them as the supreme gods, the rulers of
the universe." Bunsen thinks the sense of this passage is "that the forms and movements of serpents
were employed in the invention of the oldest letters,

which represent the gods." He says, however, that " the alphabet does not tally at all with the Phœnician names," and the explanation given by Philo, although curious as showing the ideas anciently associated with the serpent, is reliable only so far as it confirms the connection between that animal and the inventor of the written characters. According to another tradition, the ancient theology of Egypt was said to have been given by the Agatho-dæmon, who was the benefactor of all mankind.

The account given of the serpent by Sanchoniathon, as cited by Eusebius, is worth repetition as showing the peculiar notions anciently current in connection with that animal. The Phœnician writer says: " Taautus first attributed something of the divine nature to the serpent and the serpent tribe, in which he was followed by the Phœnicians and Egyptians; for this animal was esteemed by him to be the most inspired of all the reptiles, and of a fiery nature, inasmuch as it exhibits an incredible celerity, moving by its spirit without either hands or feet, or any of those external members by which other animals effect their motion, and in its progress it assumes a variety of forms, moving in a spiral course, and darting forwards with whatever degree of swiftness it pleases. It is, moreover, long-lived, and has the quality not only of putting off its old age, and assuming a second youth, but of receiving at the same time an augmentation of its size and strength, and when it has fulfilled the appointed measure of its existence it consumes itself, as Taautus has laid down in the sacred books; upon which account this animal is introduced in the sacred rites and mysteries." In India at the present day some Brahmans always keep the skin of a nâg, or snake, in one of their sacred books, probably from some idea connected with the casting by the serpent of its skin referred to in the preceding passage.

We have now seen that the serpent was anciently the symbol of wisdom, life, and healing, and also that it was thought to have power over the wind and rain. This last attribute is easily understood when the importance of rain in the east is considered, and the ideas associated by the ancients with the air and moisture are remembered. The Hebrew tradition which speaks of the creative spirit moving over the face of the waters embodies those ideas, according to which the water contains the elements of life and the wind is the vivifying principle. The attribute of wisdom cannot so easily be connected with that of life. The power of healing is certainly an evidence of the possession of wisdom,[1] but as it is only one phase of it, probably the latter attribute was antecedent to the former, or at least it may have had an independent origin. What this origin was may perhaps be explained by reference to certain other ideas very generally entertained in relation to the serpent. Among various African tribes this animal is viewed with great veneration, under the belief that it is often the re-embodiment of a deceased ancestor. This notion appears to be prevalent also among the

---

[1] According to Gaelic and German folklore, the white snake when boiled has the faculty of conferring medicinal wisdom. The white snake is venerated as the king of serpents by the Scottish Highlanders as by certain Arab tribes, and it would appear also by the Singhalese of Ceylon.

Hindus, who, like the Kafirs, will never kill a serpent, although it is usually regarded with more dislike than veneration. Mr. Squier remarks that "many of the North American tribes entertain a superstitious regard for serpents, and particularly for the rattlesnake.[1] Though always avoiding they never destroy it, 'lest,' says Barham, 'the spirit of the reptile should excite its kindred to revenge.'" Mr. Squier adds that, "according to Adair, this fear was not unmingled with veneration. Charlevoix states that the Natchez had the figure of a rattlesnake, carved from wood, placed among other objects upon the altar of their temple, to which they paid great honour. Heckwelder relates that the Linni Linape called the rattlesnake 'grandfather,' and would on no account allow it to be destroyed. Hemy states that the Indians around Lake Huron had a similar superstition, and also designated the rattlesnake as their 'grandfather.' He also mentions instances in which offerings of tobacco were made to it, and its parental care solicited for the party performing the sacrifice. Carver also mentions an instance of similar regard on the part of a Menominee Indian, who carried a rattlesnake constantly with him, 'treating it as a deity, and calling it his great father.'"

The most curious notion, however, is that of the Mexicans, who always represented the first woman, whose name was translated by the old Spanish writers "the woman of our flesh," as accompanied by a great male serpent. The serpent is the sun-god *Tonacatlcoatl*, the principal deity of the Mexican Pantheon,

---

[1] The snake is one of the Indian tribal *totems*.

and his female companion, the goddess mother of mankind, has the title *cihua-cohuatl*, which signifies " woman of the serpent." With the Peruvians, also, the principal deity was the serpent-sun, whose wife, the female serpent, gave birth to a boy and a girl from whom all mankind were said to be descended. It is remarkable that the serpent origin thus ascribed to the human race is not confined to the aborigines of America. According to Herodotus, the primeval mother of the Scyths was a monster, half woman and half serpent. This reminds us of the serpent parentage ascribed to various personages of classical antiquity.[1] Among the Semites, Zohak, the traditional Arabian conqueror of Central Asia, is represented as having two snakes growing at his back; and Mr. Bruce mentions that the line of the Abyssinian kings begins with " The Serpent," *Arwe*, who is said to have reigned at Axum for 400 years, showing that the royal descent was traced from this animal. From the position assigned to the dragon in China, it probably was formerly thought to stand in a similar relation to the Emperor, of whom it is the special symbol.

The facts cited prove that the serpent superstition is intimately connected with ancestor-worship, probably originating among uncultured tribes, who, struck by the noiseless movement and the activity of the

---

[1] Pausanias, iv., 14, mentions Aristodama, the mother of Aratus, as having had intercourse with a serpent, and the mother of the great Scipio was said to have conceived by a serpent. Such was the case also with Olympias, the mother of Alexander, who was taught by her that he was a god, and who in return deified her.—*Le Mythe de la Femme et du Serpent*, par Ch. Schoebel, 1876, p. 84.

serpent, combined with its peculiar gaze and power of casting its skin, viewed it as a spirit embodiment. As such, it would be supposed to have the superior wisdom and power ascribed to the denizens of the invisible world, and from this would originate also the ascription to it of the power over life and health, and over the moisture on which those benefits are dependent. The serpent-spirit may, however, have made its appearance for a good or a bad purpose, to confer a benefit or to inflict punishment for the misdeeds of the living. The notion of there being good and evil serpent-spirits would thus naturally arise. Among ancestor-worshipping peoples, however, the serpent would be viewed as a good being who busied himself about the interests of the tribe to which he had once belonged. When the simple idea of a spirit-ancestor was transformed into that of the Great Spirit, the father of the race, the attributes of the serpent would be enlarged. The common ancestor would be relegated to the heavens, and that which was necessary to the life and well-being of his people would be supposed to be under his care. Hence the great serpent was thought to have power over the rain and the hurricane, with the latter of which he was probably often identified.

When the serpent was thus transferred to the atmosphere, and the superstition lost its simple character as a phase of ancestor-worship, its most natural association would be with the solar cult. It is not surprising, therefore, to find that *Quetzalcoatl*, the divine benefactor of the Mexicans, was an incarnation of the serpent-sun *Tonacatlcoatl*, who thus became the great father, as the female serpent *Cihuacoatl* was the great mother, of the human race. It is an interesting inquiry how far the sun-gods of other peoples partook of this double character. Bunsen has a remarkable passage bearing on the serpent nature of those deities. He says that "Esmun-Esculapius is strictly a Phœnician god. He was especially worshipped at Berytus. At Carthage he was called the highest god, together with Astarte and Hercules. At Babylon, according to the above genealogy of Bel, Apollo corresponded to him. As the snake-god he must actually be Hermes, in Phœnician Têt, Taautes. . . . In an earlier stage of cosmogonical consciousness he is Agatho-dæmon-Sôs, whom Lepsius has shown to be the third god in the first order of the Egyptian Pantheon." The serpent deity who was thus known under so many forms was none other than the sun-god Set or Saturn, who has already been identified with Siva and other deities having the attributes usually ascribed to the serpent. Bunsen asserts that Set is common to all the Semites and Chaldeans, as he was to the Egyptians, but that "his supposed identity with Saturn is not so old as his identity with the sun-god, as Sirius (Sôthis), because the sun has the greatest power when it is in Sirius." Elsewhere the same writer says that "the Oriento-Egyptian conception of Typhon-Set was that of a drying-up parching heat. Set is considered as the sun-god when he has reached his zenith, the god of the summer sun."

The solar[1] character of the serpent-god appears

---

[1] Mr. Robert Brown, jun., says that the serpent has six principal points of connection with Dionysos:—1, As a symbol of,

therefore to be placed beyond doubt. But what was the relation in which he was supposed to stand to the human race? Bunsen, to whose labours I am so much indebted, remarks that Seth " appears gradually among the Semites as the background of their religious consciousness," and not merely was he " the primitive god of northern Egypt and Palestine," but his genealogy as " the Seth of Genesis, the father of Enoch (the man), must be considered as originally running parallel with that derived from the Elohim, Adam's father." Seth is thus the divine ancestor of the Semites, a character in which, but in relation to other races, the solar deities generally agree with him. The kings and priests of ancient peoples claimed this divine origin, and " children of the sun" was the title of the members of the sacred caste. When the actual ancestral character of the deity is hidden he is regarded as " the father of his people" and their divine benefactor. He is the introducer of agriculture, the inventor of arts and sciences, and the civiliser of mankind; " characteristics," says Faber, " which every nation ascribed to the first of their gods or the oldest of their kings." This was true of Thoth, Saturn, and other analogous deities, and the Adam of Hebrew tradition was the father of agriculture, as his representative Noah was the introducer of the vine.

Elsewhere I have endeavoured to show that the name of the great ancestor of Hebrew tradition has

and connected with, wisdom; 2, As a solar emblem; 3, As a symbol of time and eternity; 4, As an emblem of the earth-life; 5, As connected with fertilising moisture; 6, As a Phallic emblem.—*The Great Dionysiak Myth*, 1878, ii., 66.

been preserved by certain peoples who may thus be classed together as Adamites. He appears, indeed, to be the recognised legendary ancestor of the members of that division of mankind whose primeval home we can scarcely doubt was in Central Asia, answering in this respect to the Seth of the Semites. According to the tradition, however, as handed down to us by the Hebrews, Seth himself was the son of Adam. From this, it would seem to follow that, as Seth was the serpent sun-god (the Agatho-dæmon), the legendary ancestor of the Adamites must himself have partaken of the same character. Strange as this idea may appear it is not without warrant. We have already seen that the Mexicans a scribed that nature to *Tonacatlcoatl* and his wife, the mother of mankind, and that a similar notion was entertained by various peoples of the old world. The Chaldean god *Héa* who, as the " teacher of mankind," and the "lord of understanding," answers exactly to the divine benefactor of the race before referred to, was " figured by the great serpent which occupies so conspicuous a place among the symbols of the gods on the black stones recording Babylonian benefactions." The name of the god is connected with the Arabic *Hiya*, which signifies a serpent as well as life, and Sir Henry Rawlinson says that " there are very strong grounds indeed for connecting him with the serpent of Scripture, and with the Paradisaical traditions of the tree of knowledge and the tree of life." The god Héa was, therefore, the serpent revealer of knowledge, answering in some respects to the serpent of the fall. He was, however, the Agathodæmon, and in the earlier form of the legend doubtless answered to the great human ancestor himself. It is curious that, according to Rabbinical tradition, Cain was the son, not of Adam, but of the serpent-spirit Asmodeus, who is the same as the Persian Ahriman, "the great serpent with two feet."[1] In the name of Eve, the mother of mankind, we have, indeed, direct reference to the supposed serpent-nature of our first parents. Clemens Alexandrinus long since remarked that the name *Hevia*, aspirated, signifies a female serpent. The name Eve is evidently connected with the same Arabic root as that which we have seen to mean both "life" and "a serpent," and the Persians appear to have called the constellation *Serpens* "the little Ava," that is *Eve*, a title which is still given to it by the Arabs. But if Eve was the serpent mother, Adam must have been the serpent father. In the old Akkad tongue *Ad* signifies "a father," and the mythical personages with whom Adam is most nearly allied, such as Seth or Saturn, Taaut or Thoth, and others, were serpent deities. Such would seem to have been the case also with the deities whose names show a close formal resemblance to that of Adam. Thus the original name of Hercules was *Sandan* or *Adanos*, and Hercules, like the allied god Mars, was undoubtedly often closely associated with the serpent. This notion is confirmed by the identification of Adonis and Osiris as *Azar* or *Adar*, according to Bunsen the later Egyp-

---

[1] Mr. Cooper states (*loc. cit.*, p. 390) that prominent in the Egyptian religious system was the belief in a monstrous *personal* evil being typically represented as a serpent, and that the principle of good was there likewise represented by an entirely different serpent, a constant spiritual warfare being maintained between the two.

tian *Sar-Apis*, who is known to have been represented as a serpent. The *Abaddon* of St. John, the old dragon Satan, was probably intended for the same serpent-god. It is interesting to compare the ideas entertained as to the great dragon in the Book of Revelation and those held by the Chinese in relation to probably the same being. Mr. Doolittle says : "The dragon holds a remarkable position in the history and government of China. It also enjoys an ominous eminence in the affections of the Chinese people. It is frequently represented as the greatest benefactor of mankind. It is the dragon which causes the clouds to form and the rain to fall. The Chinese delight in praising its wonderful properties and powers. It is the venerated symbol of good."

This was probably the view originally taken by the Egyptians, who were all followers of the serpent cult. In Egypt two kinds of serpents were the objects of peculiar veneration, and of an almost universal worship. All the gods were more or less symbolised or crowned by serpents, while all the goddesses were hieroglyphically represented by serpents. The animal used for these purposes was the cobra de copello, or uræus, which, according to Mr. W. R. Cooper,[1] "from its dangerous beauty, and in consequence of ancient tradition asserting it to have been spontaneously produced by the rays of the sun," was universally assumed as the "emblem of divine and sacro-regal sovereignty." The uræus appears to be always represented on the Egyptian monuments, in

[1] "The Serpent Myths of Ancient Egypt," published in the "Transactions of the Victoria Institute," vol. vi., 1872.

the feminine form, and it was used as a symbol of fecundity, agreeably to which idea the generative power of the solar beams is typified by pendent uræi. The uræus, moreover, symbolised life and the power of healing, and it was the emblem of immortality. Mr. Cooper remarks that in the Egyptian religious system the principle of good was typically represented by a serpent, while under the form of an entirely different serpent was figured a monstrous *personal* evil being who maintained a constant spiritual warfare with the spirit of good. The serpent embodiment of the principle of evil was called Hof, Rehof, or Aphôphis, and it was a species of coluber of large size. It is described as "the destroyer, the enemy of the gods, and the devourer of the souls of men;" and it was thought to dwell in the depths of "that mysterious ocean upon which the Baris, or boat of the sun, was navigated by the gods through the hours of day and night, in the celestial regions." The idea of an antagonism between the giant serpent Aphôphis and the good serpent, as the "soul of the world," constantly occurs in the Ritual of the Dead, and the aid of every divinity in turn is sought by the deceased in his conflict with the evil being. It is remarkable that the "soul of the world," Chnuphis, or Bait, is represented as a coluber, and that it appears to be identified with Aphôphis in one chapter of the Ritual. Mr. Cooper states that, although a large coluber which is figured as being worshipped resembles Aphôphis, it cannot be him, as there is no example of direct worship paid to Aphôphis, "unless, indeed, we identify it with Sutekh, as the Shepherd Kings, the last but one of whom was named Aphôphis, appear to have done." The serpent Aphôphis is sometimes represented with the crown of Lower Egypt upon his head, and at one period he was identified with Set or Seth, the national deity of the Hyksos or Shepherd tribes. All traces of the worship of Set was obliterated from the Egyptian monuments, but one representation has been preserved in which Set is figured with Horus, united as one divinity, between the triple serpent of good. This shows that Set, and probably, therefore, his serpent emblem, was originally not considered evil. Lower Egypt was largely populated by Semitic peoples, whose national deity was their legendary ancestor Seth, and the detestation with which the Egyptians regarded Set and the serpent Aphôphis identified with him was probably the result of national enmity. Mr. Cooper points out that the serpent of good is always represented by the Egyptians as upright and the serpent of evil as crawling, this being generally the only distinction made. The god Chnuphis, the " soul of the world," is usually figured as a Serpent (Coluber) walking upon two human legs, and curiously enough this is the form taken by the evil principle of Persian mythology, the great serpent walking on two feet. A similar inversion of ideas occurs in the religious mythology of the Naga peoples of the East. Near the ruined temples of Cambodia, as on the Buddhist Topes of India, are sculptured gigantic serpents with voluminous folds supported by human figures, as the gigantic Aphôphis is represented on the Egyptian monuments. There must have been some special reason why the great serpent was regarded so differently by various peoples, and this was probably the result of race antagonism.

It is remarkable that one of the most ancient people of whom we have any written record—the primitive inhabitants of Chaldea—not only bore the name of the traditional father of mankind, but were especially identified with the serpent. The predecessors of the *Akkad*, in Chaldea, were the Medes, or *Mad*, of Berosus, and the distinctive title of at least the later Medes was *Már*, which in Persian means " a snake." This Sir Henry Rawlinson supposes to have given rise " not only to the Persian traditions of Zohák and his snakes, but to the Armenian traditions, also, of the dragon dynasty of Media." The Medes of Berosus belonged almost certainly to the old Scythic stock of Central Asia, to whom the Chaldeans, the Hebrews, and the Aryans have alike been affiliated by different writers. When, therefore, Mr. Fergusson says that serpent-worship characterised the old Turanian Chaldean Empire, he would seem to trace it to the old Asiatic centre. Probaby to the same source must be traced the serpent tradition of the Abyssinian kings. Bryant long since asserted that that superstition originated with the Amonians or Hamites, who also would seem to have been derived from the Scythic stock. The facts brought together in the preceding pages far from exhaust the subject, but they appear to justify the following conclusions :—

First, The serpent has been viewed with awe or veneration from primeval times, and almost universally as a re-embodiment of a deceased human being, and as such there were ascribed to it the attributes of life and wisdom, and the power of healing.

Secondly, The idea of a simple spirit re-incarnation of a deceased ancestor gave rise to the notion that mankind originally sprang from a serpent, and ultimately to a legend embodying that idea.

Thirdly, This legend was connected with nature—or rather sun-worship—and the sun was, therefore, looked upon as the divine serpent—father of man and nature.

Fourthly, Serpent-worship, as a developed religious system, originated in Central Asia, the home of the great Scythic stock, from whom all the civilised races of the historical period sprang.

Fifthly, These peoples are the Adamites, and their mythical ancestor was at one time regarded as the Great Serpent, his descendants being in a special sense serpent-worshippers.

Note.—At page 88, the Malagasy idol Ramahavaly is spoken of as still existing. As a fact, however, in 1869 all the Malagasy national idols were, by order of the Government, publicly burned. Many other idols and charms were at the same time destroyed by their owners.—*Madagascar and its People*, by the Rev. James Sibree, Jun., p. 481.

CHAPTER IV.

THE ADAMITES.

MUCH has from time to time been written as to the distinction between the Adamites and the pre-Adamites, although little has been done to identify the members of the two great divisions into which the human race has been thus divided. Those who accept the Deluge of Noah as a historical fact, stated however in terms too wide, may say generally that all the descendants of this patriarch are, as such, Adamites, while the pre-Adamites comprise the peoples of the primitive area inhabited by the dark races, supposed by some writers to be referred to in the Hebrew Scriptures under the term *ish*, " the sons of man," as distinguished from the sons of Adam.   Little value, however, can be attached to such a general statement as this.   Supposing Noah to have been a second common father of the race, we are still ignorant as to what peoples are to be classed among his descendants. No doubt the *Toldoth Beni Noah* of Genesis throws considerable light on the question.   According to that genealogical table the whole earth was divided after the Flood among the families of the three sons of Noah—Shem, Ham, and Japheth. It is not necessary here to identify the peoples described as the descendants of these patriarchs. It will suffice to say that Professor Rawlinson, who differs only in one or two particulars from other recent authorities, writes as to the distribution of those peoples: "Whereas the Japhetic and Hamitic races are geographically contiguous, the former spread over all the northern regions known to the genealogist—Greece, Thrace, Scythia, most of Asia Minor, Armenia, and Media; the latter over all the south and the south-west, North Africa, Egypt, Nubia, Ethiopia, Southern and South-eastern Arabia, and Babylonia—so the Semitic races are located in what may be called one region, that region being the central one, lying intermediate between the Japhetic region upon the north and the Hamitic one upon the south."

Supposing the Toldoth to give an exact statement of the descendants of the three sons of Noah, it by no means follows that the peoples there referred to are alone entitled to be classed as Adamites, and I propose, therefore, to see whether the latter can be identified by other evidence. Almost intuitively we turn, in the first place, to that region known as Chaldea, which has furnished in our own days material so important for the reconstruction of the annals of civilised man in the earliest historical period. Professor Rawlinson, indeed, at the Liverpool meeting of the British Association, held in 1870, sought to establish that the Garden of Eden of the Hebrew writers was none other than Babylonia; a hypothesis which certainly agrees with Sir Henry Rawlinson's statement that *Héa*, the third member of the primitive Chaldean triad, may be connected with the Paradisaical traditions of the tree of knowledge and the tree of life. This would point to Chaldea as the original home of the Adamites, unless, indeed, the traditions were derived from a still earlier centre, and it will be well to ascertain whether there is anything in the history of Babylon which directly connects its people with the Adamic stock.

If we were to accept with Chwolson the great antiquity of "The Book of Nabathæan Agriculture," there would be no difficulty in assigning such a position to the Chaldeans. For this book not only expressly declares that they were the descendants of Adam, but in it Adam appears as the founder of agriculture in Babylon, acting the part of a civiliser, and hence named "The Father of Mankind." This agrees well with the Old Testament account of Adam as the first cultivator of the ground. M. Renan, however, would seem to have conclusively established the late date of the so-called Nabathæan work, showing that it contains legends as to Adam, Seth, Enoch, Noah, and Abraham, "analogous to those which they have in the apocryphal writings of the Jews and Christians, and subsequently in those of the Mussulmans," Adam being known to all the Moslem East as "The Father of Mankind."

We must seek, therefore, for some more reliable record of early Chaldean history; and this we have in the stone monuments on which its annals were engraved. Sir Henry Rawlinson, on their authority, says of the Chaldeans of Babylonia that they were " a branch of the great Hamitic race of *Akkad*, which inhabited Babylonia from the earliest times. With this race originated the art of writing, the building of cities, the institution of a religious system, the cultiva-

tion of all science, and of astronomy in particular."
The race affinity of the *Akkad* is hardly yet settled,
but some information as to this point may be gained
from the name by which they were designated. This
appears to be composed of two words *Ak(k)-Ad*, the
latter of which may be identified with the first syllable
of the name Adam. As to the word *Ak*, some light
may probably be thrown on its meaning by reference
to the Celtic languages. Baldwin, without seeing its
full bearing, makes the remark that the Dravidians of
Southern India use *Mag*, as the Berbers and Gaels
use *Mac* (*Mach*), the former word denoting "kindred"
in all the Teutonic languages. Now, it could be
proved by many examples that the letter *M*, which is
found at the beginning of certain words in various
eastern languages, is often simply a prefix. This is
especially the case in Hebrew and Arabic, and, therefore, probably in the more ancient languages with
which they are allied. Such, at least, must be the
case with the initial letter of the word *mach*, "son," as
in Erse the *m* is wanting, and in Welsh the related
word, having the sense of "a root or stem, lineage,"
is also simply *ach*. Thus *Ak(k)-Ad* may well be
"the sons or lineage of Ad;" as Mac-Adam in Gaelic
is "son of Adam." That the first syllable of this
word had the signification here assigned to it is
rendered extremely probable by another circumstance.
It is well known that the Welsh equivalent for *Mach*,
in the sense of "son," is *Ap;* and so also we find that
in Hebrew "son" is rendered by *ben* (the Assyrian
ban), while in Arabic it is *ibn*. In these words the *b*
is the root sound, and if son was expressed by *ak* in

the old Akkad tongue, this would bear the same relation to the Semitic languages as the Welsh does to the
Gaelic and Erse—*ak* and *ben* in the one class answering
to *ach* and *ap* in the other. Nor is this view without
positive support. The Hebrew has a word *ach* which
expresses, not only the sense of "a brother," but also
"one of the same kindred." In Assyrian *uk* means a
"people," while *ak* signifies a "Creator;" these words
being connected with the old Egyptian *uk*, and also
ahi, "to live."

Nor is the idea that the Chaldean *Akkad* were literally "the sons of *Ad*" without historical basis. According to Berosus, the first Babylonian dynasty was
Median. What people were referred to by this name
is still undecided. Professor Rawlinson supposes that
they were really the same as the so-called Aryan
Medes of later history, while Sir Henry Rawlinson,
although treating the later Medes as Aryan, yet considers those of Bersosus to have belonged to a
Turanian, or at least a mixed Scytho-Aryan, stock.
Elsewhere Professor Rawlinson seems inclined to
identify the Chaldean *Akkad* with these Medes, as a
Turanian people who at a very early date conquered
the Babylonian Kushites and mixed with them. This
is, in fact, the conclusion which appears to be required
by other considerations. The name by which the
Medes are first noticed on the Assyrian monuments is
Mad. But if the initial labial is removed, this name
is reduced to the more simple form *Ad ;* and, supposing the explanation given of the primitive name of the
Chaldean race to be correct, the (*M*)*ad* who preceded
them would really be the parent stock from which the

Akkad, or Chaldeans, were derived. Confirmation of this notion may be supplied from another source. Among their Aryan neighbours the later Medes had the distinctive title of *Már*. This, Sir Henry Rawlinson supposes to have given rise, "not only to the Persian traditions of Zohák and his snakes, but to the Armenian traditions also of the dragon dynasty of Media, the word *Már* having in Persian the signification of a snake." But this must have been through ignorance of the real origin of the title, which had reference rather to the lion than to the snake. The Arab historian, Massoudi, in accounting for the application to the city of Babylon of the name of *Iran-Sheher*, observes that, "according to some, the true orthography should be *Arian-Sheher*, which signifies in Nabathæan, "the city of Lions," and that "this name of Lion designated the kings of Assyria, who bore the general title of Nimrud." Sir Henry Rawlinson thinks that the title *Már* is Scythic, and, if so, there can be little doubt of its signification. The primitive meaning of *Ar* was "fire," from which the lion, as the symbol of the Sun-god was called *ari*, the Sun-god himself having a name *Ra*. Strictly, therefore, *Már* would denote "fire-worshippers," a title which, as is well-known, was especially applicable to the ancient Medes. The *Aryans* generally appear to have been Sun- or Fire-worshippers, and probably they received their name from this fact. This would seem to be much more probable than the ordinary derivation of the name Aryan from the root *ar*, "to plough;" and it would include the sense of "noble" preferred by Mr. Peile, "children of the Sun" being usually a special title of the priestly or royal caste.

Connected with this question is that of the origin of the name of the Greek god *Ares* (the Latin *Mars*). Among other grounds for inferring the Asiatic origin of this deity is his connection with Herakles. The Latin myth of Hercules and Cacus would seem, moreover, to require the identification of the former with Mars. Such would appear to be the case also in Chaldean mythology. The Babylonian Mars was called *Nergal*, which is probably the same name as "Hercules," and Sir Henry Rawlinson suggests that the only distinction to be made between that deity and *Nin*, or Hercules, as gods of war and hunting, is that the former is more addicted to the chase of animals and the latter to that of mankind. That Hercules, or Herakles, was of Phœnician or Assyrian origin has been fully established by the learned researches of M. Raoul-Rochette, who has shown, moreover, that the proper name of that deity was *Sandan* or *Adanos* (*Adan*), a name which not only reminds us of Aduni, supposed by Professor Rawlinson to be a primeval Chaldean deity, but also recalls that of the Median *Ad*, and even of the Hebrew *Adam*.

A remark made by Lajard strongly confirms the idea that the Latin war-god was derived from a similar source. This learned French writer accounts for the rapidity with which *Mazdëism*, better known as the worship of Mithra, spread among the Romans, by supposing that it was in some way connected with their national worship. Probably a key to this connection may be found in the curious figures of Mithra which appear to have been peculiar to the Roman phase of Mazdöism. These figures, which are encircled by a serpent, unite to the human body and limbs, the head of the lion, and they might well be taken to represent Mars himself, since the title *Már*, which was distinctive of the Medes, not only conveyed the idea of a serpent, but was also, and more intimately, associated with the lion symbol of the Sun-god.

If the alliance thus sought to be established, through the title *Már*, between the Medes or *Mad*, and the other peoples of the so-called Aryan stock be correct, we may expect to find traces among some, at least, of these peoples of the primeval *Ad*. Nor will such expectation be disappointed. The Parsis of Bombay have a book called the "Desatir," the first part of which is entitled "the Book of the Great *Abad*," who is declared to have been the first ancestor of mankind. The authenticity of this book has been denied, as Mr. Baldwin thinks, however, on insufficient grounds. It is certainly strange, on the assumption of its being apocryphal, that such a name as *Abad* should have been given to the mythical head of the race. The meaning of the name is evidently "Father *Ad*," and there is nothing improbable in the Persians preserving a tradition of the mythical ancestor, whose memory was retained in the national name of the Medes, a people with whom they were so closely connected. It simply confirms the conclusion before arrived at, that they also must be classed among the Adamites.

The Hindus themselves would seem not to be without a remembrance of the mythical ancestor of the Adamic stock. The Puránas, which, notwithstanding their modern form, doubtless retain many old legends, refers to the reign of King *It* or *Ait*, as an avatar of Mahadeva (*Siva*), who is a form of Saturn. Assuming that the information given to Wilford as to the reign of this king in Egypt ought to be rejected; yet, as *Aetus* is mentioned by Greek writers as a Hindu, we must suppose such information to have been founded on actual statements contained in the Puránas. These certainly refer to the *Yáduvas*, descendants of Yadú, supposed emigrants to Abyssinia, whose character, as described in the Puránas, agrees well, says Wilford, with that ascribed "by the ancients to the genuine Ethiopians, who are said by Stephanus of Byzantium, by Eusebius, by Philostratus, by Eustathius, and others, to have come originally from India under the guidance of Aetus or Yátu," whom they believed to be the same as King Ait.

Nor do the Celtic peoples appear to be without a traditional remembrance of the mythical ancestor. The leading Celtic people of Gaul, in the time of Cæsar, were the *Ædin*, and Davies thought that their name was derived from *Aedd* the Great, whom he finds referred to in the Welsh triads, and whom he identifies with *Aides* or *Dis*. Cæsar, indeed, says that the god *Dis* was the mythical ancestor of the Gauls. The position occupied by this deity in the traditions of the Celtic race is very remarkable, when we consider that a divine person bearing the same name was known, not only to the Greeks, but apparently also to the Babylonians. Sir Henry Rawlinson points out that *Dis* should be one of the names of *Anu*, the first member of the leading Chaldean triad, and the deity who answered to *Hades* or *Pluto*. *Warka* or *Urka*, the great necropolis of Babylon, was especially dedicated to *Anu*, and Sir Henry Rawlinson remarks on this: "Can the coincidence then be merely accidental between *Dis*, the Lord of *Urka*, the City of the Dead, and *Dis*, the King of Orcus or Hades?" Most certainly not, as it is only one of many circumstances which prove the close connection of the Greeks and other Aryan peoples with the ancient Babylonians. The original character of *Dis*, "Lord of the Dead," was probably the same as that of the Gallic *Dis*, *i.e.*, the mythical ancestor of the race. A similar change of character has been undergone by the Hindu *Yama*.

It is very probable that in the divine ancestor *Dis*, as in the mythical King *It* of the Hindus, we have reference to the primeval *Ad*.[1] A common relationship as Adamites may be shown, as well by association with the Medes, through their title *Már*, as by preservation of a tradition of the common ancestor.

The result, so far, is that not only the Persians, Greeks, and Romans, and probably the Hindus, but also the Celtic peoples, have been connected with the Medes or *Mad*, and through them with the *Akkad*. But among the peoples supposed to be still more nearly allied to the Chaldeans, we may expect to find references to the mythical ancestor of the Adamic division of mankind. According to old tradition, indeed, *Ad* himself was the primeval father of the

---

[1] *Adonai*, "Our Lord," was converted by the Greeks into *Adoneus*, as a synomym of Pluto, *i.e.*, *Dis*. (King's "Gnostics," p. 101). Through his name, *Sandan* or *Adanos*, these deities are connected with *Hercules*, and hence with *Ares* (Mars).

original Arab stock. Moreover, the dialect of Mahrah, where pure Arab blood is supposed still to exist, is called the language of *Ad*. It can hardly be doubted that a reference to the same mythical personage is also contained in the name of the great deity of the Syrians, *Adad*, "King of Kings," whose title implies the idea of "fatherhood." Nor are there wanting traces of the primeval *Ad* among the Egyptians. Mr. William Osburn states that the name of the local god of On or Heliopolis "is written on the monuments with the characters representing the sound *a, t, m.*" This God was associated with the setting sun, and he was placed with the gods of the other cities of the Delta, a distinction he received, says Osburn, "for the triple reason, that he was the local god of the capital city, that he was the father of mankind, and that he was the ruler and guide of the sun, the common dispenser of earthly blessings to all men." *Atum* thus becomes identified with the Hebrew *Adam*, and although the description given by Osburn of the Egyptian deity may require some qualification, yet that identification is strengthened rather than weakened by other considerations. Bunsen says that the office of *Atum* in the lower world is that of a judge, and he supposes from this that at one time he may have been a Dispater. He does, indeed, bear much the same relation to man as *Dis* himself. In the Ritual of the Dead, the souls call him father, and he addresses them as children. Sir Gardner Wilkinson says that *Atum*, or *Atmoo*, is always figured with a human head and painted of a red colour. This seems to confirm the idea derived from his name, that this

deity was related to the Hebrew Adam, with whom
the idea of *ruddiness* was undoubtedly associated. The
human form of the Egyptian Atum shows, moreover, that he was considered as peculiarly connected
with man.

It has now been shown that not only are the people
mentioned in the *Toldoth Beni Noah* rightly classed as
descendants of the mythical *Ad*, but that the Asiatic
Aryans, with the allied peoples of Europe to the fur-
thest limits of the Celtic area, may also well be thus
described. The ancient *Mad* belonged, however, to
the great Scythic stock, and hence all the Turanian
peoples, including the Chinese, may doubtless be
classed among the Adamites. There is some ground,
therefore, for asserting that the Adamites include all
the so-called Turanian and Aryan peoples of Asia and
Europe, with the Hamitic and Semitic peoples of
Western Asia and Northern Africa—in fact, the yellow,
the red, and the white races, as distinguished from the
darker peoples of the tropics. But even these
limits may perhaps be extended. One of the solar
heroes of the Volsung Tale is *Atli*, who becomes the
second husband of Gudrun, the widow of Sigurd,
Sigurd himself being the slayer of the dragon Fafnir,
who symbolises the darkness or cold of a northern
winter—the Vritra of Hindu mythology. This dragon
enemy of Indra was also called *Ahi*, the strangling
snake, who appears again as *Atri*, and Mr. Cox supposes that the name *Atri* may be the same as the
Atli of the Volsung Tale. *Atli*, who in the Nibelung
song is called *Etzel*, overpowers the chieftains of
Niflheim, who refused to give up the golden treasures

which Sigurd had won from the dragon, and he throws them into a pit full of snakes.

The connection of the Teutonic hero with the serpent is remarkable; for in the Mexican mythology we meet with a divinity having almost the same name, and associated with the same animal. Humboldt tells us that the Great Spirit of the Toltecks was called *Teotl;* and Hardwicke says that *Teotl* was the only God of Central America. If so, however, he was a serpent deity, for the temples of Yucatan were undoubtedly dedicated to a deity of that nature. It is not improbable, however, that *Teotl* was really a generic term, agreeing in this respect, as curiously enough in its form, with the Phœnician *Taaut* (*Thoth*).

The God to whom the temples of Yucatan were really dedicated appears to be *Quetzalcoatl,* by some writers called the feathered serpent, a title belonging rather to his serpent-father *Tonacatlcoatl.* This *Quetzalcoatl* was the mysterious stranger who, according to tradition, founded the civilisation of Mexico, agreeing thus in his character of a god of wisdom with the Egyptian *Thoth;* reminding us of the resemblance of the name of this deity to that of the Toltecan *Teotl.* But the first part of the name of the Mexican *Quetzalcoatl* no less resembles that borne by the Teutonic deity, *Etzel.* *Co-atl* signifies the "serpent," while *quetzal* would seem to have reference to the male principle; and thus the idea expressed in the name of the Mexican god is the male principle represented as a serpent. *Quetzalcoatl,* moreover, is said to be an incarnation of *Tonacatlcoatl,* who is the male-serpent, his wife being called *Cihuacoatl,* meaning, literally, the " woman of the serpent," or " female serpent." In the identification, then, of *Atli* or *Etzel*, who consigns his enemies to the pit of serpents, with the great serpent *Ahi* himself, we have a ground of identification of the Teutonic deity with the Mexican serpent-god *Quetzalcoatl*. This view loses none of its probability if the latter is, as Mr. Squire asserts, an incarnation of the serpent-sun, or rather a serpent incarnation of the sun-god, since *Ahi* himself is a solar deity. In the religious symbols used by the Mexicans, we have another point of contact with the Asiatic deities. The sacred *Tau* of antiquity has its counterpart on the Mexican monuments. The Mexican symbol perfectly represents the cross form of the *Tau*, but it is composed of two serpents entwined, somewhat as in the caduceus of Mercury. That the *Tau* itself had such an origin we can well believe, seeing that the name of the letter *Tet* (θητα) of the Phœnician alphabet specially associated with *Thoth*, of whom the *Tau* is a symbol, is that of the God himself, as well as meaning " serpent."

If the comparison thus made between the Mexican and Teutonic mythologies is correct, the further analogies pointed out by M. Brasseur de Bourbourg may be well founded. Thus the Mexican *Votan* or *Odon*, supposed to be the same as *Quetzalcoatl*, may be in reality none other than the Scandinavian *Odin*, *Woden*, or *Wuotan*, who, if not a sun-god, was the sky-god, whose eye was the sun (Grimm's " Teutonic Mythology," translated by Stallybrass, p. 703). The snake is intimately associated with Odin in Norse mythology (Grimm, p. 685) as it is with Votan, and both these personages have been identified with the Indian Buddha god.[1]

Nor is there wanting confirmative evidence of such an affinity between the peoples of the Old and the New Worlds as that supposed. Mr. Tylor, in his work on "Primitive Culture," points out that the Roman game of *bucca-bucca*, referred to in a passage of Petronius, is still retained as the old nursery game, "Buck, buck, how many horns do I hold up?" The meaning of this formula is not given, but, from the fact that the witch's devil of the middle ages was represented as a buck or goat, we can hardly doubt that the buck or bucca of the game referred to the evil spirit. The devil was, indeed, called by the Cornish Celts *bucka* (Welsh *bwg*), a hobgoblin, a name which is evidently connected with the Russian *buka*, a sprite, and with the *Bog* of Slavonic and other allied languages. We have, no doubt, the same word in the name of the Finnic sky-god *Ukko*. Of this again we seem to have traces, not only in the Kalmuck *Búrkhan* and the Mantchoo *Ab-ka*, but also in the Hottentot *Teqoa* (Kafir, *Tixo*), the Supreme God; and in the word *yakko*, demon, the name given to the aborigines of Ceylon by their Hindu conquerors. But the root of this word is met with again among the

---

[1] *Le Mythe de Votan*, by H. de Charencey, 1871, pp. 95, 103. Gautama was only the last of the Boudhas, and the identification of Woden is therefore not necessarily with Gautama. Dr. Brinton, "in order to put a stop to such visionary etymologies" as those which connect Votan with Wodan and Buddha, derives Votan from a Maya radical (*American Hero-Myths*, 1882, p. 217). It must be noted, however, that the Maya meaning of Votan (heart *fig.* spirit) closely agrees with that of Wodan (mind) and Buddha (knowledge).

American tribes. The Hurons believe the sky to be an *oki*, or demon, this name being also that by which the natives of Virginia knew their chief god. The same word appears to enter into the name of the Algonquin god of the North Wind, *Kabibon-okka*, as also of the Muyscan Moon goddess, *Huyth-aca*. Whether the Algonquin Great Spirit, *Kitchi-Manitu*, has preserved the same word, is questionable; but it is noticeable that in the mythology of Kamtschatka the first man is called *Haetsh*, and he is the son of *Kutka*, the Creator, whose name, by the allowable change of *t* for *k*, becomes almost the same as the Finnic *Ukko*. The word *oki* may, moreover, be found, with merely the vowel change, among the Islanders of the Pacific. Thus the Polynesian fire-god is *Mahu-ika*, the last syllable of which is doubtless connected with *akua*, meaning, like the American *oki*, spirit, or demon. The same root is met with again in *Tiki*, the Rarotongan form of *Maui*, the divine ancestor of the New Zealanders, and the *Tii* of the Society Islands; also in *Akea*, the name of the mythical first king of Hawaii. *Tiki* is probably only another form of *Ta-ata*, with the change of *k* for *t* (as in *akua* for *atua*); and it is remarkable that this name of the Polynesian First Man is really that of the mythical ancestor of the Adamites, reversed, however, and with the addition of the word *ata* (*aka*), spirit, which we have shown to be connected with the name for God among so many independent races. Mr. Fornander identifies the Polynesian word *aitu* or *iku*, spirit, with the name of the great "Kushite" king It or Ait, and he states that the idea of royalty or sovereignty attached to that word is observed in old

Hawaiian tradition.—"The Polynesian Race," 1878, vol. i., pp. 44, 54.

These mythological coincidences are, indeed, so strongly supported by similarity of customs and linguistic affinities, that there can be no difficulty in classing the Mexicans and kindred American peoples, and even the lighter Polynesians, with the Adamites. This being so, a still broader generalisation than any yet attempted may be made as to the peoples to be included in the Adamic division of the human race. The simplest classification of mankind, according to cranial conformation, is that of Retzius into dolichocephali, or long heads, and brachycephali, or short heads. The Mexicans, and other peoples of the western part of the American Continent, · belong to the latter category, as do also the inhabitants of the greater part of the area of Asia and Europe. In China, and in the southern part of Asia as well as of Europe, the various peoples are chiefly long-headed, and this is the case with the Hamitic population of Northern Africa. The latter are, however, certainly much mixed with the native African element, which is purely dolichocephalic, exhibiting traces of its prognathism; and it is far from improbable that originally they were brachycephalic, like the allied peoples of Western Asia. Such also may have been the case with the Chinese and the lighter Polynesians, who are now nearly dolichocephalic.[1] Throughout all the regions where these peoples are found there would appear to have been an indigenous long-headed stock,

---

[1] M. de Ujfalvy has found that even the purest Iranian type of Central Asia is brachycephalic.

which has more or less nearly absorbed the brachy-cephalic element, which was introduced long ages ago from the vast regions of Central Asia, and which, for want of a better term, may be called Scythic. Subject to this qualification, it may probably be said that Adamic and short-headed are synonymous terms, and that among the descendants of Father *Ad* may, therefore, be classed all the peoples who are embraced in the great brachycephalic division of mankind, or who would have belonged to it, if they had not been phy-sically modified by contact with peoples of the more primitive dolichocephalic area.

How far the Adamites have trespassed on this area it is difficult to determine. That they have become mixed with the peoples of the African Continent to a much larger extent than is usually supposed may be believed. The Hottentots, at its extremest limit, are no doubt a residual deposit of such intermixture; while the great family to which the Kafirs belong furnish evidence of it in various particulars. The Adamites appear also to have spread throughout the archipelagos of the Pacific, furnishing an explanation of the many customs and myths in which the Poly-nesian Islanders agree with Asiatic peoples. Nor are the Adamites much less widely spread throughout the American Continent. Apart from what Professor Busk affirms, that a broad type of head is to be met with on the coast all round South America, peoples allied to those of Mexico and Central America would seem to have occupied many of the West Indian Islands, and to have penetrated through the central portion of North America to the Great Lakes. Wherever the

Adamites have come into contact with the long-headed pre-Adamitic stock, they have either made these to disappear, or, while having their physical structure somewhat modified by intermixture, they have established a supremacy due to their greater vigour and mental energy. It is difficult, indeed, to say where the descendants of *Ad* are not now to be met with, or where the pre-Adamite is to be found uninfluenced by contact with them.

In conclusion, it will be well to endeavour to ascertain the origin of the tradition as to *Adam* or father *Ad*. According to usually received teaching, Adam and Eve were the actual first parents of the human race, or, at all events, of the Adamic portion of it. Whether or not this idea is correct need not be further considered here, beyond stating that if, as Bunsen suggests, the existence of other antediluvian patriarchs be mythical, so also must be that of Adam from whom they are said to have sprung.

The Semitic word ADaM conveys several ideas. In the form *Adamah* or *Adami* it has reference to the *earth* or *soil*, but its primary sense was either "red" or "man." Probably a double meaning was conveyed in the name of the Egyptian god Atum, whose representation was that of a red man. It must be noted, however, that the traditional ancestor is usually styled, not *Adam* but simply *Ad;* and this primitive root may have had some other signification, analogous perhaps to that of *Eve* (*Hhavváh*), "the mother of all living." This word, which denotes "life," is from *hhayáh*, to live, to give life—the allied word in Arabic being *haywān*, and the Arabic name for Eve becoming *hawwa.* Now, in the Celtic dialects *ad* forms the root of words denoting vegetable vitality. In Welsh, moreover, *tad* is a father; the base, *ta,* denoting, among allied senses, "a supreme one," reminding us of the Chinese *ta,* great; and connected with it being *tras,* kindred, affinity. Turning, however, to Eastern languages, we find that the old Egyptian had a word *ti,* with a sense analogous to that of the Welsh *ta,* and also a verb *ta,* to give, which is found in Hebrew, as *'athah,* to come, and in Arabic as *ata,* to give, or to bring forth. It is evident that the primitive root, consisting of the dental *t* or *d,* preceded or followed by a vowel sound, had associated with it the idea of activity, and probably of paternity. In the old Akkad speech, indeed, *ad* itself signifies a "father," and we are justified, therefore, in supposing that when this word was used as the name of the mythical common ancestor, it had a sense analogous to that which "Eve" expressed, *i.e.,* "the *father* of life, or of all living." In Adam and Eve, therefore, we may have a reference to the male and female principles which, in the philosophy of the ancients, as in that of the Chinese and some other Eastern peoples, pervade all nature, and originate all things, applied particularly, however, to the human race. But Adam was not the name given at first to this mystical father of the race. The Egyptian *Atum* was originally a cosmogonic deity. Bunsen states that the name of this god may be resolved into *At-Mu,* meaning "Creator of the mother or night." The sense of this, however, is not very apparent, and it may be suggested that the term *Adam* (in Egyptian *Atum*) was formed by the combination of the primitive *akkad* words *Ad*, father, and *Dam*, mother. It would thus originally express a dual idea, agreeably to the statement in Gen. v. 2, that male and female were called " Adam." This agrees perfectly with the Persian tradition which made the first human being androgynous. When the dual idea expressed in the name was forgotten, Adam became the Great Father, the Great Mother receiving the name of Eve (Hhavváh), *i.e.*, living or life, although *Adam* in the generic sense of " Mankind," denoted both male and female.

Note.—The Turanian or rather Altaic affinity of the Akkad, referred to at page 109 above, appears to have been established by M. Lenormant, who states that their name means " Mountaineers," from *Akkad*, a mountain. It is possible, however, that the word may have had a more primitive signification. As the name of a country and not of a people, Akkad did not come into use until the Assyrian epoch, " When the Accadian had become a dead language, and the tradition of the real meaning of the word was consequently quite lost." (*Chaldean Magic and Sorcery*, p. 404.) As to the aborignal Arab people referred to at page 117, it may be mentioned that M. Lenormant (*Hist. Anc. de l'Orient*, 9th Ed. I. t. prem. p. 313), points out that the name, Adah, of the mother of the two sons of Lameckh, who were chiefs of pastoral races, is only the feminine form of that of the people of Ad.

CHAPTER V.

THE DESCENDANTS OF CAIN.

IN various parts not only of the old world continents, but also of America, and even on some of the Islands of the Pacific, are the ruins of stone buildings which, from their general character, are well called " Kyklopean." The style of architecture varies in different countries according to the uses for which the buildings were designed, or the local influences among which they were erected. Whatever their form, all those ancient buildings agree in the massive character of their structure, and most of them in the fact that the stones are put together without mortar or cement. Kyklopean architecture proper (in which large unhewn blocks are rudely put together with small stones to fill up the interstices) differs, however, from the *Polygonal* or *Pelasgian*, and from the *Horizontal* or *Etruscan*, which, in addition, has the courses scrupulously level, with joints vertical, and fitting accurately. General Forlong, the author of " Rivers of Life, or Faiths of Man in all Ages," while pointing out that distinction, remarks that those several styles do not denote different ages, and that the builders were evidently of the same race. This opinion is confirmed by the fact that all the three styles are found in the ruins of Peru, whose Kyklopean structures, moreover, are not restricted to those of rectangular formation, but sometimes take the form of round towers.

General Forlong identifies the great building race of antiquity with the Kushites or Aithiopians of the Greek historians, and with Mr. Fergusson, he supposes them to have belonged to the Turanian family of peoples. The distinguished architect and archæologist affirms, indeed, that not only were the Turanians the great architects and builders of remote antiquity, but that they were the inventors of all the arts, as well as the religions and mythologies, which were afterwards developed by the later Shemites and Aryans.

But how far does this conclusion agree with actual facts ? M. Georges Perrot, in his important work on the "History of Art," says that the ancient Oriental world has seen the birth of three great civilisations, that of Egypt, that of Chaldea, and that of China, all of which have features in common, although each preserves its own proper character. Chaldea was the *Sennaar* of the author of the Book of Genesis, the land in which were built the ancient cities of Babel, Erech, Accad, and Calneh. The mighty hunter or warrior Nimrod, to whom the erection of those cities is ascribed, was the son of Kush and the grandson of Cham, and he is thus placed by the sacred writer in the same family as the Egyptians, Aithiopians, and the Libyans, as also the Canaanites and Phœnicians. The Kushites, of whom Nimrod is the representative in Genesis, were located by the poets and classical historians in Susiana rather than in Chaldea. Both of these countries, however, adjoin the Valley of the Tigris, and the name Aithiopians applied by those writers to the inhabitants of the shores of the Persian Gulf and the sea of Oman agrees with the relationship which, according to the genealogists of the Hebrew Scriptures, subsisted between the Kushites of Asia and those of Africa. It is to the shores of the Persian Gulf that the development, if not the origin, of the Chaldean civilisation has been traced. M. Perrot calls Egypt "the ancestor of civilised nations," and he affirms that, in grouping the great peoples of antiquity to determine the part taken by each in the work of progress, it is necessary to commence with Egypt as the point of departure of all the forces which operate to that end. The Egyptians were not, however, indigenous to the Valley of the Nile. It is now almost universally acknowledged that they belonged to the white or Caucasian stock of Europe and Western Asia, from which they reached Egypt by the isthmus of Suez. Their Caucasian origin is confirmed by their language, which, with the other Hamitic idioms, had, as M. Lenormant shows, a relationship to the Semitic languages, the two families having a common mother language, the native country of which was in Asia at the east of the basin of the Euphrates and Tigris. We are thus taken to the region where the old Chaldean civilisation flourished for the place of origin of the Egyptians; but did they belong to the same Kushite stock? In endeavouring to answer this question, it is necessary to remember that before the foundation of the Empire by Menes Egypt had comprised two kingdoms, that of Lower Egypt or the country of the north, and that of Upper Egypt or the country of the south. These kingdoms must have existed a considerable period, judging from the fact that the later Monarchs carried two crowns to indicate the dominion exercised over the two great divisions of the Empire, and probably it represented some race difference in their inhabitants. The Aryan character described by M. L. Page Renouf to the Egyptian mythology, and the features of many of the figures represented on the tombs of the fourth Dynasty, might lead us to suppose that the earliest Egyptians belonged to the Aryan stock. This opinion is, perhaps, confirmed by the consideration that the earliest and most sacred towns of the Egyptians were situate in Upper Egypt.

M. Lenormant thinks that the descendants of Mizraim settled in Egypt at different epochs, and that the earliest settlers, the Anamim of the Old Testament and the Anou of the hieroglyphic inscriptions, were driven by the later ones into different parts of Egypt, but principally into Nubia. The former may, therefore, have been pure Aryans, the southern country being referred to as the home of the race; although the Empire was first established in Lower Egypt, its chief centre being Memphis, from which its culture gradually overspread the whole country. The early inhabitants of the Delta region were represented at a later date by the Hyksos, who have been identified by Professor Duncker with the Philistines of the Syrian Coast. This people are spoken of in the Book of Genesis as descendants of Mizraim, and their neighbours, the Phœnicians, stood in the same relation to the northern Egyptians as did the Kushites of Chaldea. Like the latter peoples, the Phœnicians were great builders. The remains of vast structures still exist throughout Phœnicia, which was known to the ancient Babylonians as Martu, "the west." Among modern writers,

M. Renan is of opinion that "singular relations exist between the ethnographic, historic, and linguistic position of Yemen and that of Phœnicia," as showing that there was a close relationship between the latter and the ancient people of Southern Arabia. Mr. Baldwin accepts both these views, and comes to the conclusion that the first great civilisers and builders of antiquity were the Kushites or Aithiopians of Southern Arabia, and that they colonised or civilised Chaldea, Phœnicia, and Egypt. Tradition speaks of Kepheus as one of the great sovereigns of ancient Aithiopia, whose kingdom extended from the Mediterranean to the Persian Gulf, and whose capital was Joppa, one of the most ancient cities of Phœnicia. We may well believe that this very early Kushite kingdom comprised part of Northern Africa, and therefore that it included the Delta of the Nile with the great city, Memphis, of the Egyptian pyramid builders. The similarity in many features of the Phœnician and Egyptian architecture points to a close connection between those peoples, and a portion of the Kushite race which peopled Phœnicia doubtless settled in the Delta, from whence its culture would easily spread throughout the Nile Valley. It is certain that Southern Arabia was the seat of a very primitive civilisation, which influenced all the regions around. Phœnicia, however, would seem to have been most intimately allied with Chaldea, the origin of whose civilisation, although ascribed to the fish-god Oannes, can hardly be traced to Arabia.

According to the Biblical writer, Kush was the eldest son of Ham, who was also the father of Mizraim, Phut, and Canaan. All these peoples were great builders, and it is very probable, therefore, that they, as well as the Kushites, derived their knowledge from a common source. In this case, and even if Mizraim, Canaan, and Phut were the *descendants* rather than the brethren of Kush, the civilisation with which the Kushites are accredited was, in reality, that of the earlier Hamites. The probability is that all the peoples belonging to the Hamitic stock possessed the elements of a very ancient civilisation, which was handed down in the most direct line through the Kushites of Chaldea. M. Perrot accepts the opinion of M. Oppert, that when the primitive Chaldeans first settled in the plains of Sennaar they already had a national organisation, and that they possessed writing, the most necessary industries, a religion, and a complete legislation. If this was so we shall have to seek a very primitive source for the Kushite or Hamitic civilisation. What was its origin can only be ascertained when the race ancestry of the Hamites is known. In relation to this point it must not be forgotten that Ham was the brother of Shem and Japhet, and therefore that they were all members of a common family. As the descendants of Noah, they all alike belonged to the great white or Caucasian stock. M. Lenormant, while endorsing this view, says that anciently, as in the present day, there was an anthropological distinction between the Hamites and the Shemites, which he accounts for by supposing the former to have become intermixed with a dark or black race, which they found already established in the country to which they spread, while the Shemites, who stayed behind, preserved the purity of the white race. The facts of linguistic science and anthropology can thus be made to agree, but M. Lenormant has to admit that the Eastern Kushites cannot be brought within that theory, as from the earliest historical period they have spoken a language radically distinct from those of the Shemites and the other Hamitic peoples. He adds that the coast between the Persian Gulf and the Indus appears to have been, from a remote antiquity, the point of meeting and fusion of two distinct races having brown complexions, but inclining more or less to pure black. The Eastern Kushites are thus confounded by a gradual series of transitions with the Dravidians of India. This reference to the Dravidians is perfectly just, as there is no doubt, whatever may be the case now, that originally they partook of the high qualities possessed by the peoples of the Kushite stock. As a race they were noted for their love of art and commerce, and General Forlong, after having examined minutely most of the famous shrines of India, came to the conclusion " that there is nothing to equal those of Dravidia, save some small ones in Western India, which, in their completeness, form, and conception, denote the same master builders who, as Jainas, &c., learned in Mysore and the South under those great architects." There is indeed reason to believe that the marvellous temples of Cambodia and Java, of which the ruins still exist, were erected by Dravidians from India. M. Moura, the learned author of a history of Cambodia, has established that the great architects of that kingdom were the peoples to whom the name of Khmerdoms is given by their descendants, the Khmers. They were of Hindoo origin, and emigrated from the neighbourhood of Delhi in the fifth century before Christ. Whether the original Khmers were of pure Aryan stock is, however, very doubtful, and it is extremely probable that they were Hinduised Dravidians. The Hindoos, to whom the civilisation of Java is ascribed, are spoken of as coming from Kling, by which is meant the Dravidian Telinga.

If, as M. Lenormant supposes, the Eastern Kushites became fused with a brown or black race, it does not follow that this race was originally black, or that it belonged to a negroid stock. All the Hamites, and especially the Kushites, were of a more or less dark complexion, but the black hue may have been acquired through natural influences operating during a vast period of time. The Dravidians have, at least from a linguistic standpoint, Turanian affinities, and it is now almost universally admitted that the earliest civilised inhabitants of Chaldea belonged to the great Turanian family of peoples who are usually spoken of as the yellow race. There is no doubt that a yellow race, whose languages had an affinity on the one side with the languages of the Altaic peoples, and on the other side with the Dravidian dialects, and who preceded the Shemitic and Japhetic peoples in material civilisation, existed in Eastern Asia alongside of the white race.

M. Ujfalvy supposes the Eastern Turanians to have descended the first from the plateau of the Altai; to be followed by the Western Turanians, who occupied Northern Europe from time immemorial; the children of Noah being the last to quit the primeval home. If this was so we can well understand that the average Turanian physical type must present peculiarities which distinguish it easily from that of the Caucasian races.

What we have now to do with is the origin of primitive civilisation, and everything points to the early Turanians as the people among whom it was developed. We have already seen that if the primitive Chaldeans did not belong to the Turanian stock they were intimately associated with Turanian peoples to whom they are thought to have been indebted for much of their culture. The great western division of the Turanian race appears to have possessed an advanced civilisation long before its Aryan neighbours. The Tchoudes, who are described by Ujfalvy as the most ancient people of the Altaic race, were noted metallurgists, while the Permians and the Finns are supposed to have taught art and agriculture to the Slaves and Scandinavians of Northern Europe. M. Reclus remarks that, not only did the Turanians teach their neighbours the use of iron and other metals, but they have the glory of having given to us most of our domestic animals, and probably also the greater part of our most useful cultured plants. Finally, the Turanians were, says M. Lenormant, "the constructors of the first towns, and the inventors of metallurgy and of the first rudiments of the principal arts of civilisation." He adds that they were "addicted to rites which were reproved by Yahveh, and were viewed with as much hatred as superstitious terror by the populations still in the pastoral state whom they had preceded in the path of material progress and invention, but who remained morally more pure and elevated."

This description, applied by M. Lenormant to the Turanians, has reference primarily to the Cainites, and it carries the origin of material civilisation much farther back in time than would have been thought possible a few years ago. The facts mentioned in connection with Cain and his descendants strikingly confirm the opinion that the Kushite civilisation was handed down from a period which, in relation to the Deluge of Genesis, may be called antediluvian. The tradition of the Deluge is a primitive belief of the three white races, the Aryan, the Semitic, and the Hamitic. It appears to have been originally limited to the peoples of the Caucasian stock, and this fact requires that the Turanians should be excluded from the effect of the supposed catastrophe. The yellow race, therefore, may claim an " antediluvian " descent, and as Noah, the progenitor of the white races, belonged to the Sethite stock, the common ancestor of the Turanian peoples must have been a Cainite.

The first public event recorded in the life of Cain after his exile was the building of a town, which he called Enoch, after his first-born son. This town has been identified with the city of Khotan, which is situate in the region where Cain is thought to have fixed his abode. According to Abel Rémusat the traditions of that city, preserved in the native chronicles and referred to by the Chinese historians, go back to a much earlier period than those of any other city of Central Asia. Baron d'Eckstein has, moreover, shown that

Khotan was the centre of a district in which the art of metallurgy has been practised from the remotest antiquity. This is important, for Tubal Cain, the youngest son of Lamekh, the descendant of Cain, is said in Genesis to have been "an instructor of every artificer in brass and iron."

The ancestors of the present Chinese appear not to have been acquainted with the blacksmith's art when they first descended into the plains, although it was practised by the neighbouring Tibetan tribes, who, we can hardly doubt, were allied to the Kolarian population of Eastern India, if not also to the Dravidians of the south and west. The relationship of the Dravidians to the peoples of the Altaic stock, and the practice of metallurgy by the latter particularly, would tend, however, to prove that the Jabal were not, as supposed by M. Ujfalvy, Turanians who settled in Northern Asia and Europe. Those facts would rather support the view of Knobel, which identifies the Jabal and the Jubal as a musical and pastoral race, as distinguished from a settled metallurgic race to whom the name of Tubal Cain was given.

The opinion that the ancestors of the Turanian peoples were Cainites may be confirmed by reference to certain social and religious phenomena. In the story of the slaying by Cain of his brother Abel there is evident reference to antagonism between a pastoral and an agricultural people. M. Lenormant, who sees a connection between the fratricide and the founding of the first city, has arrived at the conviction that the Chaldæo-Babylon tradition concerning the primitive days of the human race included a reference to those two actions of Cain. He says, however, " there are certain reasons for suspecting that the Chaldeans took the part of the murderer Cain against Abel, as the Romans did that of Romulus against Remus." The preference of the Chaldeans for the murderer agrees with the Cainite origin ascribed to their Turanian ancestors, among whom the polygamy and revenge attributed to Lamekh were no doubt as prevalent as among some of their descendants at the present day. The French writer sees in the fourth chapter of Genesis a condemnaton of Lamekh as the prototype of fierce vengeance, and at the same time of polygamy. The whole pre-Deluge history of man, as given in Genesis, would seem to imply the existence of an hereditary opposition between the descendants of Cain and those of Seth, who was regarded as standing in a special relation to the Shemites. It was evidently written in the same spirit as that which saw in the enmity between the Iranians and Turanians a constant conflict between light and darkness. The race of Cain are referred in the Biblical narrative as " sons of men," a title which implies a condition of religious or moral inferiority, as compared with the " sons of God" descended from Seth. That narrative says, further, that in the time of Enoch men began to call on the name of Jehovah. This statement, which has reference only to the Sethites, supposes that the Cainites invoked some other god, and in the Shamanism of the Dravidians and various Turanian peoples we have no doubt a phase of the religious worship prevalent among their Cainite ancestors.

Another point in connection with religious ideas,

which is of great importance in relation to the above subject, is the origin of serpent-worship. M. Lenormant remarks that "the Arcadians made the serpent one of the principal attributes and one of the forms of Héa." This deity, who closely resembles Waïnamoïnen, one of the three principal gods of the Finns, occupied a very important position in the Pantheon of the ancient Chaldeans. Héa, like the Finnish god, was "not only king of the waters and the atmosphere, he was also the spirit whence all life proceeded, the master of favourable spells, the adversary and conqueror of all personifications of evil, and the sovereign possessor of all science." The worship of serpent-gods is a practice to which many of the primitive Turanian tribes have been addicted. This accounts for the curious association of serpent-worship with Buddhism and Sivaism. Both of these faiths, as exhibited in the marvellous sculptures of the ruined temples of Cambodia, are intimately connected with serpent-worship. This cult was no doubt very prevalent among the native populations before the arrival of the Hindoos, as legend states that the banished Indian Prince, for whom the city of Nakon-Thom was built, married a daughter of the King of the Nagas or Serpents, and became the sovereign of the country. Serpent-worship, indeed, would seem to have been prevalent throughout Northern India. The territory of the king of the serpent city Taxila reached nearly to Delhi, and it probably extended over Kashmere and part of Afghanistan. Here was a very important centre of serpent-worship. General Forlong states that in Kashmere this cult appears everywhere, "and the records of the country point to its beautiful lake and mountain fastnesses as the earliest historic seats which we have of the faith." It is remarkable that a King of the Naga race was reigning in Magadha when Gautama was born in 626 B.C., and, according to a Hindoo legend, even the Buddha himself had a serpent lineage. If this was so, it is not surprising that his teachings should be accepted by the Naga races, who no doubt belonged to the pre-Aryan stock.

The constant introduction of the serpent, especially of the sacred Cobra, into the sculptures of the Cambodian temples, is remarkable. M. Moura states that the ancient Khmers of Cambodia recognised both good and evil serpents, the former of which lived in the water and the latter inhabited the land. The Buddhists of India and Indo-China had the same idea, and M. Moura supposes that the good serpents represented the human Nagas who became Buddhists, and the bad serpents those who refused to abandon their native serpent-worship. This explanation, however, is not necessary, as the ancient Egyptians entertained analogous ideas. No other people, except, perhaps, the Hindoos and allied races, were more thoroughly imbued with the serpent superstition than the Egyptians. Mr. Cooper, in his "Observations on the Serpent Myths of Ancient Egypt," remarks that "the reverence paid to the snake was not merely local, or even limited to one period of history, but prevailed alike in every district of the Pharian Empire, and has left its indelible impress upon the architecture and the archæology of both Upper and Lower Egypt." The Cobra di Capello of the Hindoos and Cambodians was the sacred Uræus of the Egyptians. With the latter it was used as the symbol of fecundity and immortality, and was also universally assumed as the "emblem of divine and sacro-regal sovereignty." The Uræus was always represented in the female form, and all the Egyptian goddesses were adorned with it, as the images of the Hindoo gods were often surmounted with the sacred Naga. Among the Egyptians another kind of serpent was also held in universal veneration. It was a gigantic species of Coluber, which from the earliest ages was regarded as "the representative of spiritual, and occasionally physical, evil." This was the great snake of the celestial waters, the adversary of the gods with which the soul had to contend after death. The Egyptians had thus a good and an evil serpent, the former of which was small and the latter large. Among the Cambodians the reverse was the case, as the small serpent was the representative of evil, and the great serpent, the Naga-Naga, of good.

We have already seen that the cobra occupies an important place in the Buddhist sculpture, and that the great serpent with its human supporters was represented at both Amravati and Angkor Wat. Curiously enough a similar idea to this is represented on certain Egyptian monuments. On the sarcophagus of Oimenepthah I. is sculptured a long serpent, which, says Mr. Robert Sewell, is doubled into folds just like the roll of the Buddhist frieze, and having a god standing on each fold in the places occupied by the sacred emblems of the Buddhist faith at Amravati. He supposes the long roll of the Amravati frieze to be intended to represent a serpent, and to have had its origin in Western Asian or Egyptian ideas. I had already, before meeting with this observation, been struck with the similarity between the Egyptian and the Buddhist representations, especially when considered in the light of the Cambodian sculptures which undoubtedly represent the Naga-Naga. The gigantic serpent of the celestial ocean of Egyptian mythology is Aphôphis, the spirit of evil, and in the contest between him and Horus we have, according to M. Le Page Renouf, a form of the Indra and Vritra myth. An Accadian text speaks of "the enormous serpent with seven heads," the "serpent which beats the waves of the sea . . . . . extending his power over heaven and earth." This is supposed to refer to Héa, and it reminds us of the heavenly Naga-Naga of Hindoo mythology, which, like the Accadian serpent deity, was representative of the good principle. Such was also the case among all the old Turanian nations, and it was only when, as remarked by M. Lenormant, "the Iranian traditions were fused with the ancient beliefs of the Proto-Medic religion, the serpent-god naturally became identified with the representative of the dark and bad principle." It cannot be doubted that this was the later notion, and that the Turanian belief which associated with the serpent ideas of goodness was of earlier date. Thus, the Dragon, says Mr. Doolittle, "enjoys an ominous eminence in the affections of the Chinese people. It is frequently represented as the greatest benefactor of mankind. . . . . The Chinese delight in praising its wonderful prospects and powers. It is the venerated symbol of good."

The veneration of the serpent must have been of very early origin to occupy so strong a hold over the Chinese, whose spoken language, according to M. Terrien de Lacouperie, forms a link between the Accadian and the Ugro-Finnish divisions of the Ural-Altaic languages. The art of metallurgy was practised by the peoples belonging to both these divisions, and yet, according to M. Lenormant, it was not known to the early Chinese. We must thus suppose that the latter left the common home before the invention of metallurgy, and, therefore, that they represent a very early condition of the stock from which the Turanian peoples sprang. We seem, indeed, to be carried back to the very earliest period of the legendary history of the Cainite race, and possibly to that of the legendary ancestor of the race. According to the tradition preserved in Genesis, there was a peculiar association between Adam and the serpent. This animal is there the tempter Satan, but according to another view Adam, or rather Ad, who was apparently the traditional ancestor of a portion at least of the old Turanian stock, was himself the serpent. A rabbinical tradition makes Cain the son, not of Adam, but of the serpent-spirit Asmodeus. The name Eve is connected with an Arabic root which means both "life" and "a serpent," and if Eve was the serpent mother, Ad must have been the serpent father of the race. There is reason for believing that Adam was the legendary ancestor of the Cainites, as distinguished from the descendants of Seth. The name Adam, no doubt, signifies in the Semitic languages "the man," but it has been pointed out that the name borne by the son of Seth, and therefore the ancestor of Noah, that is Enoch, is in Hebrew the exact synonym of Adam, and also signifies "the man." There is, moreover, almost an exact parallel between the descendants of Adam, through Cain on the one hand, and those of Seth through Enoch on the other, and each line is terminated by three heads of races, that of the Cainites by the sons of Lamekh and that of the Enocides by the grandsons of Lamekh. In the latter there is the insertion of one additional generation, that of Noah, between Lamekh and the division of the family into three branches. This is, however, capable of explanation. M. Lenormant shows, by a comparison of the various legends referring to the primitive age of mankind, that the number 7 or 10 was used by all the ancient nations as a round number for the antediluvian ancestors of the race. Tradition seemed to float between these two numbers until the influence of the Chaldæo-Babylonians caused the number 10, which is that of the generations of the Sethites, to dominate over the number 7, that of the Cainites. It is to that influence we would ascribe the existence among the descendants of Seth of the legendary ancestor of the three Caucasian races. The Chaldean Noah was Khasisatra, whose vessel was saved during the Flood by the god Héa. This god himself was, however, supposed to have a vessel in which he sailed over the celestial ocean. He was, in fact, the fish-god Oannes, from whom the Chaldeans were said to have derived their civilisation, and we probably have in Oannes the point of identification between Héa and Noah himself. The Caucasian races, whose fathers had been saved from the Deluge, could not have a better legendary ancestor than the divine teacher who, issuing from the Egyptian sea, was the god Héa, not only the soul of the watery element but the source of all generation. If Noah, then, be a mythological being, introduced into the Sethite genealogy under Chaldean influence, Lamekh becomes the direct ancestor of the Caucasian stock as he is of the Turanian peoples. An argument in favour of this view is furnished by the Scripture account itself. Among the sons of Noah a peculiar position is occupied by Ham. He and his son Canaan are cursed, in like manner as Cain was cursed. The sins were different, and therefore the punishments were different, but there appears to be a kind of parallelism between Cain and Canaan for which a good reason probably existed in the mind of the writer of Genesis. We have seen that the Hamites were intimately connected with peoples belonging to the Turanian stock, and they were the special recipients of the old Cainite civilisation. It is, indeed, far from improbable that they were more Cainite than Sethite. The three sons of Noah would seem to answer to the three sons of Adam, and as Ham or Canaan is a reproduction of Cain, so Japheth and Shem are reproductions of Abel and Seth. In either case the elder brothers were put on one side or cursed, that the youngest brother might enjoy the inheritance. Perhaps an explanation of this conduct may be found in the race relationships of the Semites. That they had a closer affinity to the Hamites than had the Japhethites is unquestionable, and it can hardly be less doubted that the latter were the purest branch of the Caucasian stock. The Semites were, indeed, a mixed race, but as the Hebrews professed to be the chosen people it was necessary that the Hamite and Japhethite races should be put on one side, as Abel and Cain had been, that their ancestor Shem might take the chief place. The Semites thus became the representative Caucasian people who, as children of light, stand in opposition to the Turanian Hamites, in like manner as the sons of Seth were opposed to the descendants of Cain.

We have been led to believe that the civilisation of the ancient world originated among the Cainites, of whom the Turanians are the line of descendants. We have seen reason, moreover, for supposing that the particular branch of the Turanian stock, among whom the development of the art of metallurgy first took place, was the Ural-Altaic, to which the earliest inhabitants of Chaldea belonged, and whom Dr. Topinard supposes to be the connecting-link between the fair types of Europe and the brachycephalic types of Asia. The building art was one of the earliest to be developed, as is evident from the reference in Genesis to the building of a city by Cain. The erection of the first city is connected with the slaying of Abel, and therefore the origin of architecture may be referred back to almost the earliest period of human culture, and we may well suppose that some of the least cultured Turanian tribes represent a still earlier stage of Cainite civilisation. M. Lenormant objects to Herr Knobel's theory that the Chinese and the Mongolian peoples are Cainites, that " the geographical horizon of the traditions of Genesis did not extend far enough to include them." If, however, when the Chinese first descended into the plains they were still in the stone age, they may have been true Cainites, the more so as their immediate ancestors were located much nearer than are their descendants to the primeval home of Adamite man. The remarkable influence which the veneration for the serpent has obtained among the Chinese, a superstition which was developed no less remarkably among the peoples belonging to the Western branch of the Turanian family, and through them among the Hamitic peoples, would seem to prove that it was of primeval origin. The arts of metallurgy and architecture appear to have had a later development, and to have originated among the Turanian Aithiopians or Kuths, to whom the civilisation of the ancient world was ascribed. After leaving their home in West-Central Asia they settled in Chaldea, from whence they gradually spread throughout Western Asia, Northern Africa, and Europe, where, in later years, they came in contact with the Caucasian races, who gave a higher tone to their intellectual culture and their religious ideas, the latter being especially observable in the position assigned to the great serpent as the embodiment of evil.

Note.—The legend of the slaying of Abel by his brother Cain referred to at page 138, is met with in the Mythologies of some of the American tribes. See *Monographie des Dènè Dindjié*, by C. R. E. Petitot, pp. 62-84, and for a similar legend of the Aztecs, see *American Hero-Myths*, by Daniel G. Brinton, pp. 64-68.

CHAPTER VI.

SACRED PROSTITUTION.

Mr. Darwin, in his work entitled "The Descent of Man" (vol. ii., p. 361), seems to endorse the opinion that the high honour bestowed in ancient times on women who were utterly licentious is intelligible only "if we admit that promiscuous intercourse was the aboriginal and therefore the long revered custom of the tribe,"[1] and I propose, in the present chapter, to show that the fact referred to has nothing at all to do with the custom sought to be supported by it.

The examples on which Sir John Lubbock relies have been taken from Dulaure's work on ancient religions, but they are more fully detailed in the "Histoire de la Prostitution" by M. Pierre Dufour, and they certainly form one of the most remarkable chapters in the history of morals.

According to Herodotus,[2] every woman born in Babylonia was obliged by law, once in her life, to submit to the embrace of a stranger. Those who were gifted with beauty of face or figure soon completed this offering to Venus, but of the others some had to remain in the sacred enclosure for several years before they were able to obey the law. This statement of Herodotus is confirmed by the evidence

---

[1] Sir John Lubbock's "Origin of Civilisation," 3rd ed., p. 96.
[2] Clio, sec. 199.

of Strabo, who says the custom dated from the foundation of the city of Babylon.

The compulsory prostitution of Babylonia was connected with the worship of Mylitta, and wherever this
worship spread it was accompanied by the sexual
sacrifice. Strabo relates[1] that in Armenia the sons
and daughters of the leading families were consecrated
to the service of Anaïtis for a longer or shorter period.
Their duty was to entertain strangers, and those
females who had received the greatest number were on
their return home the most sought after in marriage.
The Phœnician worship of Astarté was no less distinguished by sacred prostitution, to which was added
a promiscuous intercourse between the sexes during
certain religious fêtes, at which the men and women
exchanged their garments. The Phœnicians carried
the custom to the Isle of Cyprus, where the worship
of their great goddess, under the name of Venus,
became supreme.

According to a popular legend the women of
Amathonte, afterwards noted for its temple, were
originally known for their chastity. When, therefore, Venus was cast by the waves naked on their
shores, they treated her with disdain, and as a punishment they were commanded to prostitute themselves
to all comers, a command which they obeyed with so
much reluctance that the goddess changed them into
stone. With their worship of Astarté or Venus, the
Phœnicians introduced sacred prostitution into all their
Colonies. St. Augustine says that, at Carthage, there
were three Venuses rather than one : one of the

<hr>

[1] Bk. ii., Melpom., 172.

virgins, another of the married women, and a third
of the courtesans, to the last of whom it was that
the Phœnicians sacrificed the chastity of their daughters before they were married. It was the same in
Syria. At Byblos during the fêtes of Adonis, after
the ceremony which announced the resurrection of
the God, every female worshipper had to sacrifice to
Venus either her hair or her person. Those who preferred to preserve the former adjourned to the sacred
enclosures, where they remained for a whole day for
the purpose of prostituting themselves.

The same curious custom appears to have been
practised in Media and Persia, and among the Par-
thians. The Lydians were particularly noted for the
zeal with which they practised the rites of Venus.
They did not limit their observance to occasional
attendance at the sacred fêtes, but, says Herodotus,
they devoted themselves to the goddess, and practised,
for their own benefit, the most shameless prostitution.
It is related that a magnificent monument to Alyattes,
the father of Crœsus, was built by the contributions
of the merchants, the artisans, and the courtesans, and
that the portion of the monument erected with the
sum furnished by the courtesans much exceeded both
the other parts built at the expense of the artisans
and merchants.

Some writers deny that sacred prostitution was
practised in Egypt, but the great similarity between
the worship of Osiris and Isis and that of Venus and
Adonis renders the contrary opinion highly probable.
On their way to the fêtes of Isis at Bubastis the female
pilgrims executed indecent dances when the vessels

passed the villages on the banks of the river. "These obscenities," says Dufour, "were only such as were about to happen at the temple, which was visited each year by seven hundred thousand pilgrims, who gave themselves up to incredible excesses." Strabo asserts that a class of persons called *pellices* (harlots) were dedicated to the service of the patron deity of Thebes, and that they "were permitted to cohabit with anyone they chose." It is true that Sir Gardner Wilkinson [1] treats this account as absurd, on the ground that the women, many of whom were the wives and daughters of the noblest families, assisted in the most important ceremonies of the temple. This fact is, however, quite consistent with Strabo's statement, which may have referred to an inferior class of female servitors, and considering the customs of allied peoples, it is more likely to be true than the reverse. The testimony of Herodotus is certainly opposed to that of Strabo. But the former acknowledges that he did not reveal all that he knew of the secrets of Egyptian worship, and we must, therefore, receive with some hesitation his assertion that "the Egyptians are the first who, from a religious motive, have forbidden commerce with women in the sacred places, or even entrance there after having known them, without being first cleansed." The Greek historian adds—"Almost all other peoples, except the Egyptians and the Greeks, have commerce with women in the sacred places; or, when they rise from them, they enter there without being washed." Whatever may be the truth as to the inhabitants of ancient Egypt, at the present day

[1] "Ancient Egyptians," iv., 204.

the dancing girls of that country, who are also prostitutes, attend the religious festivals just as the ancient devotees of Astarté are said to have done.

If we test the value of Herodotus' evidence on the matter in question by what is known of Grecian customs, it will have little weight. Sacred prostitution at Athens was under the patronage of Venus Pandemos, who is said to have been the first divinity that Theseus caused the people to adore, or, at least, to whom a statue was erected on the public place. The fêtes of that goddess were celebrated on the fourth day of each month, a chief part in them being assigned to the prostitutes, who then exercised their calling only for the profit of the goddess, and they expended in offerings the money which they had gained under her auspices. At the height of its prosperity the temple of Venus at Corinth had, according to Strabo, one thousand courtesans. It was a common custom in Greece to consecrate to Venus a certain number of young girls, when it was desired to render the goddess favourable, or when she had granted the prayers addressed to her.

The ordinary Athenian prostitutes appear to have been dedicated to the public service, and they were forbidden to leave the country without the consent of the Archons, who often accorded it only on having a guarantee that they would return. There would seem even to have been a College of Prostitutes, which was declared useful and necessary to the state. The story of the social influence of the *heteræ* during the palmiest days of Greece is too well known to need repetition, and it will be found fully detailed in the pages of

Dufour. The majority of the *heteræ*, however, were far from being in the position of Aspasia, Laïs, and others, who were the friends, and even instructors, of statesmen and philosophers. Although they were allowed some of the rights of citizenship, they were often treated with implacable rigour by the Areopagus, and their children were condemned to the same ignominy as themselves. Curiously enough, the chief accusation against the prostitutes was their irreligion, and although they were priestesses in some temples, from others they were rigidly excluded.

Among the Romans the prostitute class held a much lower position in public opinion than with the Greeks, and for a long time its members were treated as below the attention of legislators, and were left to the arbitrary regulation of the police. They were classed with the slave population as civilly dead, and, having once become "infamous," the moral stain was indelible. Dufour says, as to the religious character of Latin prostitution—"The courtesans at Rome were not, as in Greece, kept at a distance from the altars. On the contrary, they frequented all the temples, in order, no doubt, to find their favourable chances of gain; they showed their gratitude to the divinity who had been propitious to them, and they brought to his sanctuary a portion of the gain which they believed they owed to him. Religion closed its eyes to this impure source of revenue and offerings; civil legislation did not intermeddle with these details of false devotion, which concerned only religion; and, thanks to that tolerance, or rather the systematic abstention from judicial and religious control, sacred prostitution preserved at Rome nearly its primitive features, with this difference, nevertheless, that it was always confined to the class of courtesans, and that, instead of being an integral part of worship, it was a foreign accessory to it." According to some Roman writers, however, Acca Laurentia (the foster-mother of Romulus and Remus), in whose honour the Lupercales were instituted, was a prostitute, and the fêtes of Flora had a similar origin. The goddess of flowers was originally a courtesan, who made an enormous fortune, which she left to the state. Her legacy was accepted, and the Senate, in gratitude, decreed that the name of Flora should be inscribed in the fastes of the state, and that solemn fêtes should perpetuate the memory of her generosity. These fêtes always preserved a remembrance of their origin, and were accompanied by the most scandalous scenes, which were publicly enacted in the circus.

The religious prostitutes of antiquity find their counterparts in the dancing girls attached to the Hindoo temples. These "female slaves of the idol" are girls who have been dedicated to the temple service, often by their own parents, and they act both as dancing girls and courtesans. Notwithstanding their calling, they are treated with great respect, and such would seem always to have been the case, if we may judge by the ancient legend which relates that Gautama was entertained at Vesali by a lady of high rank who had the title of "Chief of the Courtesans."[1] No doubt the attention paid to the appearance and education of the temple prostitutes

---

[1] Mrs. Spier's "Life in Ancient India," p. 281.

has much to do with the respect with which they are treated, the position accorded by the ancient Greeks to the superior class of *heteræ* being due to an analogous cause.

Bishop Heber says, in relation to the Bayadêres of Southern India, that they differ considerably from the Nautch girls of the Northern Provinces, " being all in the service of different temples, for which they are purchased young, and brought up with a degree of care which is seldom bestowed on the females of India of any other class. This care not only extends to dancing and singing, and the other allurements of their miserable profession, but to reading and writing. Their dress is lighter than the bundle of red cloth which swaddles the *figuranté* of Hindostan, and their dancing is more indecent; but their general appearance and manner seemed to me far from immodest, and their air even more respectable than the generality of the lower classes of India. . . . The money which they acquire in the practice of their profession is hallowed to their wicked gods, whose ministers are said to turn them out without remorse, or with a very scanty provision, when age or sickness renders them unfit for their occupation. Most of them, however, die young." The Bishop adds, " I had heard that the Bayadêres were regarded with respect among the other classes of Hindoos, as servants of the gods, and that, after a few years' service, they often marry respectably. But, though I made several inquiries, I cannot find that this is the case; their name is a common term of reproach among the women of the country, nor could any man of decent caste marry one of their number."[1] The courtesans of Hindostan do not appear to be attached to the temples, but Tavernier relates that they made offerings to certain idols, to whom they surrendered themselves when young to bring good fortune.

The chief facts connected with religious prostitution have now been given, and it remains only to show that this system has nothing to do with any custom of communal marriage, or promiscuous intercourse between the sexes, such as it is thought to give evidence of. Sir John Lubbock says that the life led by the courtesans attached to the Hindoo temples is not considered shameful, because they continue the old custom of the country under religious sanction. This statement, however, is wholly inaccurate, as the former existence of the custom referred to cannot be established. The social phenomena which are thought to establish that mankind has passed through a stage of promiscuity in the intercourse between the sexes are capable of totally different interpretation. The ease with which any doctrine or practice, however absurd or monstrous, will be accepted, if it possesses a religious sanction, would alone account for the respect entertained for religious prostitutes. But among a people who, like the Hindoos, view sexual immorality for personal gain with abhorrence, such a calling, if it were based on so barbarous a custom as communal marriage, would inevitably lessen rather than increase that sentiment. On the other hand, if the religious position accorded to the temple prostitutes is connected with ideas which have a sacredness of their own, the

[1] " Journey," iii., 219.

respect will be greatly increased. And thus, in fact, it is. Probably no custom is more widely spread than the providing for a guest a female companion, who is usually a wife or daughter of the host. Such a connection with a stranger is permitted even among peoples who are otherwise jealous preservers of female chastity. This custom of sexual hospitality is said to have been practised by the Babylonians in the time of Alexander, although, according to the Roman historian, parents and husbands did not decline to accept money in return for the favours thus accorded. Eusebius asserts that the Phœnicians prostituted their daughters to strangers, and that this was done for the greater glory of hospitality. So, also, we find that at Cyprus the women who devoted themselves to the good goddess walked about the shores of the island to attract the strangers who disembarked.

In the earliest phase of what is called sacred prostitution it was not every man who was entitled to enjoy its privileges. The Babylonian women, who were compelled to make a sacrifice of their persons once in their lives, submitted to the embraces only of strangers. In Armenia, also, strangers alone were entitled to seek sexual hospitality in the sacred enclosures at the temple of Anaïtis, and it was the same in Syria during the fêtes of Venus and Adonis. Dufour was struck by this fact, and, speaking of it, he says, " It may be thought surprising that the inhabitants of the country were so impressed with a worship in which their women had all the benefit of the mysteries of Venus." He adds, however, that the former were not less interested than the latter in these mysteries. " The worship of Venus was in some sort stationary for the women, nomadic for the men, seeing that these could visit in turn the different fêtes and temples of the goddess, profiting everywhere, in these sensual pilgrimages, by the advantages reserved to guests and to strangers."

Besides hospitality, the practice of which is, under ordinary circumstances, an almost sacred duty with uncultured peoples, there was another series of ideas associated with the system of sacred prostitution. In the East, the great aim of woman's life is marriage and bearing children. We have a curious reference to this fact in the lament of the Hebrew women for Jephthah's daughter, which appears to have been occasioned less by her death than by the recorded fact that " she knew no man." When she heard of the vow made by her father, she said to him, " Let me alone two months, that I may go up and down upon the mountains and bewail my virginity, I and my fellows." The desire of the wife, however, is not merely for children, but for a man-child, the necessity for which has given rise to the practice of adoption; another custom which Sir John Lubbock believes to support his favourite doctrine of communal marriage. In India adoption is practised when a man has no son of his own, and it has a directly religious motive. Sir Thomas Strange shows that the Hindoo law of inheritance cannot be understood without reference to the belief that a man's future happiness depends " upon the performance of his obsequies and the payment of his [spiritual] debts." He who pays these debts is his heir; and, as " offerings from sons are more effectual than offerings from other persons, sons are first in order of succession." Hence to have a son is to the Hindoo a sacred duty, and when his wife bears no children, or only daughters, he is compelled by his religious belief to adopt one. We can understand how anxious for a son women must be where those ideas prevail, and this anxiety has given rise to various curious ceremonies having for their object to prevent or cure sterility. Some of these, which have been described by Dulaure and other writers, existed in Europe down to a comparatively recent period. In India, and probably in some other Eastern countries, they are still practised both by wives who have continued childless and by newly-married women, the latter offering to the *Linga* the sacrifice of their virginity.

This desire for children led to offerings being made to ensure the coveted blessing, and to vows to be performed on its being obtained. The nature of the vow would undoubtedly have some reference to the thing desired; and, as related by an old Arabian traveller in India, "when a woman has made a vow for the purpose of having children, if she brings into the world a pretty daughter, she carries it to *Bod* (so they call the idol which they adore), and leaves it with him." The craving for children was anciently as strong among Eastern peoples as it is at the present day, and it is much more probable that this, rather than a habit of licentiousness, either of the women themselves or of the priests, led to the sacrifice at the shrine of Mylitta. If we are to believe Herodotus, the Babylonian women were in his time noted for their virtue, although at a later period they would seem to have lost that characteristic.

The desire for children is directly opposed to the feeling which would operate in the case of communal marriage, where parents and children, having no special relation, no one would have any particular interest in preserving the issue of such intercourse. Among the uncultured peoples of the present era who the most nearly approach in their sexual relations to a state of communal marriage, the indifference to children is often apparent. Infanticide is very general, and abortion is often practised by the women to enable them to retain the favour of their husbands. The sacred prostitution, which is intimately connected with the craving for children, must, therefore, have originated at a time when a considerable advance had been made in social culture.

It would not be surprising if the ancient Babylonish custom had, of itself, resulted in a system of sacred prostitution. The act of sexual intercourse was in the nature of an offering to the Goddess of Fecundity, and a life of prostitution in the service of the goddess might well come to be viewed as pleasing to her and as deserving of respect at the hands of her worshippers. We have an analogous phase of thought in the Japanese notion, that a girl who enters the Yoshiwara for the purpose of thus supporting her parents performs a highly meritorious act. In Armenia, as we have seen, children were devoted by their parents to the service of the great goddess for a term of years, and those who had received the most numerous favours from strangers were the most eagerly sought after in marriage on the expiration of that period. That dedication was in pursuance of a vow, which no doubt, like the vows of Indian women at the present day, would at first have relation to some sexual want, although thank-offerings of the same character would afterwards come to be presented by the worshippers of the goddess for blessings of any description. Thus Xenophon consecrated fifty courtesans to the Corinthian Venus, in pursuance of the vow which he had made when he besought the goddess to give him the victory in the Olympian games. Pindar makes Xenophon thus address these slaves of the goddess: "Oh, young damsels, who receive all strangers and give them hospitality, priestesses of the goddess Pitho in the rich Corinth, it is you who, in causing the incense to burn before the images of Venus and in invoking the mother of love, often merit for us her celestial aid, and procure for us the sweet moments which we taste on the luxurious couches where is gathered the delicate fruit of beauty."

The legitimate inference to be made from what has gone before is that sacred prostitution sprang from the primitive custom of providing sexual hospitality for strangers, the agents by which it was carried out being supplied by the votaries of the deity under whose sanction the custom was placed. Assuming its existence, and the strong desire on the part of married women for children, which led them to sacrifice their own virginity as an offering to the Goddess of Fecundity, or to dedicate their daughters to her service, we have a perfect explanation of the custom of sacred prostitution. The duty of these "servants of the idol" would include the furnishing of hospitality to the strangers who visited the shrines and fêtes of the deity. These pilgrims became the guests of the deity, and she was bound to furnish them with the same hospitality as that which they would have met with if they had been entertained by private individuals. The piety of her worshippers enabled her to do this, either by devoting their daughters for a limited period to this sacred service, in return for which the reward of fecundity would be looked for, or by presenting them absolutely to the goddess in return for favours received at her hands. It is not surprising that among peoples having such notions, the temple courtesans were regarded with great respect, nor that those who had acted in that capacity with success were eagerly sought after as wives. It is more difficult to understand how sexual hospitality should have come to be placed under divine sanction. The difficulty vanishes, however, when the light in which the process of generation is viewed in the East is considered. That which by us is looked upon as due to a passionate impulse, was anciently (except among certain religious sects), and is still to the Eastern mind, an act of mysterious significance. The male organ of generation was the symbol of creative power, and the veneration in which it was held led to practices which to a modern European are nothing but disgusting, although to the Semite they partake of a purely religious character.

To pursue this subject further would be to enter upon the wide field of Phallic worship. Sufficient has, however, already been said to prove that sacred prostitution is only remotely connected, if at all, with communal marriage. The only apparent connection between them is the sexual hospitality to strangers which the former was established to supply; but the association is only apparent, as the providing of that hospitality is perfectly consistent with the recognition of the value of female chastity, and is quite independent of any ideas entertained as to marriage.

In conclusion, I may add that the opinion expressed by Sir John Lubbock,[1] that the Grecian *hetæræ* were more highly esteemed than the married women, because the former were originally countrywomen and relations, and the latter captives and slaves, is not consistent with the facts of the case. Any one conversant with the social customs of ancient Greece will be able to give a totally different explanation of that phenomenon. Marriage with foreign women was forbidden, and thus captives and slaves furnished the Greeks with concubines and prostitutes, while their wives were taken from among their own countrywomen. Even such was the case in the earliest heroic ages, when, says Mr. Gladstone, the intercourse between husband and wife was " thoroughly natural, full of warmth, dignity, reciprocal deference, and substantial, if not conventional delicacy." The same writer says: " The relations of youth and maiden generally are indicated with extreme beauty and tenderness in the Iliad; and those of the unmarried woman to a suitor, or probable spouse, are so portrayed, in the case of the incomparable Nausicaa, as to show a delicacy and freedom that no period of history or state of manners can surpass."[2]

---

[1] *Op. cit.*, p. 120.   [2] " Juventus Mundi," pp. 408, 411.

CHAPTER VII.

MARRIAGE AMONG PRIMITIVE PEOPLES.

THE usual idea associated with the term "marriage" is the union in domestic life of a single pair of individuals, and with few exceptions this is the only marriage recognised by Christian peoples. We learn from the Old Testament Scriptures that the Hebrews had different ideas on that subject. They not only considered it allowable for a man to have more than one wife, but apparently they thought he might have as many wives as he chose. This system of marriage, to which the term polygamy has been usually applied, is still prevalent in most countries outside of the European area. The monogamous and polygamous forms of marriage are, however, by no means the only possible ones. Instead of a man and a woman living together, a number of individuals may thus associate, and in lieu of a man having several wives a woman may conceivably have more than one husband. Moreover, marriage may be subject to varying regulations or restrictions, causing the same system to present dissimilar features in different localities. That which is *possible* in social life may reasonably be expected to occur somewhere or other on the earth's surface; and, as a fact, all the types of marriage referred to are to be found among peoples of the Eastern Hemisphere.

It can hardly be doubted that the most civilised
races, of which we may call the modern world, have,
with the exception of the Chinese, belonged to the two
great branches of the Caucasian stock, the Aryan and
the Semitic-speaking peoples. Those races, and especially such of them as inhabit the Western part of the
Old Continent, have shown a preference for monogamy or polygamy, the former being almost restricted
to Europeans, the latter being nearly universal
among the Asiatic portion of the Caucasian stock.
The inferior races, however, possess the least advanced
systems of marriage. The natives of the Australian
Continent are usually regarded as the most uncivilised
of mankind, and among them there has been developed
a system which some persons would probably consider
not entitled to the name of marriage. In it individuals give place theoretically to groups, between
whom the marriage relation is supposed to be formed,
the individuals being treated only as members of a
group. The existence of this peculiar system has
been established by the inquiries of the Rev. Lorimer
Fison, who has shown, moreover, that Australian
marriage " is something more than the marriage of
group to group, *within a tribe.* It is an arrangement,
extending 'across a Continent, which divides many
widely-scattered tribes into intermarrying classes, and
gives a man of one class marital rites over women of
another class in a tribe a thousand miles away, and
speaking a language other than his own. It seems to
be strong evidence of the common origin of all the
Australian tribes among whom it prevails ; and it is a
striking illustration of how custom remains fixed while

language changes."[1]   An American writer, Mr. Lewis Morgan, who was the first to point out the prevalence among the less cultured races of mankind of relationship which he terms "*classificatory*," in opposition to the *descriptive* relationships of the superior races, states that, according to Australian marriage, "a group of males distinguished by the same class name are the born husbands of a group of females bearing another class name; and whenever a male of this class meets a female of the other class, they recognise each other as husband and wife, and their right to live in this relation is regarded by the tribe to which they belong." The peculiarity of this system is, not that each individual is entitled to take a wife or husband out of a particular group, but that, in theory, every individual is from birth the husband or wife of all the members of a special group.   Mr. Fison remarks further that the idea of marriage under that system is founded on the rights neither of the woman nor of the man.   It is based "on the rights of the tribe, or rather of the classes into which the tribe is divided.   Class marriage is not a contract entered into by two parties.   It is a natural state into which both parties are born, and they have to be content with that state whereunto they are called."   But what is the nature of the social organisation to which the system of group marriage belongs?   At the present time nearly all the existing Australian tribes are divided into four classes, into one of which every individual is born.   The members of each class are supposed to trace their descent to the

[1] "Kamilaroi and Kurnai," p. 54.

same common female ancestor, they are treated as of the same degrees of kinship to each other, and they are not allowed to intermarry. There is reason to believe that originally, perhaps when the ancestors of all the existing tribes resided in the same neighbourhood, each tribe consisted of only two classes. In this case, the law of group marriage, under the regulations as to marriage and descent just mentioned, would require that all the members of each class should be real or tribal brothers and sisters of each other, and the husbands and wives of all the members of the other class. The theoretical result would be, that all the men of each class would have their wives in common, and all the women of each class their husbands in common. Whether the number of individuals in each group was large or small, the result would be the same. In practice, the exercise of the extended marriage right would be restricted to a few individuals, but that its existence is generally understood is shown by the statement of a native servant, who had travelled far and wide in Australia, that "he was furnished with temporary wives by the various tribes with whom he sojourned in his travels; that his right to those women was recognised as a matter of course; and that he could always ascertain whether they belonged to the division into which he could legally marry, though the places were a thousand miles apart, and the languages quite different." This particular case might, perhaps, be explained as an extreme example of the granting of sexual hospitality; but Mr. Fison refers to several facts which prove the reality of the relationships arising out of group marriage, and therefore of this system itself.   He states that an Australian "has the rights of a brother, and he acknowledges the duties of a brother, towards every man of his own group; and he can no more marry a woman of a group which is 'sister' to his own than we can marry our own sister."   Among the Australians, as among some other races who are supposed to have had at one time a similar marriage system, a mother-in-law and a son-in-law mutually avoid each other.   This conduct is based on the fact that the mother-in-law belongs to the class of women over whom the son-in-law has a marital right, but as she is *specially* forbidden to him they must keep out of each other's way.   Again, the incidents attendant on adoption are in accordance with the reality of group relationships.   A person who is adopted into a gens or family "forthwith abandons all the relationships of his own gens, and takes those of the gens into which he is adopted," a result which is due to the fact that relationship is conceived, not between individual and individual, but between group and group.   Extraordinary as is the Australian system at the present time, when each class, or intermarrying group, embraces so many individuals, it would not appear so strange if, as was originally the case, each group consisted only of the immediate descendants of the common female ancestor.   In this case all the males in any particular generation of each family group would be the husbands of all the females in the same generation of the other family; in other words, all the men of each group would have their wives in common and all the women their husbands in common. Moreover, the actual practice of the Australian tribes differs from the theory. Every man and every woman is permanently married to an individual of the opposite sex, and often this connection is formed at an early age by arrangement between the parents of the persons concerned. In addition, however, each of these persons may be allotted by the great council of the tribe as an "accessory spouse," or *pirauru*, to some other individual. The Australian system, therefore, presents a mixture of individual marriage and group marriage, the latter of which is evidently closely connected with the right of sexual hospitality, which is considered by the savage mind as natural and of great importance.

Australian marriage is thus based on what may be theoretically termed the natural marriage between two groups of individuals whose wishes are never consulted in the matter. The same arrangement might, of course, be made among the individuals themselves, and, curiously enough, a form of group marriage, much restricted in its operation, was at one time fully recognised among the Polynesian Islands of the Pacific. This system was known as *punalua*, and it consisted in two or more brothers having their wives, or two or more sisters having their husbands, in common. Here, brothers and sisters form one group, and the wives of the one with the husbands of the other, themselves being brothers and sisters (actual or tribal), form another group answering to the intermarrying classes of the Australians. The Polynesian *punalua* and the Australian group marriage are, therefore, fundamentally the same.[1] The Australian system is

---

[1] Mr. Fison alludes to the New Zealand practice of a woman's suitors wrestling for her, which is called *punarua*. This word,

much the more comprehensive, however, as it affects all the members of a class, while the Polynesian affects only the persons immediately concerned. Each puna-luan group appears to be formed independently, with the consent of all the parties to the arrangement, and without conferring any sexual right on the children belonging to it. This is totally unlike the Australian practice, which recognises individuals only as members of particular groups, standing to each other in a certain marital relation and perpetuated by descent through their female members. The latter may be described as *hereditary* punalua, as distinguished from the Polynesian system, which is purely personal.

Mr. Morgan points out that *punalua* may be of two forms, one founded on the brotherhood of the husbands, and the other on the sisterhood of the wives, the men of each group being polygamous and the women poly-androus. Both forms of that marriage arrangement are said to have existed among the natives of America, although, when discovered by Europeans, the family with them was founded on marriage between single pairs, but without exclusive cohabitation. Thus, it was not uncommon for a man who married an eldest daughter to claim all his wife's sisters, and he appears to have occasionally allowed his brothers to participate in the matrimonial privileges. In other cases, a man married the sister of his deceased wife as a matter of course, but he did not take her in his wife's lifetime. Similar customs exist in some parts of Australia, where the old system of marriage

he says, is the Hawaiian *punalua*, which denotes the common-right of tribal brothers to certain women (*note*, p. 153).

has been almost forgotten. The polyandrous form of punalua was known to the Australians either as a feature of the group right, or in the course of its decadence. Thus, every woman had accessory husbands or paramours who associated with her temporarily, notwithstanding that she had a recognised husband with whom she habitually cohabited. Mr. T. E. Lance mentions a tribe in which most of the women are nominally the wives of elderly men, who are, however, obliged to lend them on stated occasions to the younger men of the allowed classes.

It is evident that circumstances may favour the development of either the polyandrous or the polygamous form of punalua to the exclusion of the other. A scarcity of women would tend to the establishment of the former system, as we see in the case of the Todas of Southern India. This fine race of hillmen were inveterate practisers of female infanticide down to a recent date, and it was almost the universal practice for a family of near relations to live together in one hut, having wife, children, and cattle in common.[1] The continued formation of such alliances appears to have led to a result much resembling the group marriage of the Australians. As Colonel Marshall states, "the family come to be represented mainly by a knot of brothers, half-brothers, and cousins, married to closely related kinswomen in nearly equal numbers; the men being the common fathers of all the progeny; each woman, however, the mother of her own children only."[2] The Todas

----

[1] "A Phrenologist among the Todas," by Col. William E. Marshall, p. 213.

[2] Ditto, p. 226.

have, under British influence, given up the practice of infanticide, but they have fewer female than male children, owing to a preponderance of male births, and polyandry is still customary among them. A woman is at first married with her own consent to one man, who pays the dowry. Afterwards, however, "if the husband has brothers, or very near relatives, all living together, they may each, if both she and he consent, participate in the right to be considered her husband also, on making up a share of the dowry that has been paid."[1] Notwithstanding the example of the Todas, it must not be thought that a scarcity of women is essential to the existence of polyandry. In Tibet this system of marriage is universal, and it has been so from time immemorial. Nevertheless, unmarried women are numerous, and infanticide is not practised. Mr. Andrew Wilson defined Tibetan polyandry as the marriage of one woman to two or more brothers, and these are actual brothers,—although at one time probably they may also have been tribal. The choice of a wife is the right of the elder brother, and Mr. Wilson states[2] that "among the Tibetan-speaking people it universally prevails that the contract he makes is understood to involve a marital contract with all the brothers, if they choose to avail themselves of it." Moreover, all the children of the marriage belong to the eldest brother, as the head of the family group. In Ladak,[3] however, the consent of

[1] "A Phrenologist among the Todas," by Col. William E. Marshall, p. 43.

[2] "The Abode of Snow," p. 233.

[3] "Ancient Society," by J. F. M'Lennan, p. 158.

the younger brothers is required to the marital part-
nership, although on the death of the eldest brother
his authority, with his property and his widow, devolve
upon his next brother, whether or not there has been
a polyandrous arrangement.   Mr. Wilson observes[1]
that Tibetan polyandry had the effect "of checking
the increase of population in regions from which emi-
gration is difficult, and where it is also difficult to
increase the means of subsistence."   It is due to an
artificial scarcity of *wives*, rather than of women, in
which it differs from the polyandry of the Todas,
which is the consequence of an actual scarcity of
females, caused originally by the practice of infanticide, and afterwards by a preponderance of male
births.   Both the Tibetans and the Todas trace
descent through the male line—that is, take the
family or gentile name of the father; but some peoples
of Southern India, who practice polyandry, prefer the
female line.   This is not surprising, when we find, as
among the Nairs of Malabar, that not only has a
woman several husbands, but a man "may be one in
several combinations of husbands."   Such unions,
which are governed by certain restrictions as to tribe
and caste, closely resemble the Australian group
marriage.   In Ceylon, where polyandry is very prevalent among the Kandyans, marriage is of two forms,
one termed *deega*, in which the wife goes to live in
the house and village of her husband or husbands,
the other, termed *beena*, in which the husband or husbands come to reside with her in the house of her

<hr>

[1] *Op. cit.*, p. 234.

birth.   The Tibetan polyandry may be a form of the *deega* marriage, and the Nair polyandry a form of the *beena* marriage, although it is possible that the latter may be a "mere freak," if it be true (as Mr. Wilson affirms) that the Nairs are nominally married to girls of their own caste, but never have any intercourse with their wives, who may have as many lovers as they please, provided they are Brahmins or Nairs, other than the husband.   These lovers answer to the paramours of the Australian system, but, whereas the latter occupy a secondary place, among the Nairs it is the husband who is in that position. This custom may not improbably be explained by the remarks of a Mohammedan writer, who says,[1] with regard to the marriages of the Brahmins of Malabar, "when there are several brothers in one family, the eldest of them alone enters into the conjugal state (except in cases where it is evident that he will have no issue), the remainder refraining from marriage, in order that heirs may not multiply to the confusion of inheritance.   The younger brothers, however, intermarry with women of the Nair caste without entering into any compact with them, thus following the custom of the Nairs, who have themselves no conjugal contract.   In the event of any children being born from these connections, they are excluded from the inheritance; but should it appear evident that the elder brother will not have issue, then another brother, the next to him in age, will marry."   The irregular marriages with the Nair women were, perhaps, intro-

---

[1] "Tohful-ul-Mujahideen," p. 63.

duced by the Brahmins to provide wives for the brothers of their caste who were not allowed to marry. The original Nair polyandry may have been similar to that of the carpenters, ironsmiths, painters, and other Malabar castes, who (says the same writer) "cohabit, two or more together, with one woman, but not unless they are brothers, or in some way related, lest confusion should ensue in the inheritance of property."

It is thought, from certain facts mentioned in the Mahá Bhárata, that polyandry was a recognised institution among the early Hindus, and that the eldest brother had the right, as now among the Tibetans, to choose a wife for the family. Some writers have gone so far even as to assert that all the peoples of the primitive Aryan stock, and our own British ancestors amongst them, practised the same custom or some form of group marriage. Mr. J. F. M'Lennan regarded the Hebrew law of the Levirate, which required a younger son to take his elder brother's widow if he had died childless, as having been derived from the practice of polyandry. Whether this was so, or whether it was merely a regulation to prevent the elder branch of a stock from becoming extinct, traces of polyandry have undoubtedly been met with among peoples of the Semitic stock. It would seem, however, to have been most prevalent among the tribes of Southern Arabia, and it was probably due, chiefly to the poverty of the people,[1] as among the Tibetans, who may have directly influenced the development of polyandry in Arabia. The true marriage system of

____

[1] "Kinship and Marriage in Early Arabia," pp. 128, 235.

the Semitic peoples was punalua of the polygamous form, in which several sisters had a husband in common. We have an instance of it in the marriage of Jacob with the sisters Leah and Rachel. At a later period, however, when blood or even tribal relationship between the wives was not required, the practice of polygamy become fully established. This system has attained its chief development among the Semitic races and those African peoples who are allied to them by blood. The most widely-spread forms of marriage now existing are polygamy and monogamy, and while the former may be traced to the polygamous phase of punalua or group marriage, it is not improbable that the latter is traceable to the polyandrous phase. At all events, monogamy has been established chiefly among those races who are supposed, formerly, to have been polyandrous. The Australians, among whom group marriage has reached so full a development, are said to show a tendency to the introduction of individual marriage. Descent through the female line, which was, at one time, universal among them, is giving place to descent through males, where residence has become fixed and property accumulated. The change is accompanied by a weakening of the group right, and the gradual introduction of marriage " by gifts, by exchange, by capture, and by elopement, one or other of these predominating." The rights of the individual are thus substituted for those of the group, and individual marriage is recognised.

Strange as are the various marriage systems we have referred to, they are based on the very simple principle that every individual has a sexual right.

The conditions under which this right may be exercised vary among different peoples, their operation
giving rise to the peculiar married arrangements in
question. Among the Australians, almost the only
restriction on sexual unions appears to be that arising
from consanguinity. Their marriage regulations have
evidently been formed with the intention of absolutely
prohibiting unions between persons near of kin.
Although marriage with a sister of the half-blood is
often permitted, and for special reasons marriage with
a full sister may be allowed, the objection to consanguineous unions may be declared to be universal
among peoples of a low degree of culture. Their marriage regulations, however, are generally intended to
have certain positive results. The chief result aimed
at would seem to be the prevention of over-popula-
tion. This fact, combined with the recognition of the
sexual rights of man, accounts for the polyandry of
the Tibetans and the Hindus, and the attainment of
it is in many cases aided by the practice of infanticide.
Polygamy, on the other hand, has no apparent relation to the question of population. It is connected
rather with the rights of the gens or family to which
the women belong, the man having, in many cases,
certain duties to perform before he can obtain his
wife or wives. The development of polygamy is,
moreover, attended with an invasion of the sexual
rights of individuals; as the appropriation of the
women by the rich or powerful often renders the
obtaining of wives by the poor or weak difficult, if not
impossible.

The objection entertained by peoples of a low

degree of culture to the marriage of persons near of kin is a strong ground of objection to Mr. Morgan's theory that consanguineous unions were the earliest to be formed; in other words, that "promiscuous inter-marriage between brothers and sisters and others of the closest kin" was, at one time, customary. Mr. Fison refers to various practices which he thinks point to the former existence of such a state of things among the Australians. In reality, however, they are merely incidents of the group marriage which has been developed by that race, or at most, the result of temporary suspension under special circumstances of the restrictions which that system enforces. They are, indeed, cases of licentiousness similar to what is often met with among many peoples during religious and other festivals. The occurrence of a temporary condition of lawlessness on various occasions, such as the death of a chief or the celebration of an important event, is not unknown even to civilised nations. Mr. Morgan's opinion as to the former prevalence of consanguineous marriages derives no real support from the fact mentioned by Mr. Fison, and as I have elsewhere[1] shown, marriages of that character are not required to account for the phenomena exhibited in the classificatory system of relationship which exists among the primitive races of mankind.

---

[1] "Journal of the Anthropological Institute," vol. viii. (1879), p. 144, *et seq.*

CHAPTER VIII.

MARRIAGE BY CAPTURE.

VARIOUS attempts have been made to account for the prevalence among peoples of all degrees of culture of what has been called " marriage by capture," or of rites which furnish evidence of its former existence. Mr. M'Lennan traces it to infanticide, which by " rendering women scarce, led at once to polyandry within the tribe, and the capturing of women from without." On the other hand, Sir John Lubbock ascribes the origin of " marriage by capture" to a desire on the part of individuals to acquire women for themselves, " without infringing on the general rights of the tribe." According to this view, communal marriage was replaced by special connections, accompanied by the introduction of a foreign element, giving rise to the practice of *exogamy.* The reference to this practice (the necessity for which must, if Mr. M'Lennan's idea is correct, have preceded " marriage by capture," instead of the latter originating it) unnecessarily complicates the question under discussion.

Although exogamy is often associated with forcible marriage, the two things are perfectly distinct, and they have had totally different origins. Mr. Morgan very justly connects the former with certain ideas entertained by primitive peoples with regard to blood relationship, and it can be explained most simply and rationally as *marriage out of the clan*, it having sprang from the belief that all the members of a clan are related by blood, and therefore incapable of being united in marriage. This view is confirmed by the fact that tribes which are *endogamous* in relation to other tribes are *exogamous* in the sense that they comprise several clans, the members of none of which can intermarry among themselves. We have a curious example of this limited exogamy in the Chinese, among whom persons bearing the same family name are not permitted to intermarry. True endogamy would seem to exist among very few peoples, and when it is practised the custom is probably due to special circumstances, which, giving prominence to a particular clan, have enabled them to claim a caste privilege, or it may be owing to a necessity arising from the complete severance of the members of a clan from their fellows. The scarcity of women, whether occasioned by infanticide or polygamy, may have rendered exogamy more requisite, and it may have been complicated by forcible marriage, but none of these have any real bearing on its origin.

It could be shown without difficulty that the opinion entertained by the writers I have referred to, that the primitive condition of man was one of communal marriage, is untenable, and if I am correct in this conclusion, there will be no occasion to consider the argument that "marriage by capture" depended on such a social condition. The idea that "marriage by capture" originated in the necessity for exogamy, arising from infanticide or some other practice, is more plausible, and such an explanation of the custom may be accepted where it is not universal in a tribe, but resorted to only in particular cases or under special conditions. The capture of wives among the Australian aborigines is expressly accounted for by Oldfield as being due to the scarcity of women. But where forcible marriage can be traced to the action of individual caprice it must be treated as exceptional, and some other explanation must be sought for the widespread practices which are supposed to prove the former prevalence of that custom. From this standpoint Mr. M·Lennan's explanation is far from satisfactory, as may be shown by analysis of the incidents attendant on "marriage by capture," as practised by different peoples.

It is true that sometimes the carrying off of the bride is resisted by her friends, and is attended in some cases, as among the Welsh down to a comparatively recent period, by a sham fight between them and the friends of the bridegroom; although among other peoples, as with the Khonds of India, the protection of the bride is left to her female companions. In the great majority of cases cited by Sir John Lubbock, however, the suitor forcibly removes the bride without any hindrance from her friends. Occasionally, as with the Tunguses, the New Zealanders, and the Mandingos, she strongly resists. Among other peoples, as with the Esquimaux, the resistance is usually only pretended, and is thus analogous to the sham fight already referred to. In all these cases alike, however, it is the girl only who has to be conquered, and if the resistance were real it would depend on herself whether or not she should be captured. There are other incidents of this forcible marriage which have more significance than has hitherto been attached to them. Among the New Zealanders, if the girl who is being carried off can break away from her captor and regain her father's house, the suitor loses all chance of ever obtaining her in marriage. So, also, among the Fijians, if a woman does not approve of the man who has taken her by force to his house, she leaves him for some one who can protect her. Among the Fuegians the girl who is not willing to accept her would-be husband does not wait to be carried off, but hides herself in the woods, and remains concealed until he is tired of looking for her. According to Mongol custom, the bride hides herself with some of her relations, and the bridegroom has to search for and find her. Something like the Fuegian custom is practised by the Aitas, among whom the bride has to conceal herself in a wood, where the suitor must find her before sunset.

In these cases the will of the bride-elect is a very important element, and it is equally so in those cases where she is captured and carried off only after a prolonged chase. Thus, with the Kalmucks, according to Dr. Clarke, the girl gallops away at full speed, pursued by her suitor, and if she does not wish to marry him she always effects her escape. An analogous custom is found among the uncultured tribes of the Malayan Peninsula. Here, however, the chase is on foot, and generally round a circle, although sometimes in the forest, and, as Bourien (quoted by Sir John Lubbock) says, the pursuer is successful only if he " has had the good fortune to please the intended bride." A similar custom is found among the Koraks of North-

Eastern Asia.   Here the ceremony takes place within
a large tent containing numerous separate compart-
ments (*pologs*), arranged in a continuous circle around
its inner circumference.   Mr. Kennan (in his " Tent Life
in Siberia ") gives an amusing and instructive description
of such a ceremony.   The women of the encampment,
armed with willow and alder rods, stationed themselves at the entrances of the pologs, the front curtains
of which were thrown up.   Then, at a given signal,
" the bride darted suddenly into the first polog, and
began a rapid flight around the tent, raising the
curtains between the pologs successively, and passing
under.   The bridegroom instantly followed in hot
pursuit, but the women who were stationed in each
compartment threw every possible impediment in his
way, tripping up his unwary feet, holding down the
curtains to prevent his passage, and applying the
willow and alder switches unmercifully to a very
susceptible part of his body as he stooped to raise
them. . . .   With undismayed perseverance he pressed
on, stumbling headlong over the outstretched feet of
his female persecutors, and getting constantly en-
tangled in the ample folds of the reindeer-skin curtains, which were thrown with the skill of a matador
over his head and eyes.   In a moment the bride had
entered the last closed polog near the door, while the
unfortunate bridegroom was still struggling with his
accumulated misfortunes about half way round the
tent.   I expected," says the traveller, " to see him
relax his efforts and give up the contest when the
bride disappeared, and was preparing to protest
strongly on his behalf against the unfairness of the

trial; but, to my surprise, he still struggled on, and with a final plunge, burst through the curtain of the last poióg, and rejoined his bride," who had waited for him there. Mr. Kennan adds that "the intention of the whole ceremony was evidently to give the woman an opportunity to marry the man or not, as she chose, since it was obviously impossible for him to catch her under such circumstances, unless she voluntarily waited for him in one of the pologs."

Judging only from the element of force observable in what are termed "marriages by capture," the explanation of them given by Mr. M'Lennan appears reasonable. But, although capture may be an incident of exogamy, the customs under consideration are really connected with endogamy, in the sense that the parties to them belong to a common tribe. Moreover, those customs are wanting in another of the elements which would be necessary to justify their being classed as "survivals" of an earlier practice of forcible exogamy. This pre-supposes the absence of consent on the part of the relatives of the bride, but the so-called marriage by capture is nearly always preceded by an arrangement with them. The only exception among the various examples of such marriages mentioned by Sir John Lubbock is that of the inhabitants of Bali, where the man is said to forcibly carry off his bride to the woods, and to *afterwards* effect reconciliation with her "enraged" friends. It is not improbable, however, that rage may be simulated in this case as in others, and that the capture is arranged beforehand with them. Sir John Lubbock himself explains an apparent act of lawless violence among the Mandingos as an incident of "marriage by capture," on the ground that the bride's relatives " only laughed at the farce, and consoled her by saying that she would soon be reconciled to her situation ;" and it appears that her mother had previously given her consent to the proceeding. A mere general understanding, if universally recognised, would indeed be as efficacious as a special consent, and whether the consent of the parent has to be obtained previously to overcoming the opposition of the bride, or whether this has to be overcome as a condition precedent to the consent being given, is practically of no importance. We seem to have an example of the latter in the marriage customs of the Afghans as described by Elphinstone. Among this people wives are always purchased, and the necessity for paying the usual price is not done away with, although a man is allowed to make sure of his bride by cutting off a lock of her hair, snatching away her veil, or throwing a sheet over her, if he declares at the same time that she is his affianced wife.

The facts just mentioned lead to the conclusion that the " capture" which forms the most prominent incident in the marriage customs under discussion, has a totally different significance from that which is connected with exogamy in the sense supposed by Mr. M'Lennan and Sir John Lubbock. In the latter case force is resorted to to prevent the possibility of opposition by the tribe to whom the victim of the violence belongs ; but in the former, as the consent of the woman's relatives had already been given, expressly or by implication, the force must be to overcome the possible opposition of the woman herself, whether this may arise from bashfulness or from an actual dislike to the suitor. We have here an important distinction, and it points to a state of society where women have acquired a right to exercise a choice in the matter of marriage. Before this right could be fully established the suitor would be allowed to obtain her compliance by force, if necessary, as with the Greenlanders, among whom, according to Crantz, the bride, if, after she has been captured by the old women who negotiated the marriage, she cannot be persuaded by kind and courteous treatment, is "compelled by force, nay, sometimes by blows, to change her state." But even among the Greenlanders, if a girl had great repugnance to her suitor, she could escape marriage by betaking herself to the mountains. A still more efficacious plan is the cutting off of her hair, which frees her from all importunity, as it is accepted as a sure sign that she has determined never to marry. "Marriage by capture" has thus relation not to the tribe but to the individual immediately concerned, and it is based on her power to withhold her consent to the contract made between her suitor and her relatives. Among some uncultured peoples the opposition of the bride-elect is effectually overcome by force, but it is seldom that she is not allowed the opportunity of escaping a marriage which she dislikes. When once it has become usual for the bride to show a real or simulated opposition to the proposed marriage, as might easily be the case among peoples who, although uncultured, esteem chastity before marriage, it would in course of time be firmly established as a general custom. Thus, when a Greenland young woman is asked in marriage she professes great bashfulness, tears her ringlets, and runs away. When the show of opposition had become a matter of etiquette, it would, notwithstanding that the marriage had been previously arranged, be joined in by the friends of the bride, who, by a fiction, is being carried off against her will. Hence the customs of having a sham fight before the bridegroom is allowed to gain possession of his prize, and the placing of impediments in the way of his catching her in the chase, neither of which has any relation to a supposed primitive practice of forcible abduction from a hostile tribe.

It will be said, however, if the relations of the bride have consented to her marriage, why do they oppose the carrying into effect of their agreement? Much light is thrown on this point by the description given by Colonel Dalton of the customs of the hill-tribes of Bengal.[1] With many of the aboriginal peoples of India, and with some Sudra castes, one of the most important ceremonies of marriage is the application of the *Sindur* to the forehead of the bride; this consists in the bridegroom making, usually with vermilion, a red mark between her eyes. In some places, however, particularly in Singhbum, among the Hos, the bridegroom and bride mark each other with blood, signifying that by marriage they become one. Colonel Dalton supposes this to be the origin of the *Sindrahan*, a custom which is as singular as it is widespread. With the Oraons, a Dravidian tribe, the

---

[1] The Ethnology of Bengal.

same ceremony is practised, but in secret. A veil is cast over the bridal pair, who are then covered with another piece of stuff held by some of their male relations, while others mount guard, fully armed, as though to kill any one who might approach to interfere with the ceremony. In the Singhbum villages the ceremony is modified, and the engaged couple drink beer from the same vessel. This signifies that they form only one body, belong to the same *kili*—in other words, that the woman is admitted to the clan of her husband. Dr. Hunter, in his admirable work entitled " Annals of Rural Bengal," says the great event of the life of a Santal is the union of his " tribe" with another " tribe" in marriage. No individual can marry a member of his own clan, and the woman in marrying abandons the clan of her father, as well as his gods, to adopt the clan and the gods of her husband. The ceremony by which the Santals express this separation is different from that adopted by the Hos. The husband's clansmen knot together the garments of the bridegroom and the bride, after which the women of the bride's clan bring lighted charcoal, crush it with a pestle to indicate the breaking of the old family tie, and then extinguish it with water to indicate the definitive separation of the bride from her own clan. As we have seen, this separation is effected among the Oraons in the presence of the members of the two clans, and the sham combat by which the marriage ceremonies commence is evidently intended to show that it is indispensable to obtain the consent, not only of the bride, but also of the family group to which she belongs, before the ties which bind her to the clan can be broken. After offering a pretended resistance, the clansmen of the bride express their consent in joining with the relations of the bridegroom to celebrate the formation of the fresh family tie.

At first sight, it might be thought that there is little difference between this explanation of "marriage by capture" and that given by Sir John Lubbock, but in reality they differ completely. Sir John Lubbock supposes a violent capture from another tribe without any reference to the question of clanship. On the other hand, in the explanation above proposed, there is a change in the position of the woman, but it is brought about by arrangement, the pretended combat having relation to the rights of the clan, but having no reference to the wider organisation of the tribe. The sham-fight is simply a phase of the ceremonies, destined to show the objection entertained by a family group to part with one of its members, and, what is of still greater importance, to give up the interest they possess in the future offspring of the woman who is to be cut off from the clan.   The essentially pacific character of the sham-fight is shown by the manner in which, as described by Colonel Dalton, it is conducted in Gondwana.   Among the Muasi of this district, when the cavalcade of the bridegroom approaches the house of the bride, there issues from it a merry troop of young girls, who are headed by the mother of the bride, bearing on her head a vessel full of water, surmounted by a lighted lamp. When the girls come near the bridegroom's friends they throw at them balls of boiled rice, after which they beat a retreat.   The young men pursue them to the door of the house, which, however, they cannot enter until they have made presents to its female defenders. The fact that among nearly all the peoples who have "marriage by combat," the children belong to the clan of their father, confirms the truth of the conclusion I have sought to establish, that the ceremony in question has relation to the clan, and not to the bride. Among the primitive peoples to whom it would be necessary, on the hypothesis of Sir John Lubbock, to trace the origin of that curious custom, the children usually belong to the family group of their mother. The sham-fight could be introduced when a change has taken place in the condition of women; but this would imply a phase of civilisation much more recent than that of the Australians and other barbarous tribes, to whose practice of stealing women for wives, which is mere forcible marriage, has been wrongly traced the origin of "marriage by capture."

CHAPTER IX.

DEVELOPMENT OF THE "FAMILY."

MR. M'LENNAN has remarked, in relation to the curious customs of capturing women for wives found among peoples in all parts of the world, that "in almost all cases the form of capture is the symbol of a group-act—of a siege, or a pitched battle, or an invasion of a house by an armed band, while in a few cases only, and these much disintegrated, it represents a capture by an individual. On the one side are the kindred of the husband; on the other the kindred of the wife."[1] Whatever may be the true explanation of the origin of exogamy, with which the custom referred to is connected, there can be no doubt of the truth of the statement that the wife-capture is now usually, although it sometimes has relation solely to the individual, the symbol of a group-act. This may not be in the sense intended by Mr. M'Lennan, who looks upon exogamy and polyandry as referable to one and the same cause, and who regards " all the exogamous races as having originally been polyandrous."[2] The phenomena of wife-capture prove conclusively, however, that the family group to which the woman belonged possessed, or thought themselves entitled to, certain rights over her—rights of which they resisted the invasion, whether by an individual alone, or by

---

[1] " Studies in Ancient History," p. 444.   [2] Ditto, p. 181.

a group of persons, or by an individual aided by the
other members of a group. It is important to notice
that the groups in question appear to consist, not of
strangers to each other, or to the man or woman more
immediately concerned, but of persons bound together
by certain ties of blood. This is shown to be so by
the fact that the capture is atoned for by the payment
to the relations of the woman of the marriage-price, if
this has not been agreed on beforehand.[1] It is required, moreover, by the conclusion arrived at by Mr.
M'Lennan, that the tribes among whom the system of
wife-capture prevails are chiefly those whose marriages are governed by the law of exogamy.[2] By
exogamy is meant the practice of marrying out of the
tribe or group of kindred,[3] and it is founded on a
prejudice against marriage with kinsfolk.[4] There is
some uncertainty as to the nature of M'Lennan's primitive group, but, judging from his statement that
" promiscuity, producing uncertainty of fatherhood,
led to the system of kinship through mothers only,"[5]
we may suppose that it consisted of a number of
persons, all of whom, as the result of promiscuity, were
related by blood. The first division into which he
classes uncultured peoples, according to their marriage-
rules, is that where tribes are separate, and all the
members of the tribes are, or feign themselves to be,
of the same blood.[6] Mr. Morgan very properly criti-
cises this definition, which, he says, " might answer for

---

[1] " Studies in Ancient History," pp. 54, 57.

[2] Ditto, pp. 104, 110.   [3] Ditto, p. 174.   [4] Ditto, p. 112.

[5] Ditto, p. 139.   [6] Ditto, p. 113.

a description of a gens; but the gens is never found alone, separate from other gentes. There are several gentes intermingled by marriage in every tribe composed of gentes,"[1] a fact which would seem to distinguish the primitive group of M'Lennan, although consisting of consanguinei, from a gens or clan proper. Moreover, as Mr. Morgan shows, exogamy has relation to a rule or law of a gens, considered as "the unit of organisation of a social system," and therefore the gens (of which, as an institution, the rules are prohibition of intermarriage in the gens, and limitation of descent in the female line[2]), or rather the family from which it has sprung, may be regarded as the earliest social group of which we have any knowledge.

It is of the greatest importance to the discovery of the nature of the primitive human family to understand the origin of the gens or clan. As defined by Morgan, it is "a body of consanguinei descended from the same common ancestor, distinguished by a gentile name, and bound together by affinities of blood." Mr. Morgan affirms that the gens originated in three principal conceptions, "the bond of kin, a pure lineage through descent in the female line, and non-intermarriage in the gens."[3] The most essential feature is that of tracing kinship through females only, and the discovery of the origin of this custom will throw light on that of the clan-institution itself, and therefore on the nature of the primitive family.

Mr. M'Lennan finds the origin of kinship through females only in the uncertainty of paternity, arising

---

[1] "Ancient Society," p. 512.   [2] Ditto, p. 511.   [3] Ditto, p. 69.

from the fact that, in primitive times, a woman was not appropriated to a particular man for his wife, or to men of one blood as wife.[1] The children, although belonging to the horde, remain attached to their mothers, and the blood tie observed between them would, as promiscuity gave place to polyandry of the ruder kind in which the husbands are strangers in blood to each other, become developed into the system of kinship through females.[2]. An earlier writer, Bachofen, was so much struck with certain social phenomena among the ancients, that he believed women to have, at an early period, been supreme, not only in the family but in the state. He supposed that woman revolted against the primitive condition of promiscuity, and established a system of marriage, in which the female occupied the first place as the head of the family, and as the person through whom kinship was to be traced. This movement, which had a religious origin, was followed by another resulting from the development of the idea that the mother occupied a subordinate position in relation to her children, of whom the father was the true parent. Mr. M'Lennan very justly objects to this theory that, if marriage was, from the beginning, monogamous, kinship would have been traced through fathers from the first.[3] He adds that "those signs of supremacy on the woman's part were the direct consequences (1) of marriage *not* being monogamous, or such as to permit of certainty of fatherhood; and (2) of wives

---

[1] "Ancient History," p. 124.   [2] Ditto, p. 139.
[3] *Loc. cit.*, p. 418.

not as yet living in their husband's houses, but apart from them, in the homes of their own mothers."[1] The meaning of this is, that the phenomena referred to by Bachofen were due to the former prevalence of a system of polyandry, such as still exists among the Nairs of Southern India. It is very improbable, however, that kinship through the female only could have had the origin supposed by Mr. M'Lennan. According to him one cause of the supremacy of woman referred to by Bachofen was the fact of wives living apart from their husbands in the homes of their own mothers. This custom must, therefore, have preceded the supremacy of woman, assuming this to have existed, and the tracing of kinship through females which gave rise to it. We must believe that originally women lived alone with their daughters (and their sons also, until these set up a separate establishment for themselves, taking with them probably their favourite sisters, as with the Nairs at the present day),[2] there being no male head of the family. If, however, we trace our steps back in thought to the most primitive period of human existence, we shall see that such a domestic state as that here supposed cannot have been the original one. Among savages there is never that subordination of the man to the woman which we should have to assume. We cannot suppose that the primeval group of mankind consisted of a woman and her children, and if the woman had a male companion we cannot doubt, judging from what we know of savage races, that he would be the head

[1] *Loc. cit.*, p. 419. [2] M'Lennan, p. 150.

and chief of the group.   The very notion, however, of
the family group having a male as well as a female
head is inconsistent with Mr. M'Lennan's theory, and
we must trace the origin of female kinship as a system
to a different source from the polyandry to which he
ascribed it.

The idea of a special relationship subsisting between
a woman and her children might no doubt be originated during the period when the men of a group, " in
the spirit of indifference, indulged in savage promiscuity,"[1] if such a condition of things ever existed, but
that alone would not be sufficient to establish kinship
through females only.   It may be questioned, indeed,
whether there ever was a time when the uncertainty
of paternity, which Mr. M'Lennan's whole theory requires, was so pronounced as to prevent kinship
through males being acknowledged.   Mr. Morgan
agrees with Mr. M'Lennan so far as to say that, "prior
to the gentile organisation, kinship through females
was undoubtedly superior to kinship through males,
and was doubtless the principal basis upon which the
lower tribal groups were organised."   He affirms truly,
however, that "descent in the female line, which is all
that 'kinship through females only' can possibly indicate," is only the rule of a gens, and that relationship
through the father is recognised as fully as that through
the mother.[2]   I have elsewhere, however, given
reasons for believing that this statement does not go
far enough, and that the earliest forms of the classificatory system of relationships, on which Mr. Morgan

---

[1] M'Lennan, p. 134.   [2] " Ancient Society," p. 516.

bases his special theory, require actual kinship, and not relationship merely, through the male quite as fully as through the female.

It is surprising that Mr. Morgan says little as to the origin of descent in the female line. He says: "The gens, though a very ancient social organisation founded upon kin, does not include all the descendants of a common ancestor. It was for the reason that, when the gens came in, marriage between single pairs was unknown, and descent through males could not be traced with certainty. Kindred were linked together chiefly through the bond of their maternity."[1] We have here apparently two reasons stated for the establishment of kinship through females, the absence of marriages between single pairs, and the uncertainty of paternity. Both of these conditions are found by Mr. Morgan to exist in the consanguine family groups which he supposes to have been formed when promiscuity ceased. The Polynesian peoples, among whom he finds traces of the consanguine family, have preserved the recollection of female kinship, although, according to Mr. Morgan, the gens is unknown to them.[2] The classificatory system of relationships, the origin of which he traces to the consanguine family, can, however, receive a totally different interpretation, and the existence of that family itself is very doubtful. Further, the difficulty of tracing descent through males, which Mr. Morgan supposes, is the result only of the polyandrous unions his theory requires, and if they ever really existed they could supply no further

[1] " Ancient Society," p. 67.   [2] Ditto, p. 60.

explanation of the origin of female kinship than the polyandry of the Nairs. He would have done better to have sought to connect it, as Mr. M'Lennan does, with the special relation supposed to exist between a mother and her child.

Mr. Herbert Spencer shows how this idea may have arisen. Unlike the other writers I have referred to, he does not think that promiscuity in the relation of the sexes ever existed in an unqualified form.[1] He thinks, indeed, that monogamy must have preceded polygamy, although, owing to the extension of promiscuity, and the birth of a larger number of children to *unknown* fathers than to *known* fathers, a habit would arise of thinking of *maternal* kinship rather than of *paternal*, and where paternity was manifest children would come to be spoken of in the same way.[2] Mr. Spencer adds, that the habit having arisen, the resulting system of kinship in the female line would be strengthened by the practice of exogamy.[3] The defect of this explanation lies in its requiring uncertain paternity, and I shall show that the system of female kinship has not arisen from the simple association in thought of a child with its mother in preference to its father. It is, moreover, inconsistent with the fact mentioned by Mr. Spencer himself, that where the system of female kinship now subsists " male parentage is habitually known."[4] It is true that he supposes male kinship to be disregarded, but this conclusion appears to me not to be supported by sufficient evidence.

[1] " Principles of Sociology," vol. i., p. 662.

[2] Ditto, p. 665.   [3] Ditto, p. 666.   [4] Ditto, p. 667.

That there may have been a short period of barbarism in which the intercourse between the sexes was unrestrained by any law of marriage is possible. Probably, as female chastity before marriage is even now but slightly regarded among most uncultured peoples, all sexual alliances were allowable, so long as the rule as to consanguinity was not infringed, and so long as no offspring resulted from the alliance,[1] where this was entered into without the consent of parents. This consent would be necessary in all cases where such alliances were formed by females for marital purposes, and the sanction required would be that of the family head at the early period we are treating of. Judging from what we observe among modern savages we cannot doubt that self-interest chiefly would govern the father in connection with his daughter's marriage. He would make certain requisitions as the price of his consent. Whether the marriage was to be a permanent or a terminable engagement, the father would stipulate that his daughter should continue to live with or near him, and that her children should belong to the family group of which he is the head. In this case not only would the children form part of the family to which their mother belonged, but the husband himself would become united to it, and would be required to labour for the benefit of his father-in-law.

A custom still prevalent among the New Zealanders may be cited in illustration. The Reverend Richard Taylor says: "Sometimes the father simply told his intended son-in-law he might come and live

---

[1] Lahontan, "Memoires," ii., pp. 144, *et seq.*

with his daughter; she was thenceforth considered his wife, he lived with his father-in-law, and became one of his tribe or *hapu* to which his wife belonged, and in case of war was often obliged to fight against his own relatives." Mr. Taylor adds, that so common is the custom of the bridegroom going to live with his wife's family, that it frequently occurs; when he refuses to do so, she will leave him, and go back to her relatives.[1] When the wife left her father's house to reside with her husband he had to purchase the privilege by giving her father and other relations handsome presents.[2] As among the New Zealanders, children belonged to their father's family, the fact of the wife going to reside among her husband's relations meant the loss by her father's family of the children. The presents may, therefore, be supposed to represent the price given by a man for his wife's offspring to her relations. This opinion is confirmed by reference to the marriage customs of a West African people. Mr. John Kizell, in his correspondence with Governor Columbine, respecting his negotiations with the chiefs in the River Sherbro, says: "The young women are not allowed to have whom they like for a husband; the choice rests with the parents. If a man wishes to marry the daughter, he must bring to the value of twenty or thirty bars to the father and mother; if they like the man, and the brother likes him, then they will call all their family together, and tell them, 'we have a man in the house who wishes to have our daughter; it is that which makes us call the family

---

[1] "Te Ika A Maui," p. 357.   [2] Ditto, p. 337.

together, that they may know it.' Then the friends
inquire what he has brought with him? the man tells
them. They then tell him to go and bring a quantity
of palm wine. When he returns, they again call the
family together; they all place themselves on the
ground, and drink the wine, and then give him his
wife. In this case, all the children he has by her are
his, but if he gives nothing for his wife, then the
children will all be taken from him, and will belong to
the woman's family; he will have nothing to do
with them."[1]

Mr. Taylor says that the ancient and most general
way of obtaining a wife among the New Zealanders was
"for the gentleman to summon his friends, and make
a regular *taua*, or fight, to carry off the lady by force,
and ofttimes with great violence."[2] A fight also took
place if, when a girl was given in marriage, the friends
of another man thought he had a greater right to her,
or if she eloped with some one contrary to her father's
or brother's wish. Even if all were agreeable, "it
was still customary for the bridegroom to go with
a party, and appear to take her away by force, her
friends yielding her up after a feigned struggle; a
few days afterwards, the parents of the lady, with all
her relatives, came upon the bridegroom for his pretended abduction; after much speaking and apparent
anger, it ended with his making a handsome present
of fine mats, &c., and giving an abundant feast."[3] In
this case the affair ended in the same manner as the

---

[1] "Sixth Report of the Directors of the African Institution"
(1812), p. 128.

[2] *Op. cit.*, p. 336.   [3] Ditto, p 536.

African marriage already referred to, and the idea was no doubt the same in both—the giving of compensation to the parents and relations of the woman for the loss sustained by them through her offspring being removed from the family group; probably the widespread custom of pretended forcible marriage was originally connected with the rights of the woman's relations, although sometimes the capture is due to the desire to obtain for nothing what could otherwise be acquired only by a purchase fee.

What those rights are may be ascertained from the information given us by Mr. Morgan as to the privileges and obligations associated with the membership of a gens. Among them is an obligation not to marry in the gens, mutual rights of inheritance of the property of deceased members, and reciprocal obligations of help, defence, and redress of injuries. "The functions and attributes of the gens," says Morgan, "gave vitality as well as individuality to the organisation, and protected the personal rights of its members,"[1] who, as being connected by the ties of blood relationship, may be regarded as forming an enlarged family group, or rather a fraternal association based on kinship.

The gens would, however, form too large a group for ordinary social purposes, and a smaller group would be composed of those more immediately allied by blood. Thus, although theoretically the effects of a deceased person were distributed among his gentile relations, yet Morgan admits that " practically they were appro-

---

[1] "Ancient Society," p. 71.

priated by the nearest of kin."[1] Among the Iroquois, if a man died leaving a wife and children, his property was distributed among his gentiles in such a manner that his sisters and their children, and his maternal uncles, would receive the most of it. His brothers might receive a small portion. An analogous rule prevailed when a woman died. The property remained in the gens in either case,[2] although its division was restricted to a small number of gentiles. It could not have been otherwise where the members of the gens are numerous or widely distributed. The same principle would apply in relation to rights over children, who in a low social stage are looked upon in the light of property. Among the aborigines of America each gens had personal names that were used by it alone, and, says Morgan, a gentile name conferred of itself gentile rights. Now, although a child was not fully christened until its birth and name had been announced to the council of the tribe, its name was selected by its mother with the concurrence of her nearest relatives. Morgan says nothing of any right of the gens over the marriage of its members, and it would seem not to have any voice in the matter. The formation of the alliance is usually left to the two individuals more immediately concerned or to their near relations,[3] and the marriage price belongs to the parents and near kin of the wife. This, in the absence of the marriage price, would be the case also with the children born of her marriage, on the principle that " children are

---

[1] " Ancient Society," p. 75, 528.   [2] Ditto, p. 530.
[3] See Lafitau " Les Mœurs des Sauvages," ii., p. 564, *et seq.*

the wealth of savages." Reference to the custom of blood revenge confirms the view that, for certain purposes, a smaller family group than the gens is recognised by the peoples having that organisation. Mr. Morgan thinks the practice of blood revenge had "its birthplace in the gens," which was bound to avenge the murder of one of its members. He says further that it was "the duty of the gens of the slayer, and of the slain, to attempt an adjustment of the crime before proceeding to extremities." It rested, however, with the gentile kindred of the slain person to decide whether a composition for the crime should be accepted, showing that they were considered the persons more immediately concerned. The crime of murder is, as Mr. Morgan says, "as old as human society, and its punishment by the revenge of kinsmen is as old as the crime itself."[1] This is hardly consistent with the preceding statement that the practice of blood revenge had its birthplace in the gens. It preceded the development of the gens, and originated with the smaller family group which, as we have seen, is more immediately connected with property and children and the marriage of its female members. Those who are liable to the obligations of the law of blood revenge in any particular case must be identified, and, as they can hardly comprise all the members of the gens, we must suppose them to be restricted to the smaller group consisting of near blood relations. Judging from what we know of the habits of the Australian aborigines in relation to the *lex talionis*, we cannot doubt that the persons subject

---

[1] See Lafitau, ii., p. 77, *et seq.*

to retaliation in any particular case are well defined.

The example of the Polynesian Islanders, who are said not to have risen to the conception of the gens, shows that before this was developed, not only was the *lex talionis* recognised, but the law of marriage and the rights of parents over their children were fully established. These are, therefore, not dependent on the gens, but are incidental to a simpler group of blood relations—that on which the gens itself is based. The idea of "brotherhood" is at the foundation of all these early social organisations. Mr. Morgan says, in relation to the Iroquois *phratry*, that "the phratry is a brotherhood, as the term imports, and a natural growth from the organisation into gentes. It is an organic union or association of two or more gentes of the same tribe for certain common objects. These gentes were usually such as had been formed by the segmentation of an original gens."[1] So also, a gens forms a fraternal association, as it consists of "a body of consanguinei descended from the same common ancestor, distinguished by a gentile name, and bound together by affinities of blood."[2] If we trace the ascent until we come to the common ancestor, we shall have a group of kinsmen who compose the simplest form of "brotherhood," that of a parent and his or her children. Originally this would be a mother and her daughters, as when the sons formed marriage associations the daughters only and their children would be left under the parental roof. It is evident, therefore, that the primitive family cannot have

---

[1] "Ancient Society," p. 88.   [2] Ditto, p. 63.

originated within the gens or clan. On the contrary, the clan was based on the family or group of kinsmen, without which it could not have existed. Moreover, it by no means follows that, because the common ancestor of the members of the gens or clan was a female, the primitive group of kinsmen had not a male as well as a female head. Considered as a "fraternal association," the father may have been excluded, but for the purposes of the brotherhood it was of no importance whether paternity was certain or uncertain. The result would have been the same in either case. For other than brotherhood purposes kinship to the father may have been fully recognised. The obligations of the *lex talionis*, the right to property, and the control of children in marriage, may have concerned only the kinsmen by the mother's side, but those on the father's side may have been equally affected by the law of marriage. That such was the case I have sought to establish elsewhere, as evidenced by the classificatory system of relationships, and that view is confirmed by various facts showing that kinship by the male side is fully recognised among savages.

I have already had occasion to refer to Mr. M'Lennan's admission that, if "marriage was, from its beginning, monogamous, kinship would certainly (human nature being as it now is) have been traced through fathers, if not indeed through fathers only, from the first."[1] Mr. Herbert Spencer, although apparently thinking that promiscuity in the relations of the sexes was originally extensive, yet supposes that it was accompanied by monogamic connections of

---

[1] "Ancient History," p. 418.

a limited duration. He says that "always the state of having two wives must be preceded by the state of having one," and he looks upon the preference for the maternal kinship rather than paternal kinship as a habit, arising from the fact that the former is observed in all cases, whilst the latter is inferable only in some cases.[1] Mr. Spencer's admission that where the system of female kinship now subsists, "male parentage is habitually known, though disregarded," greatly weakens his position, the more so as we are not told why or when it is disregarded.[2] Mr. Morgan goes far towards supplying an explanation of the fact, although his theory is defective. He affirms that gentile kin were superior to other kin only because it conferred the rights and privileges of a gens, and not because no other kin was recognised. "Whether in or out of the gens, a brother was recognised as a brother, a father as a father, a son as a son, and the same term was applied in either case without discrimination between them."[3] Mr. Morgan does not, however, admit of certainty of paternity, although he states that "they did not reject kinship through males because of uncertainty, but gave the benefit of the doubt to a number of persons—probable fathers being placed in the category of real fathers, probable brothers in that of real brothers, and probable sons in that of real sons."[4] This explanation is plausible but insufficient, if, as Mr. Morgan says, descent in the female line is only a rule of a gens.[5] In this case, female descent

---

[1] "Types of Sociology," pp. 665, 669.   [2] Ditto, p. 667.
[3] "Ancient Society," p. 516.
[4] Ditto, p. 515.   [5] Ditto, p. 516.

cannot have existed before the gens, and recognition of kinship through the father may have subsisted prior to the formation of the gens, together with that of the relationship between mother and child on which such descent is founded. This would seem to be required by the facts mentioned by Mr. Morgan in relation to the social institutions of the American aborigines. He says "an Indian tribe is composed of several gentes developed from two or more, all the members of which are intermingled by marriage, and all of them speak the same dialect. To a stranger the tribe is visible and not the gens."[1] Originally, therefore, the tribe consisted of two gentes, that is of the descendants from two female common ancestors, and, as the gentes are not visible to a stranger, we must suppose that the tribe originally represented the male head of the primitive family group to which the female common ancestors belonged. On this supposition the primitive group consisted of a male and two females, the former being the recognised representative of the group, although the descent of its members is traced through the latter. This view is quite consistent with the explanation I have elsewhere given of the classificatory sytem of relationship, which undoubtedly requires the full recognition for certain purposes of blood relationship through both the father and the mother.

The conclusion thus arrived at is confirmed by what we know of the opinions entertained by peoples among whom the gentile organisation is fully developed. Carver, as quoted by Sir John Lubbock, states that among the Hudson's Bay Indians, children always take

---

[1] "Ancient Society," p. 103.

P

the name of their mother. The reason they give for this is, "that as their offspring are indebted to the father for their souls, the invisible part of their essence, and to the mother for their corporal and apparent part, it is more rational that they should be distinguished by the name of the latter, from whom they indubitably derive their being, than by that of the father, to which a doubt might arise whether they are justly entitled."[1] The reason given by the Hudson's Bay Indians why children are called after their mothers shows that the system of female kinship is quite consistent with the recognition of kinship through the male. No doubt the mother is regarded by savages as having a closer physical relationship to her child than their father, but it is incredible to suppose that the latter could ever be looked upon as having no closer relationship to it than a stranger in blood. If the mother had several husbands the actual paternity may not be certain, but, as the father must be one of several well-ascertained individuals, the paternity is only rendered less certain, and the child may be regarded as having several fathers, and claim kinship through them all. If they are sons of the same father, that kinship will be with the same persons as though its mother had but one husband. Under the conditions I have supposed, however, where a woman takes, as her husband, a man who lives with her among her own relations, there would not be any uncertainty as to paternity, and therefore the stronger relationship supposed between mother and child must have originated in the close physical connection

______

[1] "Travels in Northern America," p. 378.

observed to subsist between them. This does not, however, explain the origin of clan relationship based on kinship through females only, which is connected with the fact of the members of a woman's clan possessing certain rights over her and her children. These rights would not be affected, even if the primitive custom of the woman continuing to live among her relations after marriage were departed from. Before this took place, the system of female kinship would have become firmly established, and it would be confirmed, although it could not be originated, by the idea that, as the wife may not be faithful to her husband, there is more certainty about maternity than paternity.

The fact that a man's heirs are usually his sister's children, shows that consanguinity is of great importance in the eyes of uncultured peoples, and what has been advanced is quite sufficient to account for that fact without assuming the existence of a state of promiscuity in the relations between the sexes. Such a state is not consistent with the abhorrence which even savages show to the marriage of persons of near blood relationship, and it has no support at all in the observed phenomena of savage life. The *punalua* custom of the Polynesian Islanders, which has its counterpart among the Todas of the Neilgherries, and traces of which may perhaps be found, on the one hand, in the fraternal polyandry of the Tibetans, and, on the other hand, in the sororal polygamy of the North American aborigines, is neither promiscuous nor incestuous in the proper sense of these words. The possession by several brothers of wives in common, who may themselves be sisters, or by several sisters of husbands in common, who may be brothers, may, as I have elsewhere suggested, have originally been due to the feeling that marriage has a spiritual as well as a physical significance.   Punalua was really an application of the idea of brotherhood to marriage, and it is not surprising that, among uncultured peoples, the having wives or husbands in common should be considered a high mark of friendship.

It is important to notice that among the peoples who have developed or perfected the gentile institution, a rule of which is descent in the female line, the husband is the head of the household, and the wife little more than a servant, so long as they continue to live together.   It is true, as Lahontan states,[1] that the wife has the same power of divorce as the husband, but so long as she remains in his cabin she is treated by him as a drudge and a mere child-bearer.   As women they have some influence in the tribe, but this is only when they have children to give them dignity. The Polynesian Islanders not having risen to the conception of a gens, it is, perhaps, not surprising that woman is usually regarded by them as an inferior creature.   Her position as a woman is, however, better than that of a wife, in which capacity she is cared for as little as among the American aborigines. Her condition is mitigated only under the influence of the Areoi Institution, and where she enters into the punaluan engagement.   If it is true, as Mr. Morgan states, that "the Australians rank below the Polyne-

<hr>

[1] "Memoirs," ii., p. 150.

sians, and far below the American aborigines," we cannot wonder that the position of woman among the Australian aborigines is one of great inferiority. In fact, among them wives are considered as articles of property, and not only do they suffer great privations, but they are most barbarously treated. The last-named people practice the simplest form of obtaining wives, that of capture by cunning and personal violence, but in most of their tribes descent is in the female line, and the gens or clan is developed more or less perfectly. And yet the Australian aborigines possess marriage regulations which seem formed for the express purpose of preventing the intermarriage of blood relations, and which fully recognise kinship by the male line.

A modern French writer of great authority, Fustel de Coulanges, affirms that the ancient family was con-stituted chiefly by religion, the first institution of which was marriage. The family gives rise to the gens, and " with its elder and younger branches, its servants and dependents, formed possibly a very numerous group of persons." Such a family, says de Coulanges, " thanks to the religion which maintained its unity, thanks to its special privileges which rendered it in-divisible, thanks to the laws of protection which retained its dependents, formed in time a wide-spread society under an hereditary chief."[1] This view of the primitive family possesses much truth, although it leaves out of sight one of the most essential features of the family among uncultured peoples. The same may

[1] " La Cité Antique " (6th Ed.), 1876, p. 133.

be said in relation to the patriarchal family of Sir Henry Maine. This writer says that "the earliest tie which knitted men together in communities was consanguinity or kinship," and that "there was no brotherhood recognised by our savage forefathers, except actual consanguinity regarded as a fact."[1] He adds, that "kinship, as the tie, binding communities together, tends to be regarded as the same thing with subjection to a common authority." The notions of power and consanguinity are blended, a mixture of ideas which is seen "in the subjection of the smallest group, the family, to its patriarchal head."[2] "This group," says Sir Henry Maine, "consists of animate and inanimate property, of wife, children, slaves, land and goods, all held together by subjection to the despotic authority of the eldest male of the eldest ascending line, the father, grandfather, or even more remote ancestor. The force which binds the group together is power. A child adopted into the patriarchal family belongs to it as perfectly as the child naturally born into it, and a child who severs his connection with it is lost to it altogether." The patriarchal family of Maine thus differs from the ancient family of de Coulanges in its binding force, which in the one case is power, and in the other religion, forces which are, nevertheless, reconciled by the fact that the chief element in this religion is the ancestral idea which is at the base of the patriarchal family. This view of the nature of the ancient family would be complete if

---

[1] " Early History of Institutions," pp. 64, 65.

[2] Ditto, p. 68.

it provided for the fact, revealed by the study of primitive institutions as now exhibited among uncultured peoples, that descent was originally traced by the female line in preference to the male line. The defect thus revealed will, however, be removed if it can be shown, as I have endeavoured to do, that descent through the male is, for certain purposes, recognised equally with that through the female. Mr. Herbert Spencer, in his " Principles of Sociology," refers,[1] as follows, to a suggestion made by Mr. Fiske, which contains an important truth bearing on the subject of this paper : " Postulating the general law that, in proportion as organisms are complex, they evolve slowly, he infers that the prolongation of infancy which accompanied development of the less intelligent primates into the more intelligent ones, implied greater duration of parental care. Children, not so soon capable of providing for themselves, had to be longer nurtured by female parents, to some extent indeed by male parents, individually or jointly; and hence resulted a bond holding together parents and offspring for longer periods, and tending to initiate the family. That this has been a co-operating factor in social evolution is very probable." The bond thus formed shows its influence even among the lowest savages, in the natural affection which subsists between a mother and her children, when these escape the not unusual fate of infanticide. Natural affection is less operative with male parents, but there are other feelings which have relation chiefly to male children which tend to form an equally binding tie. Mr. Spencer

[1] P. 630, *note.*

remarks that "to the yearnings of natural affection are added, in early stages of progress, certain motives, partly personal, partly social, which help to secure the lives of children, but which, at the same time, initiate differences of status between children of different sexes. There is the desire to strengthen the tribe in war; there is the wish to have a future avenger on individual enemies; there is the anxiety to leave behind one who shall perform the funeral rites and continue oblations at the grave."[1] These motives must have been influential from the earliest period at which mankind consisted of more than a few small and isolated groups, and, therefore, we must assume that in these groups the male element was equally as strong as the female element, if, indeed, they had not a male head. Mr. Spencer remarks further that those motives, "strengthening as societies passed through the earlier stages, gradually gave a certain authority to the claims of male children, though not to those of females."[2] These ideas are quite inconsistent with the notion that the family group ever consisted only of a female ancestor and her children, or that the woman was originally the head of, and supreme in, the family. The custom of tracing descent by the female line shows, however, that for certain purposes the woman occupied an important position, although it may, when the practice of wives going to reside among their husband's relations become established, have tended to confirm that of female infanticide, as the children would be lost to the

---

[1] "Principles of Sociology," p. 769.   [2] Ditto, p. 771.

mother's family group.   One of the motives referred
to by Mr. Spencer would, after the idea of special
kinship through females had become established, affect
more especially the persons bound together by a
maternal tie.   Where the gentile organisation is
established the duty of revenging private injuries is
confined to the other members of the common gens.
The duty of defence against the external enemy
belongs, however, to the *tribe*, which here undoubtedly
stands in the place of the original family group, in
which both male and female kinship, with their special
duties, was recognised, represented by its male head.
This group we must suppose, therefore, had much in
common with Sir Henry Maine's patriarchal family.
Under the head of the oldest living male ancestor, it
embraced wife or wives, children and dependents.
The repugnance to marriages between blood relations,
which seems almost instinctive to man, would prevent
such alliances between the members of the group.   The
male children, when they reached the age of manhood,
would leave the paternal roof, and obtain wives from
other groups, with which they would become associated on the principle of adoption, while, on the other
hand, young men from other groups would take their
places as the husbands of the female children.   It
would be during this primitive period that the idea of
a special relationship subsisting between a mother and
her children, on which the custom of tracing descent
through the female is founded, would become formed,
as already mentioned.   The importance attached to
female kinship would be increased by the development
of a fraternal feeling among the children of the same

mother, a feeling which would be strengthened if, as would probably not seldom be the case, men, after some years of cohabitation with their wives, left their children solely to the mother's care. Under the influence of these various ideas and circumstances the custom of tracing kinship for certain purposes in the female line would be developed by the time that the habit had been formed of wives leaving their parents to reside among their husband's family. As when this took place, the custom would be firmly established under the influence of polygamy, the development of the gentile organisation would almost necessarily follow. The primitive idea of kinship through the father would, however, still remain in full force with the attributes which originally appertained to it—namely, the headship in the family group of the eldest male ancestor, whose authority is practically represented by the tribe, and the non-intermarriage of those thus connected.

CHAPTER X.

THE SOCIAL POSITION OF WOMAN AS AFFECTED BY "CIVILISATION."

THE legend which teaches that the first woman was formed out of one of the ribs of the first man must surely be true, seeing that it agrees perfectly with the position which woman holds among all primitive peoples!

With few rights, if any, in this life, it is not surprising that her subordination is continued in the spirit world, and that if she gains admittance at all into the native heaven, it is usually under peculiar circumstances. Thus, the Fijian women are voluntarily strangled or buried alive at the funerals of their husbands, from the belief that in *their* company alone "can they reach the realms of bliss;" to which is added the idea that she "who meets her death with the greatest devotedness will become the favourite wife in the abode of spirits." What becomes after death of the women who do not die with their husbands is, perhaps, uncertain, but there is reason to believe that among many uncultured peoples as little thought is given to the future state of such unfortunates as to that of animals killed for food. In fact, among the Papuan tribes, and with many of the natives of Australia, women are highly prized for cannibal purposes.   Judging from this fact, we shall not expect to find that, during life, they are much cared for, unless it be on the principle which sometimes leads cannibals to fatten their victims before preying on them.   This is not the case, however, with the natives of Australia, and women among them not only have to endure many privations, but are most barbarously treated. Wilkes states that they are considered as articles of property.   Among few peoples is the lot of woman so cruel as with the aborigines of Australia.

In this respect, however, there is little difference with any uncultured race.   Marriages of affection are unknown to the Fijians, and women remain faithful to their husbands from fear rather than from love.   "Like other property," says Admiral Wilkes, "wives may be sold at pleasure, and the usual price is a musket. Those who purchase them may do with them as they please, even to knocking them on the head."   Thus, among the Fijians, women are, in the true sense of the word, "property," and marriage is a matter of bargain and sale.   This remark is applicable to peoples less savage than the untamed Papuan.   Among the pastoral tribes of East Africa, and also the black tribes of Madagascar, women are, if anything, thought less of than cattle.   The Kafirs, indeed, value them *in* cattle, and girls pride themselves on the price they fetch.   The condition of the Kafir wife agrees with the estimation in which she is held.   Woman occupies much the same position with the true Negro tribes, and even among the North African peoples who have embraced Mohamedanism the woman is subject absolutely to the will of her husband.   Wives do not appear to be treated with cruelty, however, and, according to Mr. Winwood Reade, they often, by force of a certain public opinion, exercise a peculiar influence over the men in domestic affairs. Among the Wahuma of East Africa, women, curiously enough, are not regarded exactly as property, and their condition is probably, on the whole, superior to what it is among the Negro or Kafir tribes.

Women occupy among the American aborigines a position of, on the whole, greater hardship. They are generally considered as inferior beings, and their lives are spent in the lowest and most laborious drudgery. Throughout both North and South America, with few exceptions, a wife is treated as the property of her husband, who will lend her to a friend with as little compunction as he would a hatchet. Moreover, as amongst most uncultured peoples, she is always liable to instant divorce. This arbitrary treatment, and the hardships which women suffer, have probably much to do with the prevalence of infanticide, especially of female children. The condition of woman among the Eskins appears to be more bearable than with the true American tribes. This is shown by the existence between husband and wife of a certain attachment, which sometimes ripens into real affection; and yet, according to Sir John Ross, the Eskino women are considered merely as property or furniture. It is not far otherwise with the Greenlanders. Crantz declares that, from their twentieth year, the life of their women is a mixture of fear, indigence, and lamentation.

Among some of the Polynesian Islanders, and particularly the Samoans, woman is more esteemed than with others, but usually she is treated in the same manner as with most uncultured peoples. As shown by many of their customs, she is looked upon as an inferior creature. Captain King remarked that at the Sandwich Islands, when these were first discovered, less respect was shown to women than at any of the other Pacific Islands which Captain Cook's expedition had visited. All the best kinds of food were forbidden them. In domestic life they lived almost entirely by themselves, and although no instance of positive ill-treatment was actually observed, yet it was evident that "they had little regard or attention paid them."

The facts stated sufficiently establish that, among primitive peoples, woman is regarded as "property." Usually female children are thought little of by their parents, and they are cared for only as having a certain exchange value. In the more advanced stage represented by the pastoral peoples they are more highly prized, because, although a man may prefer his cattle to his daughters, these, if successfully reared, will bring a certain addition to his stock. A curious relic of this primitive idea of the exchange value of woman is yet extant in Afghanistan, where crimes are atoned for by fines estimated, partly in young women, and partly in money. It is not surprising that the man who has purchased his wife should look upon her in the same light as any other chattel which he has acquired, and this *property* notion is at the foundation of most of the social habits of savage life.

It must not be thought that women, even among the

most uncultured peoples, are altogether without influence, if not over their own condition, yet over the minds of other.   The wars, if such they can be called, waged by the Australian aborigines, are generally due to the old women, who incite the men with the most passionate language to revenge any injury to the tribe, and they perform the same office among other uncivilised peoples.   It is well-known what influence over the conduct of such peoples is exercised by the sorcerers or wizard doctors, and in many parts of both Africa and America women as well as men exercise that calling.   It is not often that among the more warlike races women attain to the position of chief, but such a state of things is not unknown to the African tribes; and in Madagascar and the Polynesian Islands woman is as competent as man to occupy the throne.   With the American tribes who trace descent through females, women have great influence in the election of the chiefs.

Nor is woman exactly without *rights* among uncultured peoples.   At first these relate to the disposition of her own person before marriage, and the existence of such a right is implied in the widespread customs which have been thought to give evidence of the primitive social phase described as " marriage by capture."   Mr. Darwin, in his work, " The Descent of Man," well points out that among uncultured peoples girls have more choice in the matter of marriage than is usually supposed.

It by no means follows that the position of a woman is, among uncultured peoples, more bearable because she has managed to marry the man whom she prefers.

Where the marriage has been preceded by actual attachment, no doubt it usually is so ; and in that case, especially if she has much intelligence, a wife may have great influence over her husband.   It is probable that polygamy has been an important instrument in improving the condition of the married woman.   With most uncultured peoples who practise polygamy, a first wife is the head wife, and all the succeeding ones are under her control.   The former thus occupies a position of influence in the household; she is less roughly treated by her husband, and she gradually acquires certain rights.   Mr. Shooter says that, among the Kafirs, all the cows which a man possesses at the time of his earliest marriage are regarded as the property of his first wife, and after the birth of her first son they are called *his* cattle.   Theoretically, the husband can neither sell nor dispose of them without his wife's consent.   Cattle are assigned to each of the wives whom the husband subsequently takes, and the wife who furnishes the cattle to purchase and endow a new wife, is entitled to her services, and calls her " *my* wife."   These rights of property are, however, in reality of very slight value.   On the death of the husband, the women of his household descend to the son who is entitled to the cattle belonging to each family division, and if he dies without direct heirs, to the next male relative, who is nevertheless bound to provide for them.

It is difficult to conceive that the improvement in the position of woman witnessed among civilised peoples, can have been much affected by any change that could take place in the relation between husband

and wife, so long as the latter is treated as mere property. I am disposed, therefore, to trace that improvement to another source, and to look upon it as spring-
ing from the maternal relationship. Stern as may be
the treatment experienced by a wife, it is seldom that
a mother is not honoured. This is especially the case
among the African tribes. The same feeling is not
unknown to the Arabs, whose sacred book declares
that "a son gains Paradise at the feet of his mother."
Inconsistent as it is with our ideas, there can be little
doubt that the curious custom of strangling parents, or
burying them alive, when they have become old and
helpless, is looked upon as a mark of respect and
regard. Wilkes was assured by the missionaries that
the Fijians were kind and affectionate to their parents,
and that they considered the strangling custom as so
great a proof of affection that none but children could
be found to perform it.

The Chinese have preserved the germs of the primitive idea, according to which woman is a kind of property, and among them still a wife may be sold, although
only with her own consent, and as a wife and not as a
slave. These restrictions show a great advance, which
is evidenced also by the fact that wives possess equal
rank with their husbands. Moreover, mothers are
allowed a certain degree of influence over their sons,
who are, indeed, obliged at particular seasons to pay
homage to them, the Emperor himself not being
exempt from performing the ceremonies of the *kotow*
before his mother. Where the filial piety is so strong,
it is not surprising that ancestral-worship extends to
the mother as well as the father, and that the memory

of women celebrated for their virtues is perpetuated. Nevertheless, Chinese women are almost absolutely in the power of their fathers, husbands and sons, to whom they owe obedience as the representatives of heaven.

In some of their customs the Romans bore considerable resemblance to the Chinese. With the former, as among the latter, the father was absolute within his family, and originally a woman, as part of her husband's *familia*, could be sold or put to death by him without interference by the State. This was not so if the wife was only *uxor* and retained her own familia, in which case, however, her children belonged to her husband. The latter form of marriage, or the custom known as " breaking the usus of the year," gradually came to be the most usual, and it resulted in the emancipation of women from the control to which they had before been subjected.

The old Roman, Cato the elder, complained of their having much power in political matters, and statues were even then erected in the provinces to Roman ladies. Unfortunately the emancipation of woman among the Romans was attended with a license which had the most deplorable results, both moral and social.

In Greece the peculiar institutions established by Lycurgus gave the Spartan women much influence, and they were even said by the other Greeks to have brought their husbands under the yoke. On the other hand, among the Athenians, women were generally viewed as inferior to men, and wives were treated rather as household drudges than as companions.

Before marriage girls were kept in strict seclusion, a habit which, in the middle and higher classes, was long retained after marriage, wives seeing little even of their husbands or fathers. It would appear, however, to have been different during the heroic age, when the intercourse between husband and wife, says Mr. Gladstone, was " thoroughly natural, full of warmth, dignity, reciprocal deference, and substantial, if not conventional, delicacy."

It is to the development of the emotion of love that the full recognition of the true position to which woman is united must be traced. The parent has influence because he or she is respected, and love induces the same feeling in relation to the wife and woman in general. Thus, at least, it would seem to be with Eastern peoples, who probably closely agree in social habits with the ancient Greeks. Among the Bedouins, in whose manners we may doubtless trace those of the early Hebrews, women enjoy a considerable degree of liberty ; and hence marriages, although accompanied by the incidents of wife-purchase, are often governed by choice, and husbands make real companions of their wives. The respect paid to them is so great that, if a homicide can succeed in concealing his head under the sleeve of a woman and cry *fyardhék*, " under thy protection," his safety is insured. Pallas mentions an analogous custom as existing among the Circassians, who also highly esteem woman. The same may be said of the Afghans, among whom, although marriage is still a matter of purchase, love-matches are by no means rare. Wives often exercise great influence in Afghan households, the husband sometimes sinking into a secondary place.

How far the condition of women has been mitigated among the Bedouins and other races by Mohammedanism is an open question. According to the Koran, the Arabs were accustomed to treat them with great cruelty, while one of the chief features of Mohammed's teaching is the high position accorded to them. In permitting polygamy, Mohammedan law accomodates itself to the habits of an earlier stage of social progress, and tends to perpetuate many of its objectionable features. As remarked by Lord Kames, polygamy is intimately connected with the treatment of woman as a slave to be purchased even in marriage. But, great as are the evils attending that custom, they depend in great measure on special circumstances, and they are capable, as Mohammedan teaching shows, of considerable mitigation. Probably the practice of polygamy has never, among a civilised people, been accompanied by more baneful results than it exhibits in modern Egypt, if we can accept the testimony of Miss Martineau. This lady somewhat unjustly remarks that, "if we are to look for a hell upon earth, it is where polygamy exists; and that, as polygamy runs riot in Egypt, Egypt is the lowest depth of this hell." Polygamy has not in India so degrading an effect, but, of the six qualities ascribed to woman by the code of so-called Gentoo laws, all are bad ones. A really good wife is, however, so highly esteemed that, if a man forsake her of his own accord, he is to receive the punishment of a thief. Perhaps the scarcity of such wives accounts for the fact mentioned by Bishop Heber, that throughout India anything is thought good enough for women, and that " the roughest words, the poorest garments, the scantiest alms, the most degrading labour, and the hardest blows, are generally of their portion." No doubt women of the lower castes are here referred to, and it cannot be supposed that all women are thus treated. The Abbé Dubois, indeed, affirms that among the Hindoos the person of a woman is sacred, and that, however abject her condition, she is always addressed by every one by the term "mother." If we may believe the Abbé, who lived for thirty years among the natives, the position of Hindoo women is far superior to what Europeans in general believe. He says, " To them belong the entire management of their household, the care of their children, the superintendence over the menial servants, the distribution of alms and charities. To them are generally entrusted the money, jewels, and other valuables of the family; to them belong the care of procuring provisions and providing for all expenses; it is they also who are charged, almost to the exclusion of their husbands, with the most important affairs of procuring wives for their sons, and husbands for their daughters, and in doing it they evince a nicety of attention and wisdom which are not certainly surpassed in any other country; while in the management of their domestic business, they in general show a shrewdness, a savingness, and a foresight, which would do honour to the best housekeepers in Europe. . . . . In short, although exposed outwardly in public to the forbidden frowns of an austere husband, they cannot be considered in any other view than as perfect mistresses in the house.

The influence of the Hindoo females on the welfare of families is so well known, that the successes or misfortunes of the Hindoo are almost entirely attributed to the good or bad management of the former; when a person prospers in the world, it is the custom to say that he has the happiness to possess an intelligent wife, and when any one runs to ruin, it is the custom to say that he has the misfortune to have a bad wife for a partner."

Judging from the Abbé's description, the properties of a good wife, according to the compiler of the " Book of Proverbs," would doubtless meet with the perfect approval of the Hindoo.

Much as the emancipation of woman is aided by the development of love between the sexes, she is indebted to religion for its completion. The description given by Tacitus of the high honour in which women were held by the ancient Germans, as being in some sense holy and as having the gift of prophecy, may be somewhat exaggerated; but if it is true that the safest mode of binding that people to their political engagements was to require as hostages women of noble birth, we may well believe that their regard for the female sex had a religious basis. Tacitus adds, that the care of house and lands and of the family affairs, was usually committed to the women, while the men spent their time in feasting, fighting, and sleeping. A happy commentary this on the question whether the former is capable of managing her own affairs! The true position of woman, however, is not that assigned to her by the ancient Germans, who gave her a fictitious superiority based on superstition. We

must look to the peoples among whom have flourished
the religions which have permanently influenced the
world, for evidences of the continued improvement of
that position.   That which has had the most striking
and lasting effect over the social status of women in
the East is undoubtedly Buddhism.   Gautama preached
salvation to all human beings alike, rich and poor,
male and female, and some of his first converts were
women.   His teaching went to the root of the prejudice so powerful in the East, which leads man to
consider woman his inferior,[1] and she was at once
raised to a level with him.   Hence, in most Buddhist
countries, women are treated as man's companions,
and not as his slaves.   The fact that the former are
allowed to take monastic vows reveals the true source
of female emancipation.   It is a recognition of the
capability of woman to attain to the spiritual re-birth,
and, as a consequence, not only to escape from the
material life with its continued evils, but to secure
supreme bliss in another state.   The idea of the
spiritual re-birth was at the foundation of the ancient
mysteries, and therefore the admission to them of
woman was a sign of her emancipation.   The Zend-
Avesta places men and women on the same footing,
and among the ancient Persians the latter sometimes
occupied even high sacerdotal positions.   She was,
moreover, freely admitted to the secret mysteries.
M. Lajard says that the monuments show us women

---

[1] I have not forgotten the so-called *Mutterrecht*.   Whatever
the influence of woman, as head of the family or household,
however, her position in society was a secondary one, except
under the conditions referred to in the chapter on " Sacred
Prostitution."

not only admitted as neophytes to the celebration of the mysteries, but performing there sometimes the part of god-mother (marraine), sometimes that of priestess and arch-priestess. In these two characters they assist the initiating priest, and they themselves preside at the initiation, assisted by a priest or an arch-priest. The learned French writer concludes, therefore, that " women among the peoples endowed with the institution of the mysteries found themselves thus placed in a condition of equality with man." That which had been begun by Buddhism and Mazdaism was continued by Christianity, which knows no distinction of sex or position, however much its principles may from time to time have suffered at the hands of ignorant or irrational legislators.

CHAPTER XI.

SPIRITISM AND MODERN SPIRITUALISM.

WHETHER what is known as Modern Spiritualism is true or false, it must have an equal influence on those who believe it to be true.   As being, then, influential for good or for evil over the lives of thousands of people, its phenomena are deserving of most careful attention.   For the same reason the analogous phenomena which have been from time to time observed among uncultured peoples are also worthy of study. There is little doubt that nearly everything which has been done by modern Spiritualists has been performed from time immemorial by the Shamans, or sorcery doctors, of the Turanian and allied tribes of the American and African Continents.   The two great essentials required in either case are the existence of disembodied spirits and mediums through whom they can communicate with man.   As to the former, it is doubtful whether there is any race of uncivilised men who are not firm believers in the existence of spirits or ghosts.   In most cases, and probably in all originally, these are the spirits of dead men, who are thought, for a time at least, to wander about the scenes of their material life, and occasionally to make their presence known by sounds or by a visible appearance.   So great is the dread of ghosts among many of such peoples that they will hardly venture out of their huts after dark, and when any person is compelled to do so he invariably carries a light, although he would not have the slightest difficulty in finding his way without its aid. Nor is the medium wanting among the uncivilised races. The most influential man in the tribe is the sorcery doctor, except where he is merely a tool in the hands of the chief, and all his influence is due to his supposed control over, or, at least, communication with, the denizens of the spirit world. By their aid he is able to bewitch his own enemies or those of the persons who seek the exercise of his natural power, and, on the other hand, to discover the origin of the disease under which the sick man is wasting away, and to remove it from him should the spirits be propitious. The sorcery doctor of an African tribe, like the Shaman of the Mongol, is in fact a very oracle through his supposed power of receiving communications from his immaterial assistants. Moreover, the means by which he becomes *en rapport* with the spirit world are exactly the same as those employed by the Spiritualist, although the mode in which the mediumistic condition is induced may often be very different. Whether arrived at by a process of mesmerism, or by means of a ceremony attended with great physical and mental excitement, or, on the other hand, induced by extreme exhaustion, or whether it is caused by a kind of intoxication, the condition required is one of trance. The most simple mode of attaining it is probably the *self-mesmerism* of the Zulus of Natal, an intense concentration and abstraction of the mind, giving the clairvoyant faculty.

Canon Calloway states that this process of "inner divination" is commonly practised by herd boys for the purpose of finding cattle which have strayed; and it is even used as a means of escape by those who are threatened with destruction by a jealous chief.

This clairvoyant power, which is intimately connected with Spiritualism, is by some peoples ascribed to spirit communication. Thus, says Scheffer, among the Laplanders, "When the devil takes a liking to any person, in his infancy, he haunts him with several apparitions. . . . Those who are taken thus a second time see more visions and gain great knowledge. If they are seized a third time they arrive to the perfection of this art, and become so knowing, that without the drum (the magic drum which answers to the tambourine of the Mongol and the rattle of the American Indian), they can see things at the greatest distances, and are so possessed by the devil, that they see them even against their will." Scheffer adds that on his complaining against a Lapp on account of his drum, the Lapp brought it to him, "and confessed with tears that, though he should part with it, and not make him another, he should have the same visions as formerly;" and he instanced the traveller himself, giving him "a true and particular relation" of whatever had happened to him in his journey to Lapland. He complained, moreover, that "he knew not how to make use of his eyes, since the things altogether distant were presented to them." According to Olaus Magnus, the Lapland Shaman "falls into an ecstacy and lies for a short time as if dead; in the meanwhile his companion takes great care that no gnat or other living creature touch him, for his soul is carried by some ill genius into a foreign country, from whence it is brought back, with a knife, ring, or some other token of his knowledge of what is done in those parts. After his rising up he relates all the circumstances belonging to the business that was inquired after."

Among the special spiritualistic phenomena which are recognised among uncultured peoples are spirit-rapping, spirit-voices, and the cord-unloosening, which, when first exhibited, created in England so much astonishment. The last-named phenomenon is not unknown to the North American Indians, and is practised by the Greenlanders and by some of the Siberian Shamans. Thus, among the Samoyedes, "The Shaman places himself on the ground upon a dry reindeer skin. Then he allows himself to be firmly bound, hands and feet. The windows are closed, and the Shaman calls upon the spirits, when suddenly a noise is heard in the darkened room. Voices are heard within and outside the court; but upon the dry reindeer skin there is regular rhythmical beating. Bears growl, serpents hiss, and squirrels seem to jump about. At last the noise ceases. The windows are opened, and the Shaman enters the court free and unbound. No one doubts that the spirits have made the noise and set the Shaman free, and carried him secretly out of the court."

We have here the noises, voices, and rope untying which are so common in spiritualistic *séances*. These find a still closer parallel in the curious rites of Green-land Shamanism, the object of which is to enable the spirits of the sorcerer to visit heaven or hell as occasion may require.　The historian Crantz thus describes the ceremony :—

"First the devotee drums awhile, making all manner of distorted figures, by which he enervates his strength and works up his enthusiasm.　Then he goes to the entry of the house, and there gets one of his pupils to tie his head between his legs, and his hands behind his back with a string; then all the lamps in the house must be put out and the windows shut up.　For no one must see the interview between him and the spirit; no one must stir, not so much as to scratch his head, that the spirit may not be hindered, or rather that he may not be detected in his knavery. . . . After he has begun to sing, in which all the rest join with him, he begins to sigh and puff and foam with great perturbation and noise, and calls out for his spirit to come to him, and has often great trouble before he comes.　But if the spirit is still deaf to his cries, and comes not, his soul flies away to fetch him. During this dereliction of his soul he is quiet, but, by-and-by, he returns again with shouts of joy—nay, with a certain rustling, so that a person who has been several times present assured me that it was exactly as if he heard several birds come flying, first over the house, and afterwards into it.　But if the Torngak (or spirit) comes voluntarily, he remains without in the entry.　There an Angekok (or magician) discourses with him about anything that the Greenlanders want to know.　Two different voices are distinctly heard, one as without and one as within.　The answer is always dark and intricate.　The hearers interpret the meaning among themselves, but if they cannot agree in the solution, they beg the Torngak to give the Angekok a more explicit answer. Sometimes another comes who is not the usual Torngak, in which case neither the Angekok nor his company understand him. . . . . But if this communication extends still further, he soars aloft with his Torngak on a long string to the realm of souls, where he is admitted to a short conference with the *Angekut poglit*, *i.e.*, the fat or the famous wise ones, and learns there the fate of his sick patient, or even brings him back a new soul. Or else he descends to the goddess of hell, and sets the enchanted creatures free. But back he comes presently again, cries out terribly, and begins to beat his drum; for, in the meantime, he has found means to disengage himself from his bonds, at least, by the help of his scholars, and then, with the air of one quite jaded with his journey, tells a long story of all that he had seen and heard. Finally, he tunes up a song, and goes round, and imparts his benediction to all present by a touch. Then they light up the lamps, and see the poor Angekok wan, fatigued, and harassed, so that he can scarce speak."

Except that the civilised medium attains to a state of trance without so much excitement, and does not, while in that state, take so distant a journey, the account given by Crantz would almost answer for a description of a spiritual *séance*. Most of the occasions in which the sorcerer is consulted would seem to be cases of sickness. Illness is usually supposed to be caused by the agency of spirits, who are annoyed at something having been done or omitted, and the mission of the sorcerer is to ascertain whether the sick man will live or die, and, if the former, what offering must be given to propitiate his tormentors. Among the Zulus, the diviners who eat *impepo* medicine answer, in a measure, to the Mongolian Shaman, although they do not profess to have intercourse with supernatural agents. This is reserved, apparently, for the diviners having familiar spirits. These people do nothing of themselves, sit quite still, and the answers to the questions put by inquirers are given by voices at a distance from them. Canon Calloway gives two curious instances of this mode of divining. In one of them a young child, belonging to a family from another kraal which had settled in a village of the Amahlongwa, was seized with convulsions, and some young men, its cousins, were sent to consult a woman who had familiar spirits. They found the woman at home, but it was not until they had waited a long time that a small voice proceeding from the roof of the hut saluted them. They were, of course, much surprised at being addressed from such a place, but soon a regular conversation was carried on between them and the voices, in the course of which the spirits minutely described the particulars connected with the child's illness—a case of convulsions. They then told the young man that " the disease was not properly convulsions, but was occasioned by the ancestral spirits, because they did not approve of them living in their relative's kraal, and that, on their return home, they were to sacrifice a goat (which was particularly described), and pour its gall over the child, giving it at the same time Itongo medicine." This took place in the day time, and the woman did nothing but occasionally ask the spirits if they were speaking the truth. "The young men returned home," says Calloway, "sacrificed the goat, poured the gall on the child, plucked for him Itongo medicine, and gave him the expressed juice to drink;" and the child had no return of the convulsions, and is still living. The statement that, during the interview, the woman did nothing but occasionally ask the spirits if they were speaking the truth, is somewhat suspicious, but, whatever the explanation of the case, one thing seems certain—the young men had not seen the woman before, as she lived on the coast, a day and a half's journey from them. In the other instance referred to, the ultimate result was not so favourable, as the sickness was not removed, but it was attended with an incident by which we are again reminded of the phenomena of Spiritualism. The spirits promised to dig up and bring to the diviner the secret poison which they said was causing the sickness inquired about. At the time appointed for the poison to be exhibited the old people assembled in the diviner's hut, and, after arranging themselves in a line at the request of the spirits, they soon heard, first one thing fall on the floor, and then another, until at length each person was told to take up what belonged to him and throw it into the running stream, when the disease would be carried away. On examining the things "some found their beads which they had lost long ago; some found earth bound up; others found pieces of some old garment; others shreds of something they had worn; all found something belonging to them." In this case, also, the voices came from above; but among some peoples the spirit enters into the body of the diviner, in like manner as with spiritualistic mediums. This is so in China, where the spirit of the dead talks with the living through the male or female medium, as the case may be—and with all uncultured peoples, in fact, who look upon their priests, or sorcery doctors, as oracles.

There are two phenomena known to spiritualists which we can expect to find only among cultured peoples. One of these, the so-called spirit writing, has been practised by the Chinese probably from time immemorial, and is effected by means of a peculiarly-shaped pen held by two men and some sand. The presence of the spirit is shown by a slow movement of the point of the pen tracing characters in the sand. After writing a line or two on the sand the pen ceases to move, and the characters are transferred to paper. After this, if the response is unfinished, another line is written, and so on, until the pen entirely ceases its motion, which signifies that the spirit of the divinity has taken its departure from the pen. Like the spirit drawings of modern mediums, the meaning of the figures thus obtained is often very difficult to make out. The other phenomenon is the rising and floating in the air, in which Mr. Home was so great an adept. This in all ages has been the privilege of the saints, Asiatic or European, Buddhist or Christian, who have attained to a state of spiritual ecstacy.

At the beginning of this Essay it was said that, so long as the phenomena of Spiritualism are believed to be true, they have equal influence, whether true or false. On the other hand, it must not be thought

R

that, because they are accepted as true by uncultured people, therefore they *are* false, as being merely due to fraud or superstition. To those even who believe in a spirit world, the question of spirit action in connection with the phenomena is one of the utmost difficulty ; and a possible explanation may be suggested of the most remarkable of them, based on physical facts recorded by spiritualists themselves, without the necessity of seeking spirit agency. It has been noticed that the faces which appear at the openings of the cabinet in which the Spiritualist mediums sit are usually at first, if not ultimately, much like the mediums themselves, and yet it seems to be absolutely impossible, considering how they are secured, that such could be the case. It may, however, only be impossible under the *ordinary* conditions of physical life. If certain phenomena said to have been observed were so in reality, the apparent difficulty is removed. It has frequently been noticed that colouring matter placed on a spirit hand has afterwards been found on the hand or body of the medium. This has been established by experiments tried for the purpose. Further, it is stated that occasionally, when a light has been suddenly struck, a long hand and arm have been seen swiftly drawn in towards the medium. Moreover, the body itself of the medium, absurd as such a thing appears to be, has been seen to elongate, if we are to believe the statement of Mrs. Corner, made through the *Spiritualist*, in connection with the medium, Miss Cook. The familiar spirit of this medium has been seen rising from her body, and some Spiritualists believe that the spirits usually, if not always, rise out of their mediums. In the instance just mentioned the spirit was said to have been visibly connected with the medium by cloudy, faintly luminous threads.

If we accept these statements as true, most of the phenomena of Spiritualism are explainable without reference to the agency of spirits. They would show that the human body must contain within itself an inner form, be it material or immaterial, which, under proper conditions, is able to disengage itself either wholly or partly from its outer covering. The spirit hands which appear, and which are able to move heavy weights and convey them long distances through the air, would really be those of the medium. The faces and full length figures which show themselves, holding conversations, and allowing themselves to be touched, and even permitting their robes to be cut, become the faces and figures of the mediums. This view receives confirmation from the Spiritualist standpoint, from the fact (if such it be) that the "doubles" of well-known mediums have sometimes been recognised in the presence of the originals, and (seeing that Spiritualists believe the body to be capable of elongation) it is not inconsistent with what has been observed that the spirit figure is sometimes much taller than the medium. It is consistent, moreover, with the facts, that the distance from the medium within which the spirit figures can appear is limited, and that if the hands of the medium be held closely *from the first*, many of the manifestations cannot be produced. This point has been insisted upon as proof of imposture; but assuming, for the sake of argument, the truth of what is said as to the human "double," it simply shows how intimately associated are the external covering and the inner form which has to become disengaged to show itself.

The more the subject is studied the more evident does it become that most of the phenomena in question are dependent solely on the medium himself. The evidence of Mrs. Everitt, given in the *Spiritualist*, seems to furnish the key to all such phenomena as that of the appearance of "Katie King." Mrs. Everitt stated that, when entranced, she had seen her own body[1] in a chair, and been struck with the circumstance; and she added, that in the case of such a temporary separation between the spirit and the body, these are united by a magnetic cord. We have only to imagine that when Mrs. Everitt was entranced, her spirit became visible to the persons at the *séance*, and we should have the exact phenomenon produced at Miss Cook's *séances*. Moreover, the fact of the so-called spirit and the body of the medium being visible at the same time, which has been thought to prove that they are perfectly distinct persons, thus loses its apparent significance. If Mrs. Everitt's spirit and the body which she saw belonged to the same person, so may the spirit seen at Miss Cook's *séances* belong to Miss Cook herself; an inference which is supported by the fact, that when the former disappeared, it was absorbed into Miss Cook's own organism. The magnetic cord which Mrs. Everitt referred to as uniting the spirit and body while these are temporarily separated

---

[1] A more remarkable case even than this was the appearance to Professor De Wette of his own double.

exists also, so far as can be judged from the published reports of the *séances* of Katie and Miss Cook.

A remarkable confirmation of the above theory[1] is given in a recent work by Col. Olcott, who, in 1874, at the Eddy homestead, in Vermont, U.S., witnessed the appearance of upwards of five hundred materialised figures, of the reality of which he was convinced, although they could be accounted for as proceeding from the medium himself, and not as due to the agency of departed spirits.[2]

While offering the above explanation of many of the most important phenomena vouched for by the advocates of Spiritualism, it is simply to show that such phenomena, according to the evidence of Spiritualists themselves, do not require the intervention of spirit agency, although this has an important bearing on the past history of mankind. Spiritism has a marvellous influence over the mind of uncultured man, and it has retained its influence almost unimpaired through most of the phases of human progress. A late French writer, after stating that superstition was supreme in the Roman Empire at the commencement of the Christian era, declares that magic was universally practised, with the object of acquiring, by means of "demons"—the spirits of the dead—power to benefit the person using it, or to injure those who were obnoxious to him. It is thus evident that the phenomena to which the modern term "Spiritualism" has been applied are of great interest to the Anthro-

[1] This was first published in "Anthropologia," in 1875.

[2] See "Theosophy, Religion, and Occult Science" (1885), p. 236, *et seq.*

pologist, and, indeed, of the utmost importance for a right understanding of some of the chief problems with which he has to deal. They constitute an element in the life-history of past generations which cannot be left out of consideration when their mental and moral condition are being studied; and modern *Spiritualism* may, therefore, be studied with great advantage as a key to what is more properly called *Spiritism.* Not that the former can be considered as an instance of "survival," in the proper sense of this phrase. Apart from such isolated instances as that of Swedenborg, Spiritualism is of quite recent introduction, and it appears to have had no direct connection with its earlier prototype. It is worthy of note, however, that it sprang up among the people who have long been in contact with primitive tribes, over whom Spiritism has always had a powerful influence. It is possible that intermixture of Indian blood with that of the European settlers in North America may have had something to do with the appearance of Spiritualism, which would thus be an example of intellectual reversion, analogous to the physical divergence to the Indian type which has by some writers been ascribed to the descendants of those settlers. Or the former may be merely a resemblance, instead of a reversion, dependent on the change in the physical organism. In either case, it is somewhat remarkable that many of the so-called "spirits," which operate through Spiritualist mediums, claim to have had an American (Indian) origin.

CHAPTER XII.

TOTEMS AND TOTEMISM.

AFTER treating of the nature of totems, I propose to explain the object of totemism as a system, and to show its origin. I am not aware that this has yet been attempted in an adequate manner, although the subject has been referred to, as I shall have occasion to show, by several writers of authority. The late Dr. J. F. M'Lennan, who first dealt with the subject of totemism, which indeed he made his own, did not profess to explain its origin, notwithstanding certain remarks bearing on this question made in the course of his inquiries.

The first point to be considered is the nature of a " totem," and this is shown by the meaning of the name itself. The word is taken from the language of the Ojibwas, a tribe of the widespread Algonkin stock, living near Lake Superior, in North America. It signifies the symbol or device of a gens or tribal division, that by which it is distinguished from all other such divisions. The kind of objects used as totems by the aborigines of North America may be seen from the names of the gentes into which the Ojibwa tribe is divided. These are twenty-three in number, and the totemic devices belonging to them comprise nine quadrupeds (the chief of which are the Wolf, the Bear, the Beaver, and the Turtle), eight birds, five fishes, and one reptile, the snake. There are numerous other totems among the American tribes, and they are not taken from the animal kingdom only. Thus, there are gentes with vegetable totems, such as *Corn, Potatoe, Tobacco-Plant, and Reed-Grass.* Natural objects, such as *Sun, Earth, Sand, Salt, Sea, Snow, Ice, Water,* and *Rain,* give names to other tribal divisions. Among natural phenomena, *Thunder* is widely spread as the name of a gens, while *Wind* is used among the Creek Indians; and the Omahas have a name meaning *Many Seasons. Medicine, Tent, Lodge, Bonnet, Leggings,* and *Knife,* have given titles to other gentes, and so also has *colour.* Thus, we have *Black* and *Red* Omahas, and *Blue* and *Red-Paint* Cherokees. Names denoting qualities have been taken by some gentes, such as *Beloved People* of the Choctas; *Never Laugh, Starving, Half-Dead, Meat, Fish-Eaters,* and *Conjurers* of the Blackfeet; and the *Non-Chewing* of the Delawares. How some of those ideas could be represented pictorially as totems is not very apparent, and Mr. Lewis Morgan very properly suggests, in relation to some of the terms, that nicknames for gentes may have superseded the original names; to which may be added that probably many of the totems are of comparatively modern origin.

The natives of Australia make the same use of totems as the Americans. The former have divisions of the tribe answering to the gentes of the latter, distinguished by a common device or totem; and the Australian totemic divisions are usually, like the American gentes, named after animals. Thus, the Kamilaroi tribes have *Kangaroo, Opossum, Iguana,*

Emu, Bandicoot, and *Blacksnake* totems. *Eaglehawk* and *Crow* are widely spread throughout Eastern Australia as names of Class divisions. Totems taken from the vegetable kingdom appear to be uncommon, as only two are mentioned in the Rev. Lorimer Fison's work on the Kamilaroi. The Rev. George Taplin names two others among the totems of the South Australian tribes, each of which has a "tutelary genius," or "tribal symbol," in the shape of some bird, beast, fish, reptile, insect, or substance. The divisions of a tribe in Western Victoria take their totems from natural features, such as *Water, Mountain, Swamp,* and *River,* and in North-Western Victoria the totemic divisions include *Hot-Wind* and *Belonging-to-the-Sun.*

Although no such developed totemic system as that in use by the natives of Australia and North America is known now to exist elsewhere, yet there are traces of the use of totems by many other peoples. Thus, among the Bechuanas of South Africa,[1] each tribe takes its name from an animal or plant, and its members are known as "men of the crocodile," "men of the fish," "men of the monkey," "men of the buffalo," "men of the wild vine," &c. The head of the family, which holds the first rank in the tribe, receives the title of "great man" of the animal whose name it bears, and no one belonging to the tribe will eat the flesh, or clothe himself with the skin, of its protecting animal, who is regarded

---

[1] Casalis' "Les Basoutos," p. 221. The Hottentots are said to have given animal names, such as Horse, Lion, Sheep, Ass, &c., to their children. Kolben's "Cape of Good Hope," p. 147.

as the father of the tribe. Many of the Arab tribes take their names from animals, such as the Lion, the Panther, the Wolf, the Bear, the Dog, the Fox, the Hyena, the Sheep, and many others.[1] Professor Robertson Smith, who has endeavoured to establish the existence of totemism among the early Arabs, states that the totem animal was not used as ordinary food by those connected with it. Again, some of the Kolarian tribes of India are divided into clans named after animals, and we find the Heron, Hawk, Crow, and Eel clans among the Oraon and Munda tribes of Chota-Nagpur.

A totem origin may probably be ascribed to the animal ancestry claimed by a chief or his tribe. Thus, it is said by M. M. Valikhanof[2] that "a characteristic feature in Central Asiatic traditions is the derivation of their origin from some animal." The Kastsché, or Tele people, are said to have sprung from the marriage of a wolf and a beautiful Hun Princess. The Tugas professed to be descended from a she-wolf, and the Tufans, or Tibetans, from a dog. The Chinese affirmed, moreover, that Balaché, the hereditary chief of the Mongol Khans, was the son of a blue wolf[3] and a white hind. Traces of the use of totems by the

---

[1] "Kinship and Marriage in Early Arabia," pp. 17, 192, *et seq.*

[2] Quoted by Dr. J. F. M'Lennan in the *Fortnightly Review,* vol. vi., new series, p. 418.

[3] The "Genealogical Tree of the Turks" ascribes a wolf paternity to the sons of the Princess Choyumna Khan (Miles' Translation, p. 47). Is there a totemic reference in the game of Kökburi, "green-wolf," practised by the Nomads of Central Asia in imitation of bride-racing? Vambery's "Travels in Central Asia," p. 323.

Chinese themselves are not wanting. Their expression for the people is *Pih-sing*, meaning "the hundred family names." As a fact, there are about four hundred such names in China, and the intermarriage of persons having the same family name is absolutely forbidden. The importance of this prohibition will be apparent when we come to consider the incidents of totemism. Mr. Robert Hart states[1] that some of the Chinese surnames have reference to animals, fruits, metals, natural objects, &c., such as Horse, Sheep, Ox,[2] Fish, Bird, Flower, Rice, River, Water, Cloud, Gold, &c., &c. He adds, "In some parts of the country large villages are met with, in each of which there exists but one family name; thus, in one district will be found, say, three villages, each containing two or three thousand people, the one of the 'Horse,' the second of the 'Sheep,' and the third of the 'Ox' family name." According to the rule that a man cannot marry a woman of his own family name, a 'Horse' cannot marry a 'Horse,' but must marry a 'Sheep,' or an 'Ox,' and we may suppose that these animals were originally the totems or devices of particular family groups; in like manner, as the Wolf, the Bear, and the Beaver are, among the American aborigines, totems of the groups of kin to which the term gens is applied."

The former use of totems may probably be assumed also when animal names are applied, not to tribal divi-

---

[1] "Systems of Consanguinity and Affinity," by Lewis H. Morgan, p. 424.

[2] These and nine other animals give names to the twelve years of the Mogul calendar.

sions, but to the tribes themselves, as we have seen is the case with the Arabs. Thus, when the great Hindu Epic,[1] in describing the adventures of Arjuna, one of the Pandavan Princes, says that the Nagas or Serpents were defeated with the aid of Peacocks, we must understand that a people known as Peacocks, from their totemic device, defeated a people whose badge was a serpent. The Peacock was indeed the heraldic device of the Tambouk Kings of Orissa. Probably the existence of the *Singhs* or Lions, the warrior caste of the tribes of North-Western India, may be accounted for in the same way. Dr. M'Lennan[2] refers to numerous facts to prove that many animals, among others the Serpent, the Horse, the Bull, the Lion, the Bear, the Dog, and the Goat gave names to ancient tribes, who used the animals after whom they were called as badges. He goes further than this, and supposes that all the ancient nations passed through a totem stage, in which they had animals and plants for gods. This question, however, we shall have occasion to refer to later on.

The nature of totems having been shown, the object of totemism as a system has now to be explained. The Rev. George Taplin remarks that each Narrinyeri tribe is regarded as a family, every member of which is a blood relation, and the totem borne by the Australian tribe, or rather tribal division, is thus the symbol of a family group, in like manner as the American totem is the device of a gens. The first question asked of a stranger by the Dieyerie tribe of

---

[1] Mahabharata.—Talbot Wheeler's " History of India," vol i., p. 412.   [2] *Fortnightly Review*, vol. vi., n. s., p. 563, *et seq.*

Cooper's Creek, in Central Australia, is "Of what family (murdoo) are you?" Each murdoo is distinguished by a special name, being that of some object which, according to a tribal legend, may be animate or inanimate, such as a dog, mouse, emu, iguana, rain, &c.[1] It is evident that the Australian totemic device is equivalent to a family name, a name which belongs to all the members of a particular group, and which cannot be held by any person not belonging by birth or adoption to that group, so that it is aptly termed by the Rev. Lorimer Fison[2] a "badge of fraternity." This badge answers to the "device of a gens," as the token of the American tribes is defined, and its possession by any person is proof that he belongs to a particular gens or tribal division, and that he is entitled or subject to all the rights, privileges, and obligations of its members. Schoolcraft very properly terms the gens the totemic institution, and as the rights, privileges, and obligations of the gens are attached to the totem, a consideration of them will throw much light on the subject of this paper.

According to Mr. Morgan,[3] the gens came into being upon three principal conceptions, the bond of kin, a pure lineage through descent in the female line, and non-intermarriage in the gens. Leaving out of view for the present the question of descent, the other conceptions give rise to obligations of great importance. The bond of kin assumes the positive

---

[1] "The Native Tribes of South Australia," p. 260.
[2] "Kamilaroi and Kurnai," p. 166.　　[3] "Ancient Society," p. 69.

obligation of mutual help, defence, and redress of injuries among the members of the gens; while the third conception implies the negative obligation which prevents the intermarriage of persons belonging to a common totem. The negative obligation is, however, no less than the positive obligation, based on the conception of kinship, and the totem device of the gens is, therefore, well described as the badge of a fraternal group. The obligation of mutual aid and defence implies the co-relative duty of doing nothing to injure a fellow member of the gens, in accordance with which all individuals of the same totem must treat each other as brethren. This applies not only to human beings, but also to the totem objects, although these may be killed and eaten by persons not belonging to the fraternal group, by which they are regarded as sacred. Sir George Grey says,[1] in relation to the *kobongs* or totems of the Western Australians, " a certain mysterious connection exists between the family and its kobong, so that a member of the family will never kill an animal of the species to which his kobong belongs, should he find it asleep; indeed, he always kills it reluctantly, and never without affording it a chance of escape." He adds: "This arises from the family belief, that some one individual of the species is their nearest friend, to kill whom would be a great crime, and to be carefully avoided. Similarly a native who has a vegetable for his kobong may not gather it under certain circumstances, and at a particular period of the year." So, also, the abo-

---

[1] " Travels in North-Western Australia," vol. ii., p. 229.

rigines of North America will not hunt, kill, or eat any animal of the form of their own totem.

Where, therefore, we find particular animals forbidden for food to a class of individuals we may assume that such animals have a totemic character. Thus, Bosman relates[1] that, on the Gold Coast of Guinea, each person "is forbidden the eating of one sort of flesh or other; one eats no mutton, another no goats'-flesh, beef, swines'-flesh, wild fowl, &c." He points out that this restraint is not for a limited time, but for the whole of life; and as a son never eats what his father is restrained from, or a daughter that which her mother cannot eat, the forbidden object partakes of the nature of a totem It is doubtful whether the Islanders of the Pacific ever possessed systematic totemism, although traces of the use of totems may, perhaps, be found in the names taken from plants met with in some of the islands, and even in the word "Samoa," which is said by the Rev. Wyatt Gill[2] to mean "the family or clan of the Moa," the Polynesian term for *fowl*. The Samoans entertained ideas as to particular animals, such as the eel, the shark, the turtle, the dog, the owl, and the lizard, similar to the notions associated with the totems of other peoples. They supposed those animals to be incarnations of household deities, and no man dare injure or eat the animal which was the incarnation of his own god, although he could eat freely of the incarnation of another man's god.[3]

---

[1] "Description of the Coast of Guinea," p. 129.
[2] "Life in the Southern Isles," p. 25.
[3] Turner's "Nineteen Years in Polynesia," p. 238.

Notions of the same kind were prevalent throughout the islands of the Pacific.[1] Thus, the Fijians supposed every man to be under the protection of a special god, who resided in or was symbolised by some animal, or other natural object, such as a rat, a shark, a hawk, a tree, &c. No one would eat the particular animal associated with his own god;[2] which explains the fact that cannibalism was not quite universal among the Fijians, as some gods were believed to reside in human bodies. The heathen Fijians allow souls not only to all mankind, but to animals and plants, and even to houses, canoes, and all mechanical contrivances. As soon as their parents die they are enrolled among the family gods, whose protecting care is firmly believed in.[3] It is very probable that these gods, who answer to the household deities of the Samoans, are regarded as being incarnate in the sacred animals, &c., of the tribe, towards whom, as being re-embodiments of deceased ancestors, they necessarily stand in a fraternal relation.

These ideas show a close connection between animal-worship and ancestor-worship, and they have an important bearing on the origin of totemism. We have seen that the obligations of the totemic institution are based on the conception of kinship. This is also essential to ancestor-worship, which, like

---

[1] See Tylor's "Primitive Culture," vol. ii., p. 213.

[2] Wood's "Natural History of Man," vol. ii., pp. 271, 290.

[3] "Seemann's "Mission to Viti," p. 391. On the temple at Dorey in New Guinea are sculptured the representations of the crocodile and serpent ancestors of some of the Dorean families. D'Estrey's "Papouasie," p. 132.

totemism, rests on the obligation of mutual aid and protection. The worshippers make the offerings and perform the rites required by their deceased ancestors, who in return give their protection and assistance to their descendants. This mutual obligation is associated with the superstitious regard for certain animals and other objects. The venerated animals are not killed or eaten by those who are connected with them by superstitious ties, and they are supposed, on their part, to act as protectors to their human allies, by whom they are viewed as guardian spirits. Catlin, the American traveller, gives a vivid description of the mode in which the Indian acquires such a guardian. He states[1] that every Indian must "make mystery," that is, obtain the protection of some mysterious power which is supposed to be connected with what is known as the mystery bag. When a boy has attained the age of 14 or 15 years, he absents himself for several days from his father's lodge, "lying on the ground in some remote or secluded spot, crying to the Great Spirit, and fasting the whole time. During this period of peril and abstinence, when he falls asleep, the first animal, bird, or reptile of which he dreams (or pretends to have dreamed, perhaps), he considers the Great Spirit has designated for his mysterious protector through life. He then returns home to his father's lodge, and relates his success, and after allaying his thirst and satisfying his appetite, he sallies forth with weapons or traps until

---

[1] "Manners and Customs of the Indians," vol. i., p. 36, and vol. ii., 247.

he can procure the animal or bird, the skin of which he preserves entire, and ornaments it according to his own fancy, and carries it with him through life, for good luck (as he calls it) : as his strength in battle, and in death his guardian spirit, that is buried with him, and which is to conduct him safe to the beautiful hunting grounds, which he contemplates in the world to come." In California it was thought that the Great Spirit sent, in a vision, to every child of seven years of age, the appearance of some animal to be its protector or guardian. The African fetish superstition is of much the same character, as the fetish object is worshipped solely that it may give the protecting aid which the Indian expects from his animal guardian. Mr. Cruickshank says,[1] in relation to the natives of the Gold Coast of Western Africa, that they believe "the Supreme Being has bestowed upon a variety of objects, animate and inanimate, the attributes of Deity, and that he directs every individual man in his choice of his object of worship. . . . It may be a block, a stone, a tree, a river, a lake, a mountain, a snake, an alligator, a bundle of rags, or whatever the extravagent imagination of the idolater may pitch upon." Here, although the nature of the protecting influence is apparently different from that which the Americans are supposed to obtain, it is in reality the same. In either case it is a guardian spirit, whether it is called a "mystery" animal or an object having the attributes of Deity.

Dr. M'Lennan saw a necessary connection between

---

[1] " Eighteen Years on the Gold Coast," vol. ii., p. 128.

totemism and animal-worship, and he affirms[1] that
the ancient nations passed, in pre-historic times,
"through the totem stage, having animals and
plants, and the heavenly bodies conceived as animals,
for gods before the anthropomorphic gods appeared."
By *totem*, Dr. M'Lennan evidently understood merely
the animal or plant friend or protector of the family
or tribe, and if it had any reference to *soul* or *spirit*,
it is the soul or spirit of the animal or plant. He
speaks[2] of men "believing themselves to be of the
serpent-breed derived from serpent-ancestors," and
so of other animals. He does not see in the totem
any reference to the actual progenitor of the
family, and he could hardly do so in accordance
with his view of the mental condition of men
in the totem stage, where "natural phenomena
are ascribable to the presence in animals, plants, and
things, and in the forces of nature, of such spirits
prompting to action as men are conscious they themselves possess." Professor Robertson Smith accepts,
in his work on the early Arabs,[3] Dr. M'Lennan's
views on the subject of totemism and animal-worship,
and gives as one of the three points which supply
complete proof of early totemism in any race, "the
prevalence of the conception that the members of the
stock are of the blood of the eponym animal, or are
sprung from a plant of the species chosen as totem."
When Prof. Smith comes to consider this point, however, it appears that among the Arabs certain animals

---

[1] *Fortnightly Review*, vol. vi., n. s., p. 408.
[2] Ditto, p. 569, and vol. vii., n. s., p. 214.
[3] "Kinship and Marriage," p. 186, *et seq.*

were not eaten because "they were thought to be men in another guise," that is, they were not merely animals but were men in disguise.[1]   This is very different from the animistic theory, which makes men trace their descent from animals or plants, although these may be supposed to have the same kind of spirits as their human descendants; but it is consistent with the doctrine of transmigration to which we shall have soon to refer.

Dr. M'Lennan's hypothesis may be tested by what we know of the animal-worship of ancient Egypt, where some animals were universally worshipped, while others were regarded with veneration only in particular districts, of which they were the guardians, and by whose inhabitants they were carefully protected.   We have here the operation of the idea of a special relation subsisting between certain persons and particular animals, such as we have seen to exist in connection with totemism; and that relationship must, according to Dr. M'Lennan's hypothesis that animal and plant gods were the earliest to be worshipped, have depended on the animal descent of those persons.   This explanation may appear to find some support in M. Maspero's statement,[2] that all the sacred animals of Egypt were at first adored in their animal character, and that afterwards they were identified with the gods of whom ultimately they became the incarnation or living tabernacle.   It is very improbable, however, that the gods would be identified with animals, unless such animals

[1] Kinship and Marriage," p. 204.

[2] " Histoire Ancienne des Peuples de l'Orient," 4th edition, p. 28.

were already regarded as divine, or as connected with
the peoples of whom they were the guardians—by
virtue of such a special relationship as is thought by
the Pacific Islanders to subsist between certain persons
and the sacred animals in which their ancestors are
incarnated. As a fact, the worship of animals was
established in ancient Egypt by a king of the
second dynasty.[1] Moreover, it has been shown by
M. Pierret that the Egyptian religion was essentially
monotheistic, the different gods represented on the
monuments being merely symbols. " Their very form,"
says that writer, " proves that we cannot see in them
real beings. A god represented with the head of a
bird or of a quadruped can have only an allegorical
character, in like manner as the lion with a human
head called a sphinx has never passed for a real animal.
It is only a question of hieroglyphics. The various
personages of the Pantheon represent the functions of
the Supreme God, of the only and hidden God, who
preserves His identity and the fulness of His attributes
under each of His forms." Dupuis, in his History of
Religious,[2] refers to the ancient opinion that the division
of Egypt into thirty-six nomes or provinces was in imitation of the thirty-six decans into which the Zodiac was
divided, each of which had its protector. The heavenly
guardians became the protecting deities of the Egyptian nomes which took the names of the animals there
revered as images of the patron gods. That opinion
is consistent with the view expressed by M. Pierret as
to the character of the Egyptian deities. Dr. M'Lennan

---

[1] Lenormant, "Histoire Ancienne de l'Orient," 9th edition, t. ii.,
p. 212, *et seq.*   [2] " Origine de tous les Cultes," t. i., p. 77.

supposes,[1] however, that the heavenly bodies were conceived as gods before the anthropomorphic gods appeared. He argues that, as there is nothing in the grouping of the stars to suggest animal forms, and as stars, when named, were given names that commanded respect, if not veneration, "the animals whose names were transferred to the stars or Stellar groups, were on earth highly, if not religiously, regarded," in support of which view he shows that nearly all the animals so honoured were anciently worshipped as gods. It by no means follows, however, that these animals were so worshipped before being transferred to the heavens; and possibly this had nothing to do with any special regard for such animals. Much depends on the origin and object of the constellations. There is still great uncertainty on this point, but it is probable that the signs of the Zodiac, at least, were supposed to represent certain cosmical phenomena connected with the progress of the seasons, or with day and night, half of the signs being diurnal and masculine, and the other half being nocturnal and feminine.[2]

In a very suggestive work by Mr. Andrew Lang, it is said[3] that Dr. M'Lennan gave up his hypothesis and ceased to have any view on the origin of totemism, and that its origin and determining causes are still unknown. Mr. Lang himself suggests a probable origin when he says, "people united by contiguity, and by the blind sentiment of kinship not yet brought into explicit consciousness, might mark

[1] *Fortnightly Review*, vol. vi., n. s., p. 563.
[2] Dupuis *Op. cit.*, t. iii., " De la Sphere," p. 19.
[3] " Custom and Myth," 2nd edition, p. 262.

themselves by a badge, and might thence devise a name, and later might invent a myth of their descent from the object which the badge represented;" the meaning of which appears to be that, before blood relationship was recognised, persons living together marked[1] themselves to enable their common origin to be remembered. Mr. Lang adds, however, that "the very nature of totemism shows that it took its present shape at a time when men, animals, and plants were conceived of as physically akin; when names were handed on through the female line; when exogamy was the rule of marriage, and when the family theoretically included all persons bearing the same family name, that is, all who claimed kindred with the same plant, animal, or object, whether the persons are really akin or not." According to this view, kinship was fully recognised when totemism was established; as descent in the female line is based on that recognition, and exogamy was the result of the objection entertained by the lower races to the intermarriage of persons nearly related by blood or adoption. This feeling could hardly be so strong when totemism took its present shape, which is probably its original shape, if, when totems were invented, kinship was not recognised. The very nature of the totem is the conception of a special relation between men and certain animals and plants, and it is this conception, together with that of the totem as a protecting influence, which have to be explained.

[1] As to supposed use of the totem as a tattoo mark, see M'Lennan, *loc. cit.*, p. 418, and Smith's "Kinship and Marriage in Early Arabia," p. 213, *et seq.*

According to Sir John Lubbock,[1] totemism is the stage of human progress in which natural objects, trees, lakes, stones, animals, &c., are worshipped, and it is regarded as equivalent to *nature-worship.* Totemism, again,[2] is the deification of classes, so that "the Redskin who regards the bear, or the wolf, as his totem, feels that he is in intimate, though mysterious, association with the whole species." The explanation given by Sir John Lubbock[3] of the phase of totemism which relates to the worship of animals is, that it originated "from the practice of naming, first individuals, and then their families, after particular animals. A family, for instance, which was called after the bear, would come to look on that animal first with interest, then with respect, and at length with a sort of awe." This does not go far enough, however, as it is not shown why certain animals and other objects are chosen as totems, or why such totems are not only viewed with veneration but are regarded as friends and protectors. Dr. E. B. Tylor well objects,[4] "as to animal-worship, when we find men paying distinct and direct reverence to the lion, the bear, or the crocodile, as mighty superhuman beings, or adoring other beasts, birds, or reptiles as incarnations of spiritual deities, we can hardly supersede such well-defined developments of animistic religion, by seeking their origin in personal names of deceased ancestors, who chanced to be called Lion, Bear, or Crocodile."

[1] "Origin of Civilisation," 3rd edition, p. 199.
[2] Ditto, p. 327.   [3] Ditto, p. 253.
[4] "Primitive Culture," vol. ii., p. 215.

The fundamental basis of totemism is undoubtedly to be found in that phase of human thought in which spirits are supposed "to inhabit trees and groves, and to move in the winds and stars," and in which almost every phase of nature is personified. But whether, as asserted by Dr. M'Lennan,[1] "the animition hypothesis, held as a faith, is at the root of all the mythologies," or whether the ideas of animism, as found expressed in totemism, have been derived from the doctrines of the ancient religions, is a question. According to the religious philosophy of antiquity, as expressed by Pythagoras, "the pure and simple essence of the Deity, was the common source of all the forms of nature, which, according to their various modifications, possess different properties." The Universe or Great Cause, animated and intelligent, and subdivided into a multitude of partial causes likewise intelligent, was divided also into two great parts, the one active and the other passive. Of these parts, the active comprises the Heavens, and the passive the Earth and the elements. In addition to this division was another, that of principles, of which one, answering to the active cause, was the principle of light or good, and the other, answering to the passive cause, was the principle of darkness or evil.[2] A very practical form of the ancient belief embodied in that philosophical system was entertained by the early Scandinavians, who, says Mallet,[3] supposed that "from the supreme divinity emanated an infinity of inferior deities and

---

[1] *Loc. cit.*, p. 422.

[2] Dupuis "Abrégé de l'Origine," pp. 71, 83.

[3] Ditto, p. 66.

spirits, of whom every visible part of the universe was the residence and the temple, which intelligences not only dwell in them, but also direct their operations. Each element had its intelligence or proper deity; the Earth, the Water, the Fire, the Air, the Sun, the Moon, and the Stars. It was contained also in the trees, the forests, the rivers, the mountains, the rocks, the winds, the thunder, the tempest, which therefore deserved religious worship." There is no reference here to the twofold division of nature, but it is found in the analogous beliefs of early races. Thus, Lenormant, in his work on "Chaldean Magic and Sorcery,"[1] when comparing the Finnish and Accadian Mythologies, speaks of their having "the same principle of the personification of natural phenomena, objects, and classes of beings belonging to the animated world." An idea of dualism, however, pervaded this system, which supposed that there was "a bad as well as a good spirit attached to each celestial body, each element, each phenomenon, each object, and each being," which were ever trying to supplant each other.[2] Thus, both Accadians and Finns "recognised two worlds at enmity with each other; that of the gods together with the propitious spirits, and that of the demons, respectively the kingdom of light and that of darkness, the region of good and that of evil."[3]

At first sight these ideas have no special bearing on the subject of totemism, but it is different when we

---

[1] English edition, p. 250.

[2] Ditto, p. 145.   [3] Ditto, p. 255.

consider certain notions entertained by the Australian aborigines.

The Rev. Lorimer Fison remarks,[1] "the Australian totems have a special value of their own. Some of them divide not mankind only, but the whole universe, into what may almost be called gentile divisions." The natives of Port Mackay, in Queensland, allot everything in nature into one or other of the two classes, Wateroo and Yungaroo, into which their tribe is divided. The wind belongs to one and the rain to the other. The Sun is Wateroo and the Moon is Yungaroo. The stars are divided between them, and the division to which any star belongs can be pointed out. The Mount Gambier tribe of South Australia has a similar arrangement, but natural objects are allied with the totemic subdivisions. Mr. Fison gives examples of this as supplied to him by Mr. D. S. Stewart, from which it appears that rain, thunder, lightning, winter, hail, clouds, &c., are associated with the crow totem, and the stars, moon, &c., belong to the same totemic class as the black cockatoo; while the black, crestless cockatoo subdivision includes the sun, summer, autumn, wind, &c. The native of South Australia thus "looks upon the Universe as a Great Tribe, to one of whose divisions he himself belongs; and all things, animate and inanimate, which belong to his class, are parts of the body corporate whereof he himself is part."

There is a curious parallelism between this system and the ancient doctrine of the separation of the intelli-

---

[1] *Op. cit.*, p. 167, *et seq.*

gent Universe into two great divisions, the celestial and terrestrial, or that of light and that of darkness. In the totemic system one great division includes the sun and summer, answering to the realm of light, and the other division comprises moon, stars, winter, thunder, clouds, rain, hail, answering to the realm of darkness. The American aborigines also show traces of the notion of the dual division of nature in their hero-myths, which, according to Dr. Brinton,[1] are intended to express "the daily struggle which is ever going on between Day and Night, between Light and Darkness, between Storm and Sunshine." It is not improbable that the American totem system is based on the idea of duality. Although the totem divisions or gentes are now so numerous, there is no reason to believe that, as long since mentioned by Lafitau[2] in relation to the Iroquois and Hurons, that they had at one time not more than three gentes. Mr. Morgan states, indeed, that the Iroquois commenced with two gentes, and it is possible that the original totems of all the North Americans were only two in number. The Wolf and the Bear, which probably answer to Light and Darkness,[3] are the only totems common to all the great families of tribes of that area.

The dualism of the American mythology possesses the element of antagonism between the powers of

---

[1] "American Hero-Myths," p. 65.

[2] "Les Mœurs des Sauvages," t. i., 465.

[3] See Gubernatis' "Zoological Mythology," *passim*. Dr. Brinton shows that the Great Rabbit of Algonkin Mythology is the Light God.—*Op. cit.*, p. 47.

light and those of darkness, which was met with in
the ancient mythologies.   The Australian dualism
appears to lose sight of that opposition, and to look
upon the two great divisions of nature represented by
light and darkness as forming parts of a great whole.
This idea is not wanting, however, to one phase of
what Lenormant terms the " naturalistic pantheism"
of ancient religions.   The French historian states[1] that,
although the Magi "preserved the dualistic form
which the old Proto-Medic religion must have admitted," yet they considered the antagonism between
the good and the bad spirits to be only superficial,
" for they regarded the representatives of the two
opposing principles as consubstantial, equal in power,
and emanating both from one and the same pre-
existent principle."   Lenormant finds traces of this
notion in the old Accadian system, and he affirms[2]
that Magism goes further than the perception of a
common principle from which both the evil and the
good principles emanated, seeing that it did not bind
itself to the worship of the latter, but rendered equal
homage to the two principles.   This fact has an important bearing on the worship of the Evil Being
so prevalent among the lower races, in combination
with the simple recognition of the existence of a
Good Being.

What has been said throws great light on the fundamental ideas of totemism, but it does not account
for the notion of protection, which forms the real
practical feature of that system.   This notion can,

---

[1] " Chaldean Magic," p. 228.   [2] Ditto, p. 231.

however, be found in certain doctrines of the ancient Persian religion. Dr. M'Lennan refers,[1] in support of his hypothesis, that animal gods were prolongations of the totems, to the opinion said to have been entertained by the Peruvians, that "there was not any beast or bird upon the earth whose shape or image did not shine in the heavens, by whose influence its similitude was generated on the earth, and its species increased." From this he assumes "that the celestial beings were conceived to be *in the shape* of the animals, and to have special relations to their breed on the earth." The Peruvian notion is, however, rather a phase of the ancient belief, expressed in the cosmogony of Zoroaster, that all things on earth had celestial prototypes which emanated from the Deity. As Lenormant remarks,[2] "stars, animals, men, angels themselves—in one word, every created being had his Fravishi, who was invoked in prayers and sacrifices, and was the invisible protector who watched untiringly over the being to whom he was attached." The Mazdian *fravishis* answer to the personal spirits of nature-worship, and, according to the Accadian Magical Table, every man had "from the hour of his birth a special god attached to him, who lived as his protector and his spiritual type."[3] We have here the

---

[1] *Fortnightly Review*, vol. vii., n. s., p. 212.　　[2] *Op. cit.*, p. 199.

[3] This idea survives in the personal patron saints of the Greek Church. The special god was of a peculiar character, "partaking of the imperfections and foibles of human nature," and, like the Mazdian *fravishi*, it was part of the man's soul. Lenormant says, however, that in the Mazdian books, "the conception rose to a higher degree, detaching itself from the materiality and imperfections of the terrestrial nature."

idea of guardianship by a mysterious being which is so
important in connection with the totem, but there is
no suggestion that the *fravishi* itself ever became embodied in a terrestrial form, although there does not
appear to be any reason why it should not do so.

We have, in the doctrine of transmigration of souls,
however, a sufficient explanation of the special association between a particular totem and the members
of the gens or family group to which it gives name.
According to that doctrine,[1] as stated in the Hindoo
code, known as the Laws of Menu (chap. xii.), " with
whatever disposition of mind a man shall perform in
this life any act, religious or moral, in a future body
endued with the same quality, shall he receive his
retribution."   Numerous animals are named as proper
for such re-incarnation, and even vegetables and
mineral substances appear among them.   Transmigration seems to have been considered by Oriental teaching essential to the attainment of perfection by the
human soul, and the forms through which it is supposed to pass, include not only beasts, birds, and
fishes, but also trees, stones, and other inanimate
objects.   The great Gautama himself is said to have
passed through all the existences of earth, air, and sea,
as well as through all the conditions of human life,
before he became the Buddha.   Dr. M'Lennan says[2]
it is of the essence of the doctrine of transmigration
that " everything has a soul or spirit, and that the
spirits are mostly human in the sense of having once

[1] See " Evolution of Morality," vol. ii., p. 154, *et seq.*
[2] *Loc. cit.*, p. 423.

been in human bodies." We have here the key to the problem of totemism, which receives its solution in the idea that the totem is *the re-incarnated form of the legendary ancestor of the gens or family group allied to the totem.* The belief that the spirits of the dead do take on themselves animal forms is widely spread.[1] The most remarkable example of this belief is that which views certain snakes, not merely as re-incarnations of human souls, but as re-embodiments of ancestors of the people by whom such snakes are venerated. Serpent-worship is, indeed, closely connected with the worship of ancestors. The followers of the serpent believed themselves "to be of the serpent-breed, derived from a serpent ancestor," and we know that peoples have claimed to belong to the serpent race. Such a claim, or that to a monkey relationship made by some of the dark tribes of India, would be readily admitted by the savage mind, and it may be explained on the principle that the legendary ancestor of the race is supposed to have become re-incarnated in monkey or snake form, and that monkeys or snakes as well as men are his descendants.

At the same time it is very probable that some savages do not distinguish between the man and the animal incarnation, and that if they think at all of the ancestor of the race, it is under the animal form. It must be remembered, however, that what to us is a monkey or a bear is to the uncultured mind an incarnate spirit, and it is this spirit-existence which is referred to when men speak of their ancestors as

---

[1] See Tylor, *op. cit.*, vol. ii., p. 6.

animals or plants. This explanation is applicable also to the case where descent is claimed from one of the heavenly bodies. Particular stars are often identified with persons who, distinguished while on earth, are thought to be no less distinguished after death. The spirit of the dead person thus becomes identified with the star. When, therefore, a man or family claims the Sun or the Moon as an ancestor, the spirit of the luminary is really referred to. In fact, to the lower races the Sun and the Moon are great beings, and there is no apparent reason to them why a great man should not be descended from the spirit of the Sun or Moon, or after death be identified as that spirit. Perhaps, when the Egyptian Monarch was called Pharaoh, he was thought to be actually a descendant of Phra, the Sun.[1] Such may have been the case also with the Incas and other royal families who have claimed to be of solar descent. Whether the Sun was regarded as the great ancestor of the race, or only as the re-embodiment of his spirit, it would be an equally powerful totem, a remark which applies as well to the Moon or other heavenly bodies. In ancient times the Solar and Lunar races were very powerful in the East, and their representatives are still to be found in India among the Rajpoots and Jats.[2] In ancient philosophy, the Sun and the Moon would represent the two realms of Light and Darkness, into

[1] Osburn's "Egypt and Her Testimony to the Truth," p. 2. The God Amoun is said to address Sethos as "my beloved son, my lineal descendant."—Ditto, p. 49.

[2] Professor Robert Smith (*op. cit.*, p. 17) refers to Arab tribes, called "Children of the Sun" and "Children of the Moon."

which the visible Universe was divided, and as totems they probably stood at first in the same relation to other totems as those of the Australian primary classes stand to the totems of the secondary groups or gentes. It is known that various animals were anciently associated with the Sun or the Moon, or were venerated as emblems of the Solar or Lunar Deity. Thus, the Lion, the Bull, the Horse, the Elephant, the Monkey, the Ram, and the Eagle, with others, were solar animals; while, among other animals, the Cow, the Hare, the Dog, the Beaver, the Dove, and the Fish, were lunar animals.[1] An example of the process by which certain creatures became associated with those heavenly bodies is noted by Macrobius, who says of the Lion, "this beast seems to derive his own nature from the Sun, being, in force and heat, as superior to all other animals as the Sun is to the Stars." Another example, but of a different character, and taken from a very different quarter, may be cited.

The Mount Gambier tribe of South Australia, as we have already seen, divides everything in nature between two great classes, and although Mr. Stewart, who is responsible for the information, could not find any reason for the arrangement, it appears from his remarks that the natives knew to which division any object belongs. Mr. Stewart asked what division a bullock belongs to. The answer was, "It eats grass, it is Bourtwerio." He then said, "A Crayfish does not eat grass: Why is it Bourtwerio?" but the only

---

[1] See De Gubernatis, *op. cit., passim.* He states that the stag, the bear, and some other animals represent the luminous appearances in the darkness, rather than the moon itself.

reply he could get was, "'That is what our fathers said it was."[1]

We are now able to qualify the definition previously given of the totem as a " badge of fraternity," or the "symbol of a gens." We see that the totem is something more than a symbol or a badge. This description might answer for the pictorial representation of the totem, but not for the totem itself, which is regarded as having actual vitality as the embodiment or re-incarnation of an ancestral spirit. Any object is fitted for this spirit embodiment, and therefore totemism may be looked upon, not as a phase of nature-worship, but as a combination of this religion with ancestor-worship. The ancestral character of the totem accounts for the association with it of the idea of protection, which is based on the existence of a fraternal relationship between the totem and all the individuals belonging to a particular group of kin. The totem, as a badge or symbol, therefore represents the group of individuals, dead or alive, towards whom a man stands in a fraternal relation, and the protection of whom he is therefore entitled to, so long as he performs all the obligations on his part which flow from the existence of that relationship. The ideas embodied in the totem are no doubt more ancient than totemism as a developed social institution. This fact will furnish an answer to the objection that totemism is known only to peoples of a low degree of culture, who can hardly be supposed capable of rising to the con-

----

[1] " Kamilaroi and Kurnai," p. 169.

ception of nature, as a whole, on which that system is founded, or the idea of a relationship existing between all the objects in nature.

Dr. Brinton[1] answers those who object that the cosmogonical myth of the Algonkins is "too refined for those rude savages, or that it smacks too much of reminiscences of old-world teachings," that "it is impossible to assign to it other than an indigenous and spontaneous origin in some remote period of Algonkin tribal history." The same reply may be given in relation to the universal totemism of the Australians, with the qualification that the tribal history of this race would have to be carried back to a period when it was in contact, on the Asiatic Continent, with peoples among whom originated or developed the ideas on which totemism is based, if, indeed, they did not belong with them to a common stock. The existence among the natives of Australia and America of that system may have been due to the establishment of the gentile institution on the basis of female kinship, and the intermingling of the gentes or family groups, owing to wives leaving their own kin on marriage to live among their husband's kin, as the result of the practice of exogamy. Some of the Australian tribes have a legend according to which the use of totems was introduced, by command of the Supreme Being, to put a stop to consanguineous marriages. This shows that the totem was connected with marriage and kinship, but, considering how universal is the objection among savages to marriage between

---

[1] *Op. cit.,* p. 43.

near relations, it is more than probable that the legend was formed to explain an already existing phenomenon, that of totemism. As the conditions of social life were changed, totemism as a system would gradually become effete, and totems would come to be regarded chiefly as curiosities of nomenclature. The preference for kinship through males, in connection with the tracing of descent, over kinship through females, combined with the practice of wives leaving their own family to live among their husband's kin, would take from the totem one of its most important uses, as all the members of a "family" would dwell together instead of being, like the individuals belonging to the American or Australian totems, intermingled in one group. Totems would then be useful chiefly as ensigns, or as surnames to establish community of descent, and therefore the evidence of marriage disability; as with the Chinese, among whom no persons of the same family name can intermarry, however distant may be the actual relationship. When the mere possession of a common surname was no longer an absolute bar to intermarriage, and kinship came to be traced equally through both parents, totemism ceased to have any value, except so far as the study of its phenomena can throw light on the constitution and habits of ancient society.

CHAPTER XIII.

MAN AND THE APE.

THE primary object of the present essay is to ascertain whether the conclusion arrived at by Mr. Darwin and other writers as to the origin of man—that he has sprung from the ape by simple descent—can be depended on, and if not, what is the nature of man's relationship to the animal kingdom.

Without further preface, I shall proceed to consider as briefly as possible the main arguments adduced by Mr. Darwin in support of this conclusion.[1] Those which are derived from the consideration of physical data appear to me to be of comparatively small importance, since they may be admitted without seriously affecting the question at issue. They are almost all connected with the fact that man is "constructed on the same general type or model with other mammals." Thus it is with the brain, every chief fissure and fold of which is declared to be developed in the brain of the orang equally with that of man. Their constitutional habit, however, appears also to be the same. Thus man and monkeys are liable to many of the same non-contagious diseases; medicines produce the same effect on both, and most mammals exhibit the mysterious law of periodicity in various diseases. These are interesting facts, but the

____

[1] "The Descent of Man," vol. i., p. 10, *et seq.*

most important for the argument of the ape-descent of man are those which show the existence in the human body of certain rudimentary organs and structures which are fully developed with some of the lower animals. It is possible, however, to explain this phenomenon without having recourse to the hypothesis of a simple ape-descent; even if it be admitted with M. Broca, that in the parallel between man and the anthropoids, the comparison of organs shows only some slight differences.[1] This may be granted even as to the brain, and that " the immense superiority of man's intelligence depends, not on the anatomical structure of his brain, but on its volume and power."[2] But then, if such is the case, it is all the more difficult to account for the vast difference which, says Broca, a comparison of function reveals, and which led M. Gratiolet to exclaim that, although man is indeed by his structure a monkey, yet by his intelligence he is a God.[3]

While admitting that physiological considerations reveal a much wider interval between man and the anthropoid apes than anatomical data require, M. Broca would hardly allow that the former exhibits anything peculiar in his mental action. So, also, Mr. Darwin says that man and the higher mammals " have some few instincts in common. All have the same senses, intuitions, and sensations—similar passions, affections, and emotions, even the more complex ones ; they feel wonder and curiosity ; they possess the same faculties

[1] " L'Ordre des Primates," p. 173 (1870).

[2] *Ibid.*, p. 168.   [3] *Ibid.*, p. 173.

of imitation, attention, ·memory, imagination, and
.reason, though in very different degrees."[1] The faculty
of articulate speech, moreover, is said not in itself to
.offer "any insuperable objection to the belief that
man has been developed from some lower form;"
while the taste for the "beautiful" is shown not to be
peculiar to the human mind. The moral sense is
supposed by Mr. Darwin to be the most distinctive
characteristic of man; but even this is asserted to
have been developed out of the social instincts which
man and many of the lower animals have in common.[3]
Finally, self-consciousness, abstraction, &c., even if
peculiar to man, are declared to be "the incidental
results of other highly-advanced intellectual faculties;[4]
and these again are mainly due to the continued use
of a highly-developed language, which originated in
" the imitation and modification, aided by signs and
gestures, of various natural sounds, the voices of other
animals and man's own instinctive cries."[5]

If, however, all this·be true, how are we to account
for the wonderful intellectual superiority of man?
Haeckel gives an explanation which, although inge-
nious, is far from satisfactory. He says that it is owing
to the fact that "man combines in himself several
prominent peculiarities, which only occur separately
among other animals." The most important of these
are the superior structure of the larynx, the degree of
brain or soul development, and that of the extremities,
the upright walk, and, lastly, speech. But, says

---

[1] *Op. cit.*, vol. i., p. 48.   [2] *Ibid.*, p. 63.
[3] *Ibid.*, p. 70, *et seq.*   [4] *Ibid.*, p. 105.   [5] *Ibid.*, p. 56.

Haeckel, " all these prerogatives belong singly to other animals—birds with highly-organised larynx and tongue, such as the parrot, &c., can learn to utter articulate sounds as perfectly as man himself. The soul's activity exists among many of the higher animals, particularly with the dog, the elephant, and the horse, in a higher degree of cultivation than with man when most degraded. The hand, as a mechanical instrument, is as highly developed among the anthropoid apes as with the lowest men. Finally, man shares his upright walk with the penguin and other animals, while capacity for locomotion is more fully and more perfectly developed among many animals than with man." Haeckel concludes, therefore, that it is " solely the fortunate combination of a higher organisation of several very important organs and functions which raises most men, but not all, above the animals." [1] This explanation, however, appears rather to increase the difficulty than to remove it. Some of Haeckel's statements might probably be challenged with success; but even admitting their truth, what cause can be given of the marvellous combination in man, of qualities possessed separately by animals, the highest in the class to which they belong ?

Mr. Darwin justly remarks, that " the belief that there exists in man some close relation between the size of the brain and the development of the intellectual faculties, is supported by the comparison of the skulls of savage and civilised races of ancient and

---

[1] " Generelle Morphologie der Organismen," vol. ii., p. 430 (1866).

modern peoples, and by the analogy of the whole vertebrate series."[1]   There must, indeed, be a certain agreement between the brain and its intellectual products, and hence the large size of the human brain requires that the mental phenomena of man should be of a vastly superior nature to those presented by the lower animals.   Whether, according to the developmental view of the correspondence between human and brute mental faculties, the lower races of man, as compared with animals, really exhibit an intellectual superiority commensurate with the largeness of their brains, may be questioned.   Mr. Wallace, indeed, declares that they do not, and he goes so far as to say that " a brain slightly larger than that of the gorilla would, according to the evidence before us, fully have sufficed for the limited mental development of the savage."[2]   This opinion is correct, on the assumption that animal and human mental action is perfectly analogous, and Mr. Wallace would undoubtedly be right in asserting that the savage possesses a brain " quite disproportionate to his actual requirements," if by this phrase is meant his mere animal wants. But the savage is a man, and the size of brain required by him must be judged of, not by the degree of intellectual action he exhibits, but by its accompaniments—not by quantity, but by quality.

The source of man's superiority must be sought in an examination of his mental faculties, and yet the inquiry is vitiated at the very commencement, by the

[1] *Op. cit.*, vol. i., p. 145.
[2] " Natural Selection," p. 343 (1870).

assumption that the mind of man differs from that of the animal only in the degree of its activity. I am prepared to admit that the higher mammalia, at least, have the power of reasoning, with all the faculties which are essential to its exercise. But this very fact makes it utterly incomprehensible how the result of human mental activity **can be** so superior, unless some further principle or faculty than those which the animal mind possesses operates in that of man. What this principle or faculty is, may be shown by reference to certain facts connected with language. Mr. Darwin ascribes the origin of human speech to imitation and modification of natural sounds and man's own instinctive utterances.[1] That the primitive elements of man's language were thus obtained is doubtless true. Something else, however, is required to explain the phenomena presented by the languages of uncultured peoples. Such, for instance, cannot have been the origin of certain ideas which are apparently common to the minds of all peoples however savage. It has been said that these peoples, although having names for every particular object, have no words to express a class of objects. This statement must be received with caution. But if absolutely true in the sense intended, it cannot be denied that nearly all primitive languages have words denoting colours, and these by their very nature, as expressive of attributes, are applicable to a series of objects.

Now there is not the slighest reason to believe that animals have any idea of qualities, as such. Even the

---

[1] *Op. cit.*, vol. i., p. 56.

taste for the beautiful, which Mr. Darwin tells us is not unknown to various animals—especially birds, has relation to the object which attracts by its colour, &c., and not to the colour itself. But it is just this perception of the qualities of objects which is at the foundation, and forms the starting point, of all human progress. The essential instrument of intellectual development, articulate language, was first prompted by such a perception, and it was in the recognition of the qualities of actions, by reflection on their consequences, that the moral sense was gradually evolved. It can hardly be that a power which has had so wonderful an effect, and one which is so different from anything met with among the lower animals, can be referred to any of the ordinary faculties which these possess. If not, we must ascribe it to a new faculty altogether, a kind of spiritual insight, which can be explained only as resulting from the addition of a principle of activity superior to that which is the seat of the animal life. If we were to trace the beginning of every single branch of human culture, it would be found to have originated in the exercise of such a faculty of reflection as that here described. The elements of knowledge man possesses in common with the animals around him; but these have not built up any superstructure, because they have no spiritual insight such as will enable them to analyse those elements, and thus to fit them for re-combination into that wonderful series of forms which they have taken in the human mind.

It is hardly necessary to discuss here the nature of the principle which thus shows its energy in the mind of man.   Whether it is the cause or the effect of the refined organisation exhibited by the human body need not now be considered.   If the latter, however, it may be objected that—assuming the human bodily organism to have been derived by descent from a lower animal form, according to the principles of natural selection—the intellectual faculty peculiar to man must have had analogous origin.   To this it might be answered that man's special faculty could not have been derived from an animal organism which does not itself possess it ; but it is advisable rather to test that conclusion by a consideration of the physical data, and to see how far the argument for natural descent can be supported.   According to this view, the tendency to the bipedal character was the first to become operative in the gradual development of man out of the ape.   The erect form is supposed, however, to have been assumed that the arms and hands might have full play,[1] and it is evident that the free use of these would not have been of any special advantage without an increased brain-activity to guide them.   Probably the changes required in the physical structure would be concomitant, but if they had a starting point it would surely be in the brain rather than in the extremities.

The great development of the encephalon in man as compared with the monkey tribe would, in fact, require all the other supposed changes.   Thus the greatly increased size and weight of the brain and its bony case, combined with the position of the foramen

----

[1] Darwin, *op. cit.*, vol. i., p. 141.

magnum at the base of the skull, would necessitate the erect position of the body, and this would supply the arms and upper part of the trunk with the required freedom of movement. These changes would be accompaned by the modification of the pelvis and lower limbs, while the increased sensitiveness of the skin, resulting from man's more refined nervous structure, will sufficiently account for its general nakedness,[1] without supposing, with Mr. Darwin, the influence of sexual selection.[2] It is therefore in reality only the large size of the human brain that has to be accounted for, and this is by no means easy on the principle of natural selection. No doubt, with the increased activity of the mental powers, the brain would become more voluminous. But what was to determine that increased activity? It can only have been an improvement in the conditions of existence, to which man's supposed ape progenitors were subjected, for which no sufficient reason can be given. Moreover, those progenitors would be subjected to the inevitable struggle for existence—a struggle which, even with man, in an uncivilised state, has a tendency to brutalise rather than to humanise. Under these conditions it would seem to be impossible for man to have raised himself to so great a superiority over his nearest allies as even the lowest savage exhibits. "His absolute erectness of posture, the completeness of his nudity, the harmonious perfection of his hands, the almost infinite capacities of his brain, constitute," says

---

[1] See Owen's "Anatomy of the Vertebrates," vol. iii., p. 186.

[2] *Op. cit.*, vol. ii., p. 376.

Mr. Wallace, "a series of correlated advances too great to be accounted for by the struggle for existence of an isolated group of apes in a limited area,"[1] as Mr. Darwin's hypothesis supposes.

While firmly convinced, on the grounds already stated, that man cannot have been derived from the ape by descent with natural selection, I am by no means prepared to admit that he may not have been so derived under other conditions. Although man undoubtedly has a mental faculty of the utmost importance which the animals do not possess, agreeing with his superiority of physical structure, there can be no question that, both physically and mentally, he is most intimately allied to the members of the animal kingdom. Before endeavouring to furnish a solution of the difficult question of the origin of man under these conditions, I would point out, what is so ably insisted on by M. Broca,[2] that *transformism*, to use the continental term, is wholly distinct from "natural selection," or any other mode by which the transformation may be originated or effected. This is a most important consideration, and one which Mr. Darwin has incidentally referred to.[3] That man is the final term in a process of evolution, the beginning of which we cannot yet trace, appears to me to be a firmly established truth. The descent of man from the ape under the influence of external conditions is, however, a totally different proposition, and one of

[1] The "Academy," No. 20, p. 183 (1871).
[2] "Revue des Cours Scientifiques," 30th July, 1870, p. 558.
[3] "Descent of Man," vol. i., p. 152.

which no actual proof has yet been furnished, the argument really amounting to this, that the correspondences between man and the higher mammals render it more likely that he has descended from the ape than that he has been specially created. This may be true, and yet those correspondences be owing to a very different cause from the one thus supposed for them.

Mr. Herbert Spencer affirms that "successive changes of conditions would produce divergent varieties or species" of the organisms subject to them, apart from the influence of "natural selection," which, in the absence of such successive changes of conditions, would effect "comparatively little."[1] It is to the latter especially Mr. Spencer traces the gradual evolution of nature, on the process of which he has thrown so much light. Thus, when treating elsewhere of that evolution, he says, "While we are not called on to suppose that there exists in organisms any primordial impulse which makes them continually unfold into more heterogeneous forms; we see that a liability to be unfolded arises from the actions and reactions between organisms and their fluctuating environments. And we see that the existence of such a cause of development pre-supposes the non-occurrence of development where this fluctuation of actions and reactions does not come into play."[2] It is evident that this theory, like that of Mr. Darwin, supposes the occurrence of slight structural changes which, in the absence of

---

[1] "First Principles," 2nd edition, p. 447, n.
[2] "Principles of Biology," vol. i., p. 430.

knowledge as to their exciting causes, may be described as " spontaneous," and the perpetuation of which is the establishment of new forms or species. But among domestic animals, and by analogy we may assume, therefore, among wild animals, variation in the way supposed is not the only mode by which the physical structure may be modified. Various instances of sudden change have been collected which are very difficult to deal with, and they have led Mr. Huxley to remark that Mr. Darwin's position " might have been even stronger than it is if he had not embarrassed himself with the aphorism ' *natura non facit saltum,*' which turns up so often in his pages." Mr. Huxley adds " that nature does make jumps now and then, and a recognition of the fact is of no small importance in disposing of many minor objections to the doctrine of transmutation."[1] Minor objections may certainly be thus removed, but only by introducing one of much greater moment. If, as Mr. Spencer says, " natural selection is capable of *producing* fitness between organisms and their circumstances,"[2] it must be by the perpetuation of slight changes, and there does not, indeed, appear to be any room in the hypothesis of natural selection for the salutary movements which it is so necessary to explain.

The changes which organisms undergo, whether sudden or gradual, and whatever their approximate exciting cause, take place in pursuance of the evolution of organic nature, and there can be no doubt that

[1] " Lay Sermons," p. 326.
[2] " Principles of Biology," vol. i., p. 446.

this proceeds under the guidance of law. Professor Owen expresses this fact in saying that "generations do not vary accidentally in any and every direction, but in preordained, definite, and correlated courses."[1] This may be accepted as expressing a general truth, subject to some qualification of the word "preordained." It is not exactly true, however, for variations are not always regular and orderly. Within certain limits, indeed, they would seem to take place in any direction, but there is always a tendency for them to accumulate in that course along which they meet with the least resistance. This is in accordance with the principle laid down by Mr. Herbert Spencer, that everything tends towards equilibration, the state being one not of absolute but of moving equilibrium, while "throughout evolution of all kinds there is a continual approximation, and more or less complete maintenance of this moving equilibrium."[2] The ultimate result is that, "when through a change of habit or circumstance an organism is permanently subject to some new influence, or different amount of an old influence, there arises, after more or less disturbance of the old rhythms, a balancing of them around the new average conditions produced by this additional influence."[3] It is evident that the variations which have been originated before the attainment of the state of temporary stability thus established would have little chance of being perpetuated; and we have probably here the explanation of the

[1] *Op. cit.*, vol. iii., p. 808.
[2] "First Principles," 2nd edition, p. 489.   [3] *Ibid.*, p. 500.

fact that the progress of evolution reveals itself so often by sudden movements. In these cases, where the disturbing influence has rendered the equilibrium of the organism affected more or less unstable, a new centre of equilibrium will be formed, and the appearance of a fresh specific form be the result.

However fitted this explanation may be to account for the gaps which so often present themselves in developmental series of animal structures, it is far from sufficient to account for the origin of man, at least on the assumption of evolution governed merely by mechanical principles. Neither man nor animals, in fact, could have come into being at all unless there had been an organic necessity, quite independent even of the general average effects of the relations of living bodies to their environments, insisted on by Mr. Spencer. That these agencies have been very influential in the evolution of organic nature is undoubtedly true. But their influence in this respect depends altogether on the organism on which they act being in a condition of unstable equilibrium. Mr. Spencer declares, when speaking of the condition of homogeneity being a condition of unstable equilibrium, that this instability is "consequent on the fact that the several parts of any homogeneous aggregation are necessarily exposed to different forces— forces that differ either in kind or amount."[1] This may be true in relation to animal and vegetable forms, whose germs are supposed not to show the slightest trace of the future organism, although even as to these

[1] "First Principles," 2nd edition, p. 404.

Mr. Spencer can say that "doubtless we are still in the dark respecting those mysterious properties which make the germ, when subject to fit influences, undergo the special changes beginning this series of transformations."[1]   But the unstable condition of the primeval homogeneous substance of nature could not be due to the cause assigned. For it requires the impossible case of certain forces, the action of which is supposed to result in the condition of instability, existing *outside* of that substance which, as being identified with the Absolute, we must assume to be present throughout all space. The notion of an universally diffused homogeneous substance, acted on by external forces, appears to be contrary to reason ; and the proper explanation of the original condition of instability would seem to be that it is natural to the primeval substance as the result of an innate energy, the internal force which constitutes its vitality. But this substance cannot have been merely " material." There is just as little room for transition from the inorganic to the organic as from the animal to man; there is but one satisfactory starting-point—nature itself viewed as organic.

If such is the case when the changes observable in nature are viewed as strictly evolutional, much more so is it when they are traced to the lower activity of natural selection. Mr. J. J. Murphy well remarks that "the facts of variability being the greatest in the lowest organisms, while progress has been most rapid among the higher ones, shows that there is something

------

[1] *Ibid.*, p. 444.

in organic progress which mere natural selection
among spontaneous variations will not account for."[1]
Elsewhere the same writer declares that "no solution
of the questions of the origin of organisation and the
origin of organic species can be adequate which does
not recognise an organising intelligence over and
above the common laws of matter"—*i.e.*, the laws of
self-adaptation to circumstances and natural selection.[2] This organising intelligence is supposed to
have been bestowed once for all on vitalised matter
by the Creator, so as to prevent the necessity of separately organising each particular structure,[3] although
it is suggested that man's spiritual nature may be a
direct result of creative power.[4] Mr. Wallace objects
to the law of "unconscious intelligence," that "it has
the double disadvantage of being both unintelligible
and incapable of any kind of proof."[5] This is true
enough, but it has the equally serious defect of re-
introducing the notion of special "creation," with all
the difficulties attendant on the origin of matter, and
the separate existence of independent spiritual and
material substances.

Mr. Wallace himself is so much struck with the
imposing position occupied by man that he thinks
that "a superior intelligence has guided the development of man in a definite direction and for a special
purpose, just as man guides the development of many
animal and vegetable forms."[6] He supposes, more-

[1] "Habit and Intelligence," vol. i., p. 348 (1869).
[2] *Ibid.*, vol. i., p 295.   [3] *Ibid.*, vol. ii., p. 8.
[4] *Ibid.*, vol. i., p 331.   [5] *Op. cit.*, p. 360.
[6] *Op. cit.*, p. 359.

over, that "the whole universe is not merely dependent on, but actually *is*, the WILL of higher intelligences, or of one supreme intelligence."[1] It seems to me, although Mr. Wallace thinks otherwise, that this notion completely undermines the hypothesis of natural selection. If not only the whole universe, but also a particular portion of it—man—has been divinely "willed," analogy will lead us to believe that every other portion of the whole has thus originated.

The difficulties attendant on theories such as those of Mr. Murphy and Mr. Wallace, and the unsatisfactory explanation afforded by the theory of evolution, as usually understood, of the origin of man, have led me to the opinion that nature as a whole is organic, and that man is the necessary result of its evolution. Not only so, however; man must be viewed as the real object of the evolution of nature viewed as a living organism. Without him nature itself would be imperfect, and all lower animal forms must, therefore, be considered as subsidiary to the human organism, and as so many stages only towards its attainment. But if living nature is an organic whole, its several parts must be intimately connected. Hence the numerous correspondences between man and the higher mammals cannot be accidental or even merely designed similarities. They betoken an actual and intimate connection between the organisms presenting them, and such an one as is consistent only with a derivation of one from the other. This view

---

[1] *Ibid.,* p. 368.

differs from that of Mr. Darwin, not in the fact of man's derivation from the ape, but in the mode and conditions under which it has taken place. Derivation, by virtue of an inherent evolutional impulse, is totally different from simple descent, aided by natural selection. In the latter case the appearance of man may be described as in some sense accidental; in the former, not only is it necessary, but it is that for which all evolution has taken place, the only condition, in fact, under which evolution was possible.

How far such a development of organic forms as I have supposed is consistent with design is a difficult question. It is apparent that when nature is conceived of as forming an organic whole, the universe becomes identified with the Absolute, of whose being relative nature is merely an expression. But is not the possession by relative existences of intellectual faculties, and of the marvellous power of insight or reflection, evidence that the same powers belong also to the absolute Being? The possession by man of intelligence is, in fact, proof that organic nature is intelligent. Still, however, the need of design is not apparent. Granting that relative nature has been evolved out of the absolute existence, such evolution can have taken only one course—that which led to man, who could appear only when the conditions of nature were fitted for him, and who *must* appear when those conditions were so fitted. Moreover, as man was from the beginning the object of organic evolution, this must have taken place along the line which led to him, without any actually preconceived design or intention other than that which is implied in the pre-knowledge of man's appearance. It does not follow, however, that other branches of organic nature besides that which ended in man may not have reached a stage of structural perfection. No doubt they have so done, and thus we can understand how it is that certain animals seem to have been, as Professor Owen asserts, " predestined and prepared for man."   The fitness pointed out by our great anatomist " of the organisation of the horse and ass for the needs of mankind, and the coincidence of the origin of the Ungulates having equine modifications of the perissodactyle structure with the period immediately preceding, or coincident with, the earliest evidence of the human race," is certainly remarkable.[1]   I cannot see in these facts, however, anything more than a necessary coincidence arising from the progress of evolution along different planes. It is possible, however, that Professor Owen may mean little more than this, and that he would be satisfied to admit the identity between the " predetermining" agent and organic nature, acting by virtue of the laws of its own evolutional impulse. So at least may be supposed from the fact that he rejects " the principle of direct or miraculous creation," and recognises " a 'natural law or secondary cause' as operative in the production of species in orderly succession and progression."[2]   It is difficult to understand how otherwise there could be an " innate tendency to deviate from the parental type."

Before concluding, reference should be made to

____

[1] *Op. cit.*, vol. iii., p. 795.   [2] *Ibid.*, p. 789.

of the brain and the change in the position of the foramen magnum were accompanied by an alteration in the order of development, not only of the different parts of the brain, but also of the internal apparatus as pointed out by M. Pruner Bey. But the advance having once taken place, the human type can no more be lost; and although the approach to the simian type which appears in the abnormal microcephalic brain evidences the intimate connection between man and the ape, yet it furnishes no disproof of derivation, one from the other, by the agency of internal evolutional impulse.

In conclusion, I would again refer to the fact, so strongly insisted on by M. Broca, that the truth of the theory of evolution is not dependent on that of the hypothesis of natural selection. The great defect of " natural selection" as an agent in organic evolution, is that it cannot do more than perpetuate certain structural peculiarities, the appearance of which it is powerless to explain. The hypothesis is properly defined as " natural selection among spontaneous variations;" and it is the appearance of these variations which constitutes the most important part of the problem. They can be explained only on the assumption of " an internal tendency to deviate from the parental type;" and granting that this tendency results from a necessary evolution of nature viewed as an organic whole, there is no difficulty in accounting for all the facts dwelt on by Mr. Darwin without supposing the derivation of man from the ape by simple descent, although not without identifying the universe with Deity, and viewing its various manifestations as His organs.